R.

PLAYING
FOR
KEEPS

PLAYING FOR KEEPS

by

Jane Waterhouse

Macmillan Publishing Company
New York

Macmillan Publishing Company
866 Third Avenue, New York, N.Y. 10022
Collier Macmillan Canada, Inc.

Library of Congress-in-Publication Data

Waterhouse, Jane.
  Playing for keeps.

  I. Title.
PS3573.A812P5 1987   813'.54   87-7908
ISBN 0-02-624310-5

10 9 8 7 6 5 4 3 2 1

Designed by Claudia DePolo

Printed in the United States of America

PLAYING FOR KEEPS

CHAPTER

1

HOBOKEN, NEW JERSEY

Even standing on the pavement, he knew. The laughter coming from inside was different. It jangled like sleigh bells against the plate glass windows before spilling onto the street. Sleigh bells in the middle of a breaksweat night in June.

When he cupped his hands and peered through the pane, pinlights from what seemed like hundreds of little lamps hurt his eyes. He couldn't see, but he didn't have to. Gone were the greasy vinyl tablecloths, the noisy exhaust fan, the postcards from Italy taped to the bar mirror.

Go home, Hunter Murtaugh. Or go somewhere else, he said to himself.

At least he meant to say it to himself, only it came out loud by mistake. A couple pushing their way through the glassy doors looked over their shoulders. In one swift backward glance he saw himself sized to type and spit out: not one of us.

Damn right I'm not one of you, the voice in his head roared. But he was unable to summon any pride at the thought.

Where was it stamped, he wondered, this mark of a Hoboken native son—poorly educated, and, more unforgivably, in the assessing stares of strangers, poorly dressed: one of the nameless and faceless who pumped gas, sold the morning paper, waited tables, walked a beat.

Well, he was sick and tired of being looked through like a smudge on an otherwise clean window.

It's your anniversary, isn't it?, Murtaugh asked himself. Don't you always come to this place on your anniversary?

He followed the couple into the soft blur of the interior.

The waiter's nails caught reflections of light from the wall sconces. They darted and settled in spangled patterns on a list of reservations.

Something about his smile bothered Murtaugh. It was a knowing smile. A cautious smile. One of those smiles which were reserved for the dangerous or drunk. And tonight Hunter Murtaugh was feeling both.

"You still serve Italian food?" he asked.

"No, sir," the waiter answered. "We've been under new management for almost six months now." Then he added hopefully, "There's an Italian restaurant further on down the block."

Murtaugh suddenly wished he was wearing a tie. At certain moments, there was nothing better than adjusting a tie to convey just the right note of dignity and resolve. This was one of those moments. Unfortunately, he had no tie. Instead, he broke from the waiter's moist, patronizing gaze and focused on his nametag, squinting until he could read the curly script.

Damn, he needed glasses.

"Table for one . . . Donny," Murtaugh said.

"It's Doug."

There was a split second of hesitation, long enough for Doug's blond lashes to flick a charged message to the bartender.

Putting him on alert, Murtaugh thought.

So what?, the dark voice in his head needled. You've got as much a right to be here as anybody else. You were a regular. Once.

But these new frosty-haloed lamps disoriented him. He found his own reflection in the mirrors startling. The ashen crescents under his eyes (Eve always said she had a weakness for blue) made him look older than he was, younger than he felt.

Doug glided through the maze of diners.

Concentrate, Murtaugh. Think of it as a game. A pinball game. Twenty points for hitting a chair, fifty for a table. He steadied himself on the rim of a bucket where a bottle of wine was overturned in ice chips.

Tilt. You lose. Never was much of a player, were you?

The waiter stood behind a chair, extending the menu in his glittering pinchers.

"Something from the bar, sir?"

"Shot and a beer."

With a resigned sigh, Doug turned, his white shirt bobbing over tops of sleek heads and marble tables like a buoy.

The desire to run out of the room hit Murtaugh as suddenly and overpoweringly as the urge to sneeze, but his legs felt rubbery and unreliable. He searched in his pockets for a cigarette and lit up.

There was a tug at his sleeve. "If you want to do *that*, you should have asked for the smoking section," the woman next to him said, curling her lips in distaste.

The way she'd said it, said—"do *that*"—made him feel he'd been caught doing something private. Something dirty. In the absence of an ashtray, he stabbed the butt mercilessly into the bread dish.

"Whatever happened to Angelo . . . the guy who used to own this place?" Murtaugh inquired casually when the waiter brought his drinks.

3

"He died," answered the young man, just as casually, picking up the soiled dish and replacing it with one from another setting.

So that was that.

Angelo was dead. There was nothing left of him here. Eve was dead, there was nothing left of her anywhere. Even the angular tape marks tracing the curves of her body were gone from that patch of asphalt in front of the hospital. Had been, for months and months.

It had been a stupid impulse, coming in. He could have kept walking, could have gone into another bar until closing time forced him back to the cage that passed for an apartment, to the flies dotting the walls like belligerent guests refusing to leave.

Murtaugh drained the last of his drink and set it down on the table so hard that a vase of irises toppled over. He mopped up the excess water with his cloth napkin. Cloth. In Angelo's place.

Not Angelo's anymore, he reminded himself.

The liquor was sticking to his insides good and proper, and that always made him feel philosophical.

You know, Hunter boy, he thought, change isn't the hardest pill to swallow. Life's going on the same as usual—that's the real bitch.

If Eve were here, it wouldn't matter whether there was stained vinyl or starched linen like this on the table. She fit in anywhere. He had always been the odd-shaped peg.

But time had steamrolled over Eve's tracks, flattening, erasing them, even for Murtaugh. He squeezed his eyes shut, willing her face into the void. There was nothing except the neon residue of lamplight and the sound of life going on and on, like a record played long past the point of enjoyment.

Justice isn't a blindfolded goddess in regal robes, Murtaugh decided bitterly. Justice is a whore, tarted up so you don't notice what a ruin she is underneath. A cancerous hag with a twisted sense of humor.

That's why a young doctor was dead. That's why those Puerto Rican bastards who killed her were still tooling around town in their rusty old Cadillac, with the radio blaring. And why Hunter Murtaugh was left to play out a losing hand.

"Are you ready to order?" Doug stood over him, his pencil poised.

"Another. Please."

"Certainly." He smiled that annoying smile. "And for your entree?"

"Just the drinks," Murtaugh repeated stubbornly.

"Will you be dining tonight, sir?"

"No," said Murtaugh, aware that people around him were making a great show of not paying attention. "I came here to toast old times."

"I'm sorry, sir," the waiter said, his tone insinuating he wasn't, "but these tables are only for patrons having dinner. Perhaps you could do your toasting at the bar."

Murtaugh protested loudly, "I don't want to toast old times at the bar. I never *had* any old times at the bar."

The bartender came over to stand next to his friend. "Is there some kind of problem?"

"Yeah, there's some kind of problem." Murtaugh was surprised at the desperation in his voice. "It seems Donny, or Dougie, or whoever the hell he is, won't bring me my drink."

He felt the man's grip under his elbow, propelling him out of his seat and causing him to step on the foot of the non-smoking woman. It was a maneuver worth at least seventy points. Too bad the game was already over.

Happy anniversary, he sang silently as they ushered him out, with one long sweep, through the winding aisles. Happy, happy anniversary.

All in all, it was a pleasurable sensation, one which Hunter

Murtaugh would have given in to, except for another peal of sleighbell laughter coming from a couple at the bar.

"Hoboken's local color, no doubt," one said to the other.

The words, the ringing, and the double glass doors confronted him simultaneously.

Doug tossed a warning into the darkness for good measure. It thrummed inside Murtaugh's head, like the snap of a wet towel: "Next time, we'll call the police."

The doors shut soundlessly.

"I *am* the police, you asshole," Murtaugh cried softly. Then more loudly, "I *am* the fucking police."

On the street, a group of young Hispanics passed. They were laughing, too, only theirs was wild and raucous.

And really, it was pretty funny when he thought about it— a cop who no longer believed in right and wrong. A cop who was an outsider in his own territory. Pretty funny. Pretty goddamn funny.

* * *

He slammed the receiver so hard that the telephone made a little ringing noise.

"Randall—Randall, d'ya hear me?"

The other detectives paused, letting Murtaugh's voice ripple the rhythm of their work.

"Is there something I can do for you, Sergeant?"

He had to hand it to her. She was a cool number. He watched her toe tap the linoleum with the regularity of a heartbeat. Except for that, you wouldn't know she cared a bit.

Eve once said if you wanted a clue about a person's bank account to look at his shoes. Alison Randall wore leather pumps that creased softly, like a smiling face. They were dead giveaways. The woman came from money.

Something about her pencil-slim good looks provoked him

to anger. She reminded him of the young woman who'd bought the home he once shared with Eve. And yet, feature for feature, they didn't look anything alike.

"You're the Operations Analyzer, aren't you?" he asked, simply to needle her.

Alison Randall stopped tapping her foot. "Analyst. I'm the Operations Analyst. And if you have a problem, Sergeant, perhaps we'd better discuss it privately."

Bromsky snickered suggestively from his desk on the other side of the room. The reaction was so totally predictable it blended imperceptibly with other comfortable morning sounds—the drip of the coffeemaker, the ticking of the clock.

"Not privately, lady. Here and now," Murtaugh persisted. "Since when am I off the Quiles case?"

She looked steadily into his eyes. "Since announcements. They begin at eight. You really should try and make them occasionally."

Randall turned on those heels that were neither too high nor too low.

He stopped her with his voice. "You owe me, Randall. You owe me an explanation."

Bonelli began shuffling papers into his desk. The metal drawer catching made everyone aware of how quiet the room had become.

"All right," Randall said. "Okay."

She was next to Murtaugh now, talking in almost a whisper. "The Captain and I agree that everything possible should be done to avoid a repeat of the Bremmar incident."

Davy O'Connell cleared his throat as though he was going to say something. But before he did, Murtaugh spoke.

"So that's it," the Sergeant smiled grimly, at no one in particular.

Alison Randall stood for a moment, as if considering how unprotected her back would be in retreat. But the detective took no notice, so she walked quickly to the door, leaving nothing but the sound of efficient heels clicking down the hallway.

O'Connell sat down on the corner of Murtaugh's desk. "A regular little charmer, isn't she?"

The telephones began to ring again, as they had every day since the disappearance of the Quiles boy last week. Crank calls, phony tips, worried parents afraid for their children— nothing that had made any difference to the investigation, up to this point; but all having to be answered, recorded, followed through by a member of the Department.

Well, it wasn't his concern anymore. Dead or alive, little Tomas Quiles was no longer his responsibility.

They wanted him out. Housecleaning, Rourke would call it. Murtaugh could almost hear him.

"Time for us old dinosaurs to take a powder, Hunt. College kids and computers, they're where it's at these days."

Ironic, really. It was common knowledge that the only reason Rourke made it out of Saint Catherine's was because the Sisters of Charity finally showed some. And yet here he was, giving orders to earnest young men with degrees in psychology, criminology, sociology.

Whenever one of them screwed up, he smacked his lips with the satisfaction inherent in having the upper hand of one's betters, and said, "Guess they didn't teach 'em that at the university."

After all, Rourke was used to dealing with detectives who thought they were smarter than they really were. Detectives like Hunter Murtaugh. And the smarter they thought they were, the harder they fell.

Murtaugh had to hand it to the son of a bitch. Rourke was patient, and he had an infallible sense of timing. It couldn't have been easy, containing his animosity all these years. At school, on the playing field, at the Academy, Murtaugh had been so goddamn *visible*. But Rourke always managed to pat him on the back, smiling with teeth arched over his gums like a dog's on a bone.

"There's our golden boy," he'd say. "The one with all the aces."

A more careless man would have gone for the jugular when Murtaugh began his downward slide. Not Rourke. He was sympathetic. Almost paternal.

"You'll never get another like her, Hunt," he said sadly at the funeral. Murtaugh felt himself falling a little further with each word.

No doubt about it. Rourke had known how to bide his time. The angry outbursts and drunken stupors were too pathetic. It wouldn't have looked right, kicking a man when he was down. So Rourke took the Sergeant's part, long after everyone else's patience had been tried, waiting for the moment when all his aces were spent.

The Bremmar incident.

Murtaugh wondered why they bothered going back that far. Surely there were other, more recent complaints on the book.

It had been his first hit-and-run since Eve. The boy's mother was only a kid herself. She followed the detective with half-crazed eyes as he paced around the small covered heap on the street.

He remembered the freakishly hot October day. He remembered how his shoes seemed to sink below the pavement, rooting him in black, gummy pitch.

So he'd kept moving. To stop from sinking, to stop from thinking. Thinking about the dark-skinned punks who'd be waking up the next morning, while Billy Bremmar lay motionless under his plastic sheet. Thinking about bending over his wife's crooked head to pluck a perfect autumn leaf from her hair.

Murtaugh kept moving until the moment Mrs. Bremmar intercepted him and began hitting his chest with her clenched fists.

"Where's your respect?" she demanded hysterically. "He's not some dead animal you can put in a bag and take away. He was my son! He's my baby!"

And before he was able to control himself, Hunter Murtaugh had found himself shaking the woman's shoulders until they folded like paper under him. "And what about you, lady? Where were you when a kid still in diapers was out playing in the street? Where the hell were you?"

The Bremmars filed a complaint. Murtaugh was put on an open-ended leave. Then one day the knock came at the door of his brownstone on Hudson Street.

She said, "You're probably going to think I'm awfully pushy, but my husband and I have fallen in love with this block. And we were wondering . . . uh, you don't happen to know of anyone who's planning to sell any time in the near future, do you?"

If he'd been sober, Murtaugh might have wondered then, as he had in more lucid periods since, whether they'd been tipped off. Or worse yet, if they'd been scouring the obituaries. But it probably wouldn't have mattered either way.

He sold his home to a couple of attractive strangers, riding in their BMW with New York plates up and down the street in search of a dream house.

One week later Murtaugh took Eve's cat to the animal shelter to be destroyed and moved into the basement apartment. For the sake of traveling light, he left all his books on the stoop next to the trash.

Sometimes, reinforced by false hopefulness and the first drink of the day, Murtaugh fantasized that a kid, fresh out of school, had picked those volumes—philosophy, theology, law, the biographies of great men—off the stoop and read them.

10

He played out the whole scenario, up to its inevitable happy ending when, years from now, the kid sat at Murtaugh's own desk and people stopped to talk with him, clapping him on the back.

Later, when the certainty of the liquor had dulled him, he decided the books were in ashes somewhere, scattered in a great windswept garbage dump.

That's how he felt today.

Rourke would win. Maybe not this time or the next, but he would win just the same. Because, for all Murtaugh's golden beginnings, what was he but a drunken Irish cop—a cartoon, the stuff of cheap fiction and barroom jokes, no different than a thousand other down-at-the-heel detectives going to seed?

He gripped the corners of his desk, his mind reeling. That might be how I look, but goddammit, I *am* different, he wanted to scream.

I'm Hunter Murtaugh, most valuable player, head of the class, top of the line, thrifty, brave, clean, and reverent. Hunter Murtaugh who gets the man in his investigations and the woman of his dreams. Or at least I used to be.

It hit him with a jolt that used to be didn't count.

Murtaugh got up suddenly, thinking now was as good a time as any for his first of the morning.

Lou Bonelli touched his sleeve. "We just had a call."

"The boy?"

Bonelli shook his head. "A woman, same neck of the woods. Sounds like an ugly one."

There wouldn't be time for a quick drink after all, and this made Murtaugh angry.

CHAPTER

2

THE MURDER was extraordinary in several respects. After all, such things didn't ordinarily happen in Hoboken.

Murtaugh first heard this disclaimer from the young uniform on duty in front of the woman's house. He was tempted to ask the kid why Hoboken should be any different from other places. Instead, he sucked in an involuntary grin and reached for the cellophane in his pocket, balling the wad up between his thumb and forefinger, without saying a word.

Later, though, after seeing the body, he admitted to himself they were the same words to run through his own head when he looked into Rose Walsh's dead eyes.

People had already gathered behind the police barricade. There was a sense of excitement, tinged with boredom, like a movie set with everyone waiting for the star to enter. But the star, in this case, Murtaugh knew, wouldn't enter. She'd exit, on a trolley. He supposed such an exit would be enough for this particular audience.

A woman with metal clips in hair the color of an Orange Julius leaned over to grab his arm, but the detective moved away, silently cursing her for reminding him of his thirst.

Murtaugh knew the block well. It was, he thought, pretty representative of the whole can of beans. The papers called it gentrification. In a town of Hoboken's size—a mile long, and just as wide—all that amounted to was social warfare.

The Italians, the Irish, the Poles—they'd be quick to tell you who was here first. They kept a wary eye on any newcomers, from their porches and their stoops, from behind cretonne curtains or Sears drapes.

Hordes of intruders, that's what they considered them. Intruders from two islands—Puerto Rico and Manhattan. One group lowered property values, the other hiked them up, along with taxes. It was all the same to the old guard in the neighborhood. They were outsiders, to be tolerated but not trusted.

With a glance, Murtaugh could label each of the attached rowhouses and put them into three neat categories. If Hoboken's Darwinian struggle was going to go to the fittest, then this block was an indication of the winners.

They lived in renovated brownstones, with windowboxes of geraniums and stripped oak doors with gleaming brass handles. They moved in with their Conran kitchens and their platform beds, with their gym equipment and their Cuisinarts.

You passed them on the street carrying hunks of cheese and golden sticks of bread in net bags. Or they passed you as they ran along the river in suitably worn Nikes. But mostly, they stayed to themselves—doing business at particular shops, frequenting certain new restaurants, as though they'd checked it out among each other at the beginning of each day.

People like Murtaugh only caught glimpses of them, as fleeting as the glimmer of fine prints and modern paintings in lit windows, behind raised Levelors, through paintboxbright shutters. Or as swift as the sound of tinkling laughter taken with him into the night air.

He winced with the memory of last night's bender. It had been a new low, and that frightened him. Because he was beginning to realize just how many levels there were to that hackneyed phrase, "the depths of despair."

In order to abandon this train of thought, the Sergeant forced himself to count the housefronts which were still old-world ethnic.

Five, plus the two buildings where the Hispanics lived on the end.

Unlike their neighbors, they stayed on home ground, away from the police barricades. The older people sat in clusters on the front steps, while young girls in bright summer clothes leaned out of windows, like exotic flowers arching toward the sun. A radio, tuned to a Spanish station, was playing. You could hear it clearly all the way down the block.

Murtaugh found himself wondering whether Maria Quiles was looking down at that moment, thinking that the police were bringing news of her little son.

But Murtaugh had no news of Tomas, and anyway, he wouldn't be the one to bring it now. He was unfit to deal with a situation demanding compassion or tact. They sent him to an old woman who'd probably been cooled because some creep wanted her color television.

Forget about the neighbors, Murtaugh told himself. There would be plenty of time for them later. He directed his attention to Number 518. Rose Walsh's house.

The windows, bereft of shutters and bracketed in aluminum storms, gaped blankly onto the street. Someone, presumably the dead woman herself, had pushed a vase of plastic flowers and a large porcelain donkey up against the glass. A plastic shade, tasseled and yellowing, acted as the backdrop in a dumb show.

Although he'd never met her, Murtaugh knew this woman. He understood the intimate details of her existence—the lace bonnet for mass, folded and creased neatly at the bottom of her purse; the clock radio, tuned to an AM talk station beside her bed; the ivory antimacassars smelling of mothballs on the armchairs.

"Living room," a patrolman out front told Murtaugh. He took the steps, two at a time.

There were flies in the Walsh house, but they were different from those plaguing his apartment. These were the small, nervous variety, the kind found in restaurants serving greasy food.

As soon as he walked in, Murtaugh smelled the kitchen: the stench of leftover casseroles, of pots too long in the sink. He fancied he could even make out the sticky-sweet odor of blood, although he knew this was part imagination and part the cloying taste in his mouth from last night.

The short climb up the steps winded him, so he stood in the foyer for a moment, taking in Rose's stale cooking and letting his eyes adjust to the light. From the door he could look straight down the hallway which led to the kitchen.

The glare from the white sky, refracted in the big back window, shattered everything into unnaturally dark or unnaturally brilliant planes. In front of him, Bonelli and Lowenstein, the medical examiner, were talking softly. The brightness was so dazzling he couldn't make out their features, only Lowenstein's massive slouch and the slender question mark of Bonelli's spine.

That's when he first noticed the silence. Unusual for the Pathology guys, whose jobs undermined any traditional notions of hushed respect for the dead.

Lowenstein met him at the archway. "A new one on me," he said as they shook hands.

Bonelli was writing in a notepad. From this point on, he

wouldn't be without it, Murtaugh knew. Not because he was overly efficient. He just didn't have a sponge for a brain like young Davy O'Connell. Lou Bonelli kept a detailed list of facts in longhand. But he seldom took his eyes off the goddamn pad long enough to really *see* anything.

"Husband's in the kitchen," he told Murtaugh, as he turned over a clean sheet.

"How's he taking it?"

Bonelli shrugged, averting his eyes. "Hard to say."

They followed Lowenstein through the open arch.

Murtaugh's first thought was how silly the men looked, crammed into the over-furnished room, attempting to keep on the plastic runners that stretched over the blue nylon carpet like a thin layer of ice over a lake.

The image of these guys, well-fed and sweating in their shirtsleeves, tippytoeing on the roller rink of Rose Walsh's parlor, was pleasing to him.

He was on the verge of cracking a smile when he saw her.

Mrs. Walsh was seated on the sofa, its fake satin cloth protected, as was everything else in the room, by a shimmering veneer of vinyl. She sat, symmetrically poised between two end tables with their matching lamps and scalloped shades, and the coffee table in front of her.

He could imagine a tea service there, and that these sweating skaters were her guests for tea. He could imagine that, if it wasn't for her unusually erect posture and the odd, open-armed way in which she appeared to greet her visitors.

Because, Murtaugh noticed, that was how she'd been pinned to the sofa.

Arms extended, unable to ever pour tea again, fastened with long, graceful needles (hat pins, Murtaugh wondered, like his mother had worn?)—fastened cleanly, artfully, so there was only a buckle in the plastic slipcover and a slight trickle of crimson, like a ribbon at her palms.

The motif—for there was something decorative about the composition of Rose Walsh's corpse—was repeated at the feet, where ankles were modestly, coquettishly, crossed and pinned together in the same manner.

From the side, you could see that the body lurched forward slightly. The Sergeant guessed she'd been moved to the sofa after being killed, and that rigor mortis had set her into forced angles.

It was the face which spoiled the general picture of tranquillity. Rose Walsh was smiling: orange lipstick smearing past her mouth in a repulsive, almost suggestive smirk; the amber blood in its creases like some fashionable cosmetic which might be featured on the pages of a magazine.

Her hair was shoulder length, dishtowel white, and she was wearing one of those stretchy headbands popular in the sixties—thick and pink against her forehead.

The eyes, probably quite protrudent in life, now popped out, cartoon-style, as if to say, look at my necklace, look at my necklace.

Murtaugh knew it wasn't a necklace, but in a crazy way the slender needles, with their pearly tops dotting Mrs. Walsh's thin, so vulnerably thin neck, gave her an elegance which the out-of-date headband and brightly colored housedress couldn't.

"Jesus," Bonelli muttered. "Never thought to see anything like this in Hoboken."

The Sergeant merely nodded, as if this was something profound.

"Those pins look like the kind used to secure wigs. They may even have belonged to the deceased, because she's got a curly number on a Styrofoam stand in the bedroom upstairs. Not an exact match, but . . ." Lowenstein shrugged.

"They what killed her?"

Lowenstein took off his glasses and wiped them with spit.

God, Murtaugh thought, why was it these Pathology guys were always such slobs?

He watched as the glasses were adjusted again. "I'd say they were put in later. See how the blood has congealed, here and here?"

The detective turned away from the body. "Any idea about time of death?" he asked.

"For now, let's put it at between nine and midnight." He gave Murtaugh a mock salute. "I'll call you. We'll do lunch."

Bonelli wrote furiously in his pad while Murtaugh walked around the room, stepping aside for the men who were settling into the lull of their duties.

A phrase from some old movie keep going through his mind: "The room had not been disturbed."

Once again, the Sergeant fought to keep from smiling. *This* room had never been disturbed. People like Rose Walsh and her husband went through life just making ends meet. They scrimped and saved to buy a roomful of furniture, then they covered it with a vinyl dropcloth and never went near it.

Murtaugh wouldn't have been surprised if the first time Rose sat on that sofa had been her last time.

Bonelli appeared at his side. "The husband's in the kitchen."

"What's his story?"

"They had a disagreement last night. Nothing new, according to a Mrs. Libretti across the street. He left around nine—can't say exactly—and spent the night wandering the streets."

"Wandering?"

"He's a real mess." Murtaugh was conscious of Bonelli's embarrassment, although he didn't understand it.

"Name?"

"Patrick Walsh. Retired."

They stood in the hallway now, within clear view of the kitchen. Cops and the medical examiner people were milling around; and at the table, head bowed so low it almost touched the Formica, sat the dead woman's husband.

"Retired from what?" Murtaugh asked, automatically feeling in his pocket for a cigarette. He wouldn't light up until he got outside, but somehow the touch of the cellophane, the proximity of it to his fingers, relaxed him.

Bonelli smiled for the first time. "That's a debatable question, Hunt. The neighbors can't remember him ever holding a job, and him—he hasn't given too many straight answers."

It wasn't until Murtaugh got close to the man that he discovered the cause for Bonelli's discomfort. With the tact of someone avoiding the word "fat" in the presence of obesity, Bonelli was skirting the fact that Patrick Walsh was so drunk he could barely stand, although he made an attempt to do so when Murtaugh introduced himself.

"Have a seat, Mr. Walsh. I realize this has been a shock."

The man swayed visibly, but looked the detective straight in the eye as if to dare him to mention his condition. It was a trick Murtaugh occasionally used himself.

"I'm fine, Sergeant. You sit, if you feel the need."

Murtaugh fingered the cellophane. He couldn't have a drink, but he might have a cigarette, only the room was too claustrophobic, too filled with this man's breath and the smell of cooking and violent death.

"I believe you found your wife, Mr. Walsh."

Patrick Walsh began to cry, his rheumy eyes and red nose, his whiskey breath and long limbs all turning liquid at once. He sat.

"A sainted woman. Who could have done such a thing, Sergeant?" His head went limp. "Forty-three years of married bliss, and I tell you in all that time, she never done nothin' to no one. A saint. A Christian martyr, she was."

Murtaugh was certain, at that moment, that Patrick Walsh had hated his wife.

"I know this is painful for you, but could you tell me exactly what happened last night?"

The muscles in Walsh's face hardened involuntarily. He looked angry, cranky as a child. But when he caught Murtaugh's determined inflection, he covered his first impulse.

"I've told your partner there everything I know," he whined. "He wrote every bit of it down, too."

"I realize that, Mr. Walsh," the Sergeant said evenly. "But I'd like to hear it in your own words. I know you want to help us find out who did this terrible thing."

Walsh simpered as he shifted in his seat. "A real saint. Anyone'll tell you."

Murtaugh turned his head in the direction of two men who had just finished dusting the kitchen for prints.

"Give us a minute?"

They left, and Bonelli followed them out, with a sympathetic nod toward the old man.

The counter was caked with crumbs and the rings from coffee cups. Rose Walsh hadn't been much of a housekeeper.

Shanty Irish, to use his mother's words. And everyone knew there was a world of difference between Shanty Irish and Lace Curtain Irish. As poor as they were, the Murtaughs always had clean curtains in the windows and a good linen tablecloth for company.

His mother had called him Hunter because it sounded to her like the name of someone who would be successful. She hadn't lived long enough to know what a burden the name would be for a cop.

"You were saying, Mr. Walsh. About last night." Murtaugh moved to the cabinet area.

He knew he would get nowhere by crowding this man. Walsh was one of those drunks who could get belligerent and mask it under a guise of illness or fatigue.

The old bugger began to cry again. Crocodile tears fell in blobs onto his rumpled shirt.

"Please, Mr. Walsh. Let's just try to remember. What did you do last night?"

"I went out," he sniffled.

"About what time was that?" Murtaugh asked, feigning interest in the china cabinet with its spindly glasses, mementos from weddings etched in ghostly letters. "Frank and Irene. March 14, 1963."

"Nine, or a bit earlier, I think."

"And that was the last time you saw your wife alive?"

The man leaned forward on thin elbows. His flesh clung in loose folds around the bone. "I never thought I wouldn't see her again . . . I never knew it would be the last time."

Murtaugh believed him.

"And us having words, and not even a right good-bye at all."

Poor bastard. He found himself annoyed that this sniveling wreck had sparked something in him he hadn't felt for months. Compassion.

"Mr. Walsh—"

"It's Paddy, sir. Just Paddy."

"Paddy. You and your wife argued last night. Can you tell me what it was about?"

Walsh lifted his head, and his face was flushed an obscene red by the sunlight that streamed through the picture window behind him.

"Ahh, that signified nothing," he said, as he wiped his eyes with the back of his hand. "She was only perturbed on account of my not keeping up with the chores, that's all. She was edgy, so I took off."

He began to cry again, but this time Murtaugh was sure it was simply for effect.

21

"Where did you go, Paddy? Where did you go so late at night?"

"Only walking. I like to walk," Walsh said defensively. "Is there anything wrong with that?"

"No," Murtaugh assured him, all the while rubbing the cellophane pacifier in his pocket. "I'm just trying to get everything straight. Could you help me, do you think?"

Walsh softened. "Sure. Sure. I'll do what I can. That's what I told your man before. I'll do what I can."

Murtaugh sat across from him. "Did anyone see you last night? After you left here?"

The old man hesitated, as if to weigh the consequences of the truth.

"Well," he said, in a confidential tone, "I stopped into the tavern on the corner for a little."

"That's Paulie's?"

"Sure. I know the bartender. Dominick. Grand fellow."

"So you stopped for a talk with Dominick," Murtaugh coaxed him.

Walsh beamed. "Yes. I stopped for a talk."

"And what was doing there?" the Sergeant asked easily.

"Ahh, not much." Paddy was speaking freely now, realizing perhaps that no sharp voice would ever reprimand him again.

"We watched the game, you know, sat around shootin' the breeze for a while, till Dom closed down."

"He closes about two, doesn't he?" Murtaugh smiled genially at the man, knowing if he got past this, they'd be home free. "I've often thought what this town needs is a good after-hours place, know what I mean? For those times when you're just not ready to go home."

Walsh was still drunk enough not to realize the impropriety of his wink. "Do I ever. It was a terrible warm night last night, if you remember. A devil for sleeping, especially since herself can't stand air conditioners, and the fan she says makes too much noise. That's why I decided to stay out in the open air."

"Really?" Murtaugh tried to picture him sacked out on some bench in the park, using his thin jacket to shield the six-pack, a sort of rustic pillow, a security blanket. "Camping out, were you?"

Paddy Walsh grinned. "Slept like a babe." Then, remembering his dead wife in the other room, he added, "And never knowing that poor woman was being . . . being murdered in her own parlor."

"We don't know that it happened in the parlor, Mr. Walsh. There's a possibility that she was—set there—after."

"Murdered in her bed? Could it be true? Ahh, if only I'd come home. If only I'd let the silly quarrel run its course—"

Murtaugh knew this tangent would take the man too close to the edge.

He cut him short. "I doubt you could have done anything to stop the killer we're dealing with, Paddy."

Walsh looked grateful. "Then I'm not at fault?"

Murtaugh sidestepped his question by putting another one to him. "What time did you say you found your wife?"

"A little after ten this morning, I'd think."

"Now, Paddy, no matter how soundly you sleep in the great out-of-doors, it's hard to believe you got up that late."

He hung his head, this time a little sheepishly. "You're a smart man, Sergeant, and a man of the world, too, I can see. So I don't mind telling you that I was guilty of indulging in an eye-opener this morning. Just to get the juices flowing."

And the courage up, so you might have nerve enough to face the old bitch, Murtaugh thought.

He said very softly, "What happened, Paddy, when you came home this morning?"

Paddy ducked his head again. Murtaugh could hear gurgling

sounds. "Take your time . . . try to remember everything."

"I didn't see her at first. I walked in, and I didn't even see her."

Murtaugh backtracked. "The door, Paddy. Was the door open, or did you use your key?"

"Huh?" The man looked as if he'd been roused from a stupor. "The door? Yes, it was open."

"And you didn't think that was unusual?"

Walsh seemed to relax. He could think about the door, and the keys, and the mundane objects in his home; they didn't bother him. It was only when he thought of his wife, fastened to the sofa like a puppet, that the tears came. And yet Murtaugh knew they weren't tears of grief.

He shook his head. "No, no, we always left the door unlocked during the day. Wasn't till the Spics moved in that we locked up a'tall."

"So you opened the door and walked into the foyer without looking into the living room?"

"That's right," Paddy told him, on the defensive again. "We never used the parlor much. I wouldn't 'a thought to look for her there. But then I wasn't looking anyway. I just had a mind to fix myself a cup of coffee, so I come right here in the kitchen."

"Did you notice anything? Anything that would suggest to you that someone had been in the house?"

"Nothing." They both knew he'd been too drunk.

"Did you notice anything later?"

"No, sir."

"All right." Murtaugh walked behind the table and peered into the yard.

The Walshes weren't gardeners either. The only thing that caught his attention was a large structure, perhaps once a carriage house, now covered with cheap siding. He made a mental note to have it checked out, if it hadn't been already.

He smiled encouragingly at the man next to him. "Can you remember what happened after you came into the kitchen?"

"I put the coffee on and sat for a bit while it got hot. Then Daisy started to bothering me."

"Daisy?"

"Her dog." He turned around in the chair to indicate a bloated old mongrel lying so still in the hot sun that Murtaugh hadn't even noticed her.

"I thought it was wantin' its breakfast, and that's not my department. But the damn animal kept pestering me, so I opened the door, and what does it do but go all over the floor."

He looked at a patch of linoleum where the Sergeant was standing. Murtaugh moved away.

Walsh continued. "Well, that was the last straw. I went calling for herself to clean up after the mutt, but I couldn't get no answer nohow."

"What made you look in the parlor?"

"I didn't set out to. I was deciding whether to go for another walk. The house smelt like hell in this heat, and I was damned if I was gonna clean it up."

Murtaugh interrupted. "You noticed her on your way out?"

Paddy looked up. His face was still red, but something in his expression had changed.

Murtaugh thought, the man is scared to death.

"Not really noticed," Walsh said slowly. "I guess you might say it was more like . . . like when you're walking down the street and you feel someone starin' at you. 'Course the strange thing was, she wasn't starin' really. I mean, she couldn't actually *see*, could she?"

"Did you touch anything?" Murtaugh asked, in a soothing tone.

"Huh?" Walsh blinked with bloodshot eyes. "No, I didn't. The dog did, I think. Brushed her with its tongue, right where she was fastened, you know . . . at the ankle . . ."

"Paddy, is there someone you'd like me to call? Someone who can come and stay with you?"

"I don't need nobody." Paddy Walsh stiffened. "There's no one."

Murtaugh was silent for a few seconds. He was trying to formulate a final question. In the interim, he imagined the old man, left alone in Number 518, with a decrepit dog, puffy with water weight, an animal he hated.

He leaned across the table so that he was nose to nose with Walsh.

"Why do you think this happened to Rose, Paddy?"

He'd avoided asking whether the woman had enemies. From this day on, the husband who had despised her in life would canonize her in death.

Paddy opened his owl eyes and stared at Murtaugh. "She was too smart, that's all. They never knew that she was too smart."

Murtaugh was intrigued. "Who never knew, Paddy?"

Walsh looked confused. The interview was over. He'd probably been fortunate to get this much out of the old bastard.

It was unbearably hot in the house now, the temperature outside having climbed past one hundred degrees for the third time in as many days. Bonelli met him at the arch to the living room, where the body was about to be moved.

"Pathetic, huh?" Lou remarked, indicating with his head the figure in the kitchen.

Murtaugh felt giddy. He knew there were things to do, but he only wanted to get out. For the length of his conversation with Paddy Walsh, he'd forgotten about wanting a drink. Now the desire came back to him, and along with it that edge that made him feel impatient with the people around him—people who were doing their jobs with self-conscious exactness, as though there were network cameras trained on them.

The body was hurried out on its narrow stretcher.

"What do you have for me?" Murtaugh asked Bonelli. "Friends, relatives, neighbors. Possible enemies."

"She was, you know, the lady on the block everyone loved to hate. Eccentric, maybe, but not murder material."

Murtaugh laughed and clapped him on the back. "Not this kind of murder, anyway," he nodded. "Too glamorous for our Rosie. Too stylish by a mile."

Lou thought it was a tasteless way to put it, but he had to agree with Hunt. It wasn't what anyone would expect in a town like this, to a woman like this.

They watched in silence as the body was loaded into the ambulance. Lowenstein, deep in conversation with one of the reporters, spat on his glasses again.

Murtaugh seemed engrossed in the cigarette he was lighting. He repeated his question to Bonelli distractedly.

"No relatives," he replied. "No contact with anyone at all, except maybe the people on the block and the whatnot at the local taverns."

There was a shift in the crowd now that the ambulance had pulled away. A television remote crew was interviewing the inhabitants of the neighborhood. The woman with the Orange Julius hair had removed the clips and put on bright lipstick.

"Like I told the officer," she was saying, looking directly, expertly, into the camera, "in all the years I knew Rose, I never thought something like this—"

"Mrs. Libretti," Bonelli told Murtaugh.

He appeared not to hear. "Got the time?"

"It's almost noon."

"I want to check out Paulie's down the end of the block. Maybe have some lunch."

The Sergeant moved past the crowd, stopping when he

realized Bonelli hadn't fallen in with him. "Aren't you coming?"

Lou looked surprised. "You want me to go with you?"

Time was when they'd shared a few brews together, but in recent months it was understood that Hunt drank alone.

"Get it in gear. And bring your pad." Murtaugh continued down the street, pushing away the microphones that were being stuck in his face.

He wondered, vaguely, why he suddenly felt so good.

CHAPTER

3

THE DOOR to Paulie's was open, its barroom darkness leaving a seductive patch of shade on the sidewalk. The air-conditioning wasn't working. Three old men sat at the bar, a stool between each of their own, drinking beer and pretending to look at the television.

They picked a table near the door. Bonelli studied his notes while Murtaugh went to the bar to place an order. Lou made a conscious effort not to give Hunt the impression he was watching him too closely. Still, he couldn't help noticing that Hunt downed a shot as he stood elbow to elbow with the bartender.

"They have three kinds. Ham. Cheese. And ham and cheese," Murtaugh announced happily, putting a tray on the table.

Lou took the cheese. It was Friday, and old habits died hard in these neighborhoods.

"Find out anything?"

"Only that our friend Paddy was here from about nine until

29

two last night, and he came in again at eight this morning."
Murtaugh was eating as though he hadn't tasted food in a long
time. "Pretty much his usual hours it sounds like. Who else
have we got?"

Bonelli read down the list.

"The Walshes' downstairs tenant is a Martin Fellows. Mrs.
Libretti says he's one of them homosexuals." He pronounced
the word self-consciously, as though it tainted his tongue, then
hurried on. "Some kind of lighting designer in New York. He
usually gets back about seven."

"They own the building, then?"

"It was left to Rose by her mother."

"Check into that," Murtaugh said, pouring them both more
beer. "Money. Wills. The whole nine yards."

Bonelli shrugged and made a note. "Don't expect 'em to
have the crown jewels stashed away, do you, Hunt?"

Murtaugh said, "You never know. What about the neighbors?"

"Number 516's owned by a couple. Jake Florian and, uh,"
he flipped through the pad, "Rebecca Lincroft."

"Married? Living together?"

"Married. You know the type that keep separate names.
They bought the building two years ago and had it completely
redone. That's his line. Architecture. She owns one of them
highfalutin stores on Washington. In at seven, too, unless they
meet for dinner somewhere, which supposedly they do a lot,
according to the Libretti dame."

"What's her store called?"

Bonelli said, "The March Hare. You figure it."

"Lewis Carroll." Murtaugh picked up another sandwich.

"Haven't come across that name yet, Hunt," Bonelli told
him as he scribbled furiously. "I thought she owned it herself."

"Forget it," the Sergeant replied, his mouth full. "It's not
important."

Bonelli resumed his reading, hoping that Hunt wouldn't interrupt with another strange comment.

"Florian and his wife rent their basement to another couple. Been there maybe a couple of months. Uh, Oakley and Dana Hall. He works for a magazine in the City. She's some kind of artist. By the way, she's usually at home so you might want to—"

"What does Mrs. Libretti have to say about them?"

Bonelli raised his eyebrows. "Only that Mrs. Hall is a few years older than the mister." He took a sip of beer to give Murtaugh a moment to absorb that salient point before going on. "Number 520, upstairs and down, are two widows. Mrs. Cappricio. Semi-invalid in her nineties. And Madie Quinn—she's downstairs—who says Rose and Paddy kept her up all hours with their shouting."

Murtaugh lit another cigarette. "A real promising bunch."

"It gets better across the street."

"What? Something hot and heavy between Paddy and the Libretti woman?"

Bonelli laughed. It was good talking to Hunt this way. It was like old times.

"Naa. But next to the Librettis, Number 519, there's a couple by the name of Rothman. He's one of those new bankers that tell you where to put your money. She used to play tennis. They got a kid . . . a girl, maybe three or four years old."

"What's the connection?"

"Well, Mrs. Libretti overheard Rose arguing with David Rothman last week. She was out walking her mutt, and when she sees the guy, she starts wagging her finger in front of his nose. Classic stuff. You know, 'I know what you're up to, and if you don't watch your step, I'm gonna tell what's goin' on . . .'"

"Tell *who* what's going on?"

"His wife, I guess. Libretti thinks Rothman fools around.

He's out most nights until late, leaving wifey waiting for him."

Murtaugh took a bite of the last sandwich, tilting his head pensively as he chewed. "So you think Rothman had motive?"

He remembered Rose Walsh, skewered to her own sofa. In his mind he saw the pins, carefully, almost delicately placed, braceleting wrists and ankles, draping her neck in a pearly chokecollar.

Bonelli seemed to read his thoughts. "Motive, maybe. But whether he'd do something like *that* . . ."

He was nervously pulling at the wire spine of his notebook. "There are some kids living in the prewar on this end who might be more what we're looking for. Puerto Ricans."

"You're talking about the place next to the Quiles' building?"

"Yeah. A group of 'em. Fifteen or sixteen years old, tops."

"A gang?"

"More like a cult," Bonelli said.

Murtaugh looked up, suddenly alert. "What do you mean, a cult?"

Bonelli was cautious. "Take it with a grain of salt. It was Mrs. Libretti's word. She said they were weirdos. Always high, mumbling crazy stuff."

"Funny, I read all the neighborhood reports for the Quiles case, and I don't remember any mention of them."

Bonelli leaned forward in his chair. "Yeah. I noticed that, too. But when I asked Libretti, she says it was because last week she just thought of 'em as smartass punks."

Murtaugh sighed. He was all too familiar with the shifting allegiances in these neighborhoods.

"So what happened since then to change her mind?"

"They cut up her cat," Bonelli said, and he closed the notebook.

* * *

In front of the building, two women sat watching several children play ball.

Murtaugh's Spanish was so halting, the younger one stopped him before he'd finished his sentence.

"Jaime Sanchez?" She was wearing a crimson sundress, cut low enough to show a plump bosom and short enough to reveal slender legs.

Like a bird, Murtaugh thought, a small, round bird with a red breast.

"The Jaime I'm looking for is about sixteen years old. His friends hang out on this block," he said, catching his voice before it raised to a shout. A lousy habit, speaking to these people as if they were deaf.

The woman nodded with her sweet, sparrow face. "Jaime Sanchez." She pointed to the small neighborhood park beyond Paulie's. "There. They go watch the basketball."

As he thanked her, Murtaugh felt a ball come soaring past him. He lunged to make the catch and missed. It bounced over the railing and into the bushes.

Jesus, Murtaugh, he thought. Your reflexes are shot to hell. And you need glasses.

"Sorry," he said to the little boy who had thrown it. He couldn't, for the life of him, remember what the word was in Spanish.

The park was a project of the fifties when the town first decided that kids needed a place other than the streets to play. Murtaugh wasn't sure it had been a good idea. Hoboken's parks were the stamping ground for more trouble than the asphalt playgrounds of his youth ever were.

It was the hottest part of the day, but every court was filled.

Murtaugh found Jaime Sanchez and his friends leaning on the wire fencing that surrounded the playing areas. They stood apart from the other spectators, not really watching the game in progress.

Each boy wore black; and despite the temperature, the tallest had on a leather jacket embroidered with a geometric design.

A band of witches, Murtaugh said to himself, as he strolled around the fence in their direction. Black hair, black eyes, black clothes, all framing pasty-white skin. Or was it makeup? Murtaugh couldn't be sure, except about one thing. These little fellows were not happy puppies. And they weren't the kind of kids you'd relish meeting on a deserted street, even in your dreams.

"Jaime Sanchez?" he asked, looking from one to the other.

There was no answer, but rather a shift in the group, a parting, so the tall boy stood alone. He shrugged.

Murtaugh presented his shield. "Sergeant Murtaugh."

Still the same stony silence.

The detective grew impatient. "Now it's your turn, Jaime. Introduce me to your pals."

Jaime's face distorted with anger. He looked as if he might spit in Murtaugh's face. Instead, he spoke in a monotone, indicating them by extending a long arm.

"Ricky Rodriguez . . . Miguel Herrara . . . Emil Velasquez . . ."

Murtaugh forced himself to look away from Jaime's hand, and his long-nailed pinky, lacquered in silver. He tried to connect the names with each sulky, staring face.

Ricky. Small and compact. The kind of kid who'd attract all the wild girls. Miguel, in a tank top that showed off his powerful build. Emil, only about thirteen, with the first fuzz of a moustache sprouting over his pouty upper lip.

Each had a different face and a different body. But their eyes, dull as black buttons on a rag doll, were remarkably the same. Nowhere in them was there the tiniest reflection of the summer sun. When a shark went in for the kill, translucent lids automatically cloaked its pupils, Murtaugh recalled. The thought made him vaguely uneasy.

The Sergeant motioned them toward a bench. "I want to talk to you about Rose Walsh."

He sensed a ripple of tension pass through them, so tentative it might have seemed a breeze if the heat were not unrelenting.

"Can't talk about somebody I don't know," Jaime said.

"Okay, then. Talk to me about Mrs. Libretti's cat."

Murtaugh was finding it difficult to keep from squinting in the harsh light, but Sanchez's gaze was steady.

"Don't know no *cats* either." He sauntered to the bench and sat, making a great show of his casualness.

The other boys snickered.

Murtaugh smiled, too. "Now that's funny, because Mrs. Libretti seems to think otherwise. She says you used to know her cat pretty well. Did you notice that I said, *used to*? That's because, according to her, a few nights ago you and your buddies here had a barbecue in her backyard."

Jaime became intent on removing a small thread from his jacket.

"*Look at me*," Murtaugh said. His voice was low, but something in it made the boy sit up stiffly.

"Mrs. Libretti says you cut up her cat and roasted its innards. She says when she woke up the next day, Fluffy was all over the garden, and his sweet little heart had been burned."

Jaime turned his dead eyes on the Sergeant and whispered, "Yeah, so what if it was? Nothin' says anybody here did it."

Murtaugh rose. The other boys made a path for him as he walked behind the bench.

"Nothing much, Jaime. Only they found something when they were collecting up the pieces of poor Fluffy, here and there. On the dirt, near the tomato plants, they said someone had drawn a picture with a stick."

Murtaugh paused, then he clapped Jaime Sanchez on the back with his big hands and said, "It looked an awful lot like that thing you've got on your jacket."

* * *

It was going to take a lot more than a dead cat to prove that Jaime and his friends had killed Rose Walsh. For one thing, they appeared to have an alibi. For what it was worth.

Jaime told him they'd been playing cards at Emil's sister's place. At about eleven o'clock they'd gone to a local club called Zoots to listen to the music. They stayed until two.

When Murtaugh remarked that it was a long time just to listen to music, the boy had only blinked his black eyes and said that, being under the drinking age, they could do nothing else. The detective understood his words were a kind of dare. Jaime cared nothing for laws. Now all Murtaugh had to do was to find out precisely which laws he and the gang had already broken.

He climbed up the stairs of Number 519 with the sinking feeling that Sanchez's story would be corroborated, true or not.

His mind kept returning to the image of Rose on the sofa, only now he thought also about a dismembered cat and a little boy missing for eight days.

What, if anything, was the connection?

The bell was answered by a tall blonde woman in her early thirties.

"Janis Rothman?"

She nodded. Murtaugh produced his shield, but it was only when she'd invited him into the living room that he recognized her.

"Janis Gillmore," he said.

She murmured softly, "I used to be."

The woman before him had a lean, bony face which didn't smile easily. Perhaps many people would read aloofness in its spare lines. Murtaugh guessed by the way her eyes momentarily sparked and then looked away that Janis Gillmore Rothman's cool was only the protective instinct of a painfully shy person.

"I was a fan of yours," Murtaugh told her. Then, impulsively, he decided to probe the wound again.

"Well, it was my wife, really. She . . . she enjoyed tennis a great deal, and she managed to get me interested."

There was an uncomfortable pause. It occurred to Murtaugh that they were both dealing with a very personal pain.

He continued, more briskly than before. "Do you still play?"

Janis Gillmore Rothman bowed her head just enough to let a strand of limp, babyfine hair fall across the face that, when it had been tanned and shining with perspiration, half of America had fallen in love with.

"No," she said. "Not very often."

A piercing shriek came from upstairs.

Murtaugh saw patches of red appear on the prominent cheekbones, like the sunburn of past days. He watched Mrs. Rothman's thin hands grasp the sofa until her knuckles were white.

"What's the matter, Melissa?" she called. Her voice was hollow, drained of any emotion or comfort.

The shrieking continued, coming closer now. Melissa Rothman entered the room wagging a coloring book in her chubby fists. The book had been torn almost to shreds.

"I went out of the lines! I went out of the lines!" the child wailed.

Janis held out her arms, robot-like, and said, "Now you know that doesn't matter, Melissa. You know I told you that was all right."

37

The child seemed to grow calmer. But when she noticed Murtaugh, the shrieking began again. This time, her mother pulled her so close that the Sergeant felt sure there'd be pinch marks left on her daughter's skin.

Mrs. Rothman was not maternal.

Well, he supposed it wasn't a prerequisite for motherhood. Eve had been a maternal woman. Murtaugh thought, not for the first time, of that baby they'd talked so much about having. In the future. Back when they both believed they'd have a future.

"Melissa, listen to me," Janis told her screaming daughter. "Mommy needs to talk to this man here, so you go into the kitchen and put on the television. You go watch your programs, okay?"

Melissa picked up her book, and with a last shudder of tears, turned and ran out of the room.

"She's a perfectionist, same as I was," Janis said. Her voice was bitter. "Can't stand to do anything wrong."

He remembered seventeen-year-old Janis Gillmore bounding up to the net for a victory handshake. What had happened?

She was talking in a rush of stillborn words, conceived in warmth but issuing cold and dead from her lips. ". . . iced tea if you'd like. I don't know what's wrong with the air-conditioning. It seems to be blowing the heat into the house. You've probably gotten used to it, though, what with the commotion across the street."

Murtaugh looked vaguely amused. "Commotion? Yes, I guess murder is as big a commotion as anyone encounters in life."

He leaned forward. "Did you know Mrs. Walsh?"

"Know?"

It was difficult to tell whether her alarm was due to tension or was simply a result of the idea that there could possibly be a link between someone like herself and old Rose.

"Any contact with her at all?"

"No, not really," Janis said. "Except maybe to say hello. Sometimes she let Melissa pet that dog of hers."

Murtaugh sat back in his chair, as if lost in thought.

"Strange . . .," he said softly.

They remained in silence until Janis couldn't stand it anymore.

"I suppose you mean—at least, I hear she died in some sort of horrible way."

She rose to straighten a crayon drawing which was on the mantel of the fireplace. All of the colors were neatly within the lines.

When she turned again, it was only to conclude with cocktail-party brightness, "It's hard to imagine the kind of person who could do something so . . . evil."

Murtaugh jerked to attention.

She'd said it. She'd said the word.

There would be no shyster lawyers this time. No hit-and-run justice. Rose Walsh's murder was a case of undiluted evil. And for Murtaugh—suddenly, clearly—what was good stood out, in sharp relief. It didn't matter if this hopeful feeling was fleeting. After all these months, that he could feel hope at all was enough.

Mrs. Rothman had stopped talking and was staring at him. Her face showed signs of strain.

"I'm sorry. You were saying—?" he inquired.

"Nothing. Only that I called to tell my husband to see if he'd come home early. He . . . he was in a meeting," she told him, averting her eyes. "But I know this will upset him."

Murtaugh picked up the ball. "He was a particular friend of Mrs. Walsh?"

"Oh, no." The suggestion seemed to strike her as funny. "I mean, he knew who she was. I just thought he'd want to know about something like this happening on our street."

Some new expression crossed her face. Irony? Humor?

"By tonight, David will have figured out if it's going to damage property values."

It was Murtaugh's turn to walk to the mantel. "Have you lived in Hoboken long, Mrs. Rothman?"

She shrugged. "About two years."

He gestured around the room, a room as elegantly un-domestic as she. "You must have had your work cut out for you. Turning an old house like this into such a beautiful home."

She flushed, obviously displeased. "That was David's doing."

Murtaugh would have asked permission to smoke, but there were no ashtrays in the room.

"Well, I won't keep you," he said. "We're just making the rounds trying to see if anyone has any information that would throw some light on what happened last night."

Janis Rothman reached for a pillow on the overstuffed sofa. Her hand was visibly shaking.

"Last night?" she asked, as if from a great distance. "But I thought it happened this morning—"

"What gave you that idea?"

For the second time in one day, Murtaugh watched as someone pulled at the thread of a fabric. Earlier it was leather, this time a brightly patterned fabric.

"I only thought—" Janis explained. "Because it was so late in the morning when the police came."

Murtaugh shook his head. "Mr. Walsh didn't discover the body until today."

When she looked away, he pressed on. "Did you notice anything unusual in the neighborhood yesterday? An unfa-miliar car? Some kind of noise, maybe?"

Janis pushed a strand of hair from her eyes. "There are always so many cars on this block. And with the air-condi-tioning, we don't hear anything outside."

His tone was paternal now. "What about your husband? Did he mention anything to you?"

"David wasn't home last night."

The words tumbled out before she could collect them. They hung in the air. Bold. Indiscreet. Embarrassing.

"I see," the detective said.

"My husband is a workaholic, Sergeant," she told him, with a forced smile. "He's home late every night. And if he did notice anything, he mustn't have thought it important enough to mention—but then you didn't tell me what time Rose was murdered."

Murtaugh noticed her use of the victim's first name, as well as the way she'd tried to force his hand.

All right, he thought. Fifteen-love.

Out loud he said, "At this early stage of the game we're projecting it was somewhere between nine and midnight."

Janis Rothman's shoulders relaxed, and when she smiled again, it was open and sincere.

"I'm afraid David won't be able to tell you anything then. He was in New York until ten," she told him. "After that, he was here, watching television with me."

* * *

On his way to the door, Murtaugh stopped to admire a photograph of the young Janis Gillmore, racket in hand.

Her mood had become expansive.

"Does your wife play?" she asked, noticing his interest.

Murtaugh dug down for the ball of cellophane, neglected for hours at the bottom of his pocket.

"I lost my wife in a car accident several months ago."

He hurried on, anxious to avoid the mandatory polite condolences. "She used to enjoy playing, though. Even tried to teach me. But you know what they say about old dogs."

41

She looked puzzled.

"I guess you could say it was too late for me to learn any new tricks," he told her.

Janis Gillmore Rothman nodded with something akin to perfect understanding.

"Yes, I know," she said, as she let him out the front door. "It's the same with David and me.

CHAPTER

4

THE FEELING of well-being which had accompanied him
since morning evaporated. On the pavement in front of the
Rothman house, he felt drained. He knew Janis' penetrating
eyes were watching him through the cracks of the oak shutters,
and at that moment he didn't care that what she saw was a
tired, middle-aged man who obviously wasn't sure of where
he was going next.

He lit a cigarette and drifted with the smoke toward the
other end of the block.

These rowhouses were as meticulously cared for as the
Rothmans'.

Mid-block and up near Paulie's, the older inhabitants still
kept shrines to the Virgin, or statues of Saint Francis, speckled
with bird droppings, on their tiny lawns. It was a simple
statement of faith, Murtaugh decided. A belief that, no matter
how narrow the patch of grass, how polluted the air, it was
put there by design, not accident.

Here, where watermarked aluminum awnings had been replaced by real canvas, striped in colonial shades of cream and blue and brick red, there was less faith and more determination at work. It was a distinctively big-city style of gardening—huge planters of sculpted concrete and wrought iron seeming to defy the ugly urban environment by being beautiful in spite of it.

Look what man hath wrought, thought Murtaugh wryly, and behold, how it's better.

The Sergeant counted four windows with building permits displayed. New plumbing, gutted walls, finished basements.

Yes, Hoboken was really turning around. Standing at this end of the block and looking down, it was like being on the goddamn threshold of the future.

A future that was doing very nicely, thank you, without the help of Sergeant Hunter Murtaugh. At exactly what point had he fallen out of step? Losing Eve had made him realize it, but hadn't it actually been long before that?

Maybe you're just one of those people doomed to slip between the cracks, Murtaugh told himself. Not quite content with the old guard, not quite cut out for the new.

All his life it seemed he'd been torn, shunted back and forth between the two.

"Hunter Francis Murtaugh, you can accomplish anything your heart desires," Sister Mary Elizabeth had said to him on the day he won the scholarship to Saint Peter's.

And young Hunter, never doubting for a moment, had replied simply, "I know, Sister."

But his heart's desire, a scholarship—the result of hours of careful planning, weeks of slaving over an essay under Sister's critical eye, and months of glorious anticipation—would have to be shelved.

He had joined the Marine Corps to fight for democracy in a place called Viet Nam, a speck on the map no bigger than

44

New Jersey. It seemed the right thing to do. The thing his father would have done. No Murtaugh had ever gone to college. He didn't suppose college would miss him.

Sister Mary Elizabeth had been quiet for a long while after he told her. He remembered thinking she must be praying, until he heard the anger in her voice. "Go with God," she said finally.

By the time he reached the door she had overtaken him with loping, ungainly strides.

"I won't let you waste that mind," she warned. Then she did something he'd always remember. She hugged him so tightly the points of her thin shoulder blades hurt his cheek. Hunter knew this show of affection had cost her something. Sister Mary Elizabeth was more at ease caning a student than comforting him.

"When you come back," she said, with a spark of the old nunnish jauntiness, "I'll get you into college yet."

But even then, he knew if he returned in one piece it wouldn't be to go to school. He wanted to be a cop. A cop in the old neighborhood, the one where his father had grown up.

Murtaugh stopped to light another cigarette. Two women in shorts and sweatsoaked T-shirts sauntered by silently, splitting up when they came to him, one on one side, one on the other, as though he were a tree growing on the sidewalk.

Could it be his imagination, or did people really talk more when he was a kid? Everyone had a word for him then. Shopkeepers, and strangers on the street, somehow always knew he was James Murtaugh's son, Jamey and Mag's boy.

They couldn't pass without stopping to recount how Jamey pitched a ball better than anybody who'd ever graduated from Saint Catherine's and pinching his cheek purple because he was the living image of his dad. They made him sit in the booth where his father once spooned icecream sodas (vanilla) and pointed out the spots where he'd proposed to young Maggie (she refused him twice).

Talk made it seem as though no one ever died in Hoboken. It was as if when you walked into a place, they'd just left. As if they were always in another part of town from where you were.

Sometimes he thought that was why he'd wanted to be a cop. Being a cop gave him a reason to patrol the neighborhoods, to keep an eye on them, to see they remained the same.

So, after his stint in the Corps he left one losing battle to join another. A pattern had emerged: an almost Pavlovian response to hopeless situations, as though, and here he shook his head at his own naïveté, there were really something noble about lost causes.

Eve always listened patiently to his exploits, kissing him on the head with a loving, albeit resigned, smile.

You made the right choice, Murtaugh, she'd say, but you may not have made the smart one.

Take the Hispanics. Young Murtaugh had ruffled more than a few feathers at Headquarters with his policy of calling a spade a spade and a bigot a bigot. He was sure the Cubans and Puerto Ricans would assimilate into the community with time. And he believed he could help them. By weeding out the bad, encouraging the good.

You arrogant bastard, the detective muttered, drawing hard on his cigarette. As if everyone existed solely as a challenge to Hunter Murtaugh, protector of this neat mile-by-a-mile world.

All those good intentions flew out the window pretty fast when a couple of the bad ones destroyed your life, didn't they?

Maybe his entire existence up until the day Eve died was nothing more than one long balancing act—on his toes, holster strapped to his chest for ballast, dancing on the narrow fence-post that separated the racists and law-and-order freaks from a netherworld of seamy lawyers and street animals. Now that she was gone, he couldn't remember why it had seemed so important to keep his balance.

"Can I help you, buddy?"

Murtaugh looked up, attempting to locate the speaker. "What's that?"

A young man had raised one of the squeaky-clean, second-floor windows of the brownstone in front of which Murtaugh stood. He leaned out over a stenciled windowbox, and adjusting his tortoiseshell glasses, peered through the peonies.

"Can I help you?" repeated the strident voice.

Murtaugh wondered what had kept this fellow at home today. A cold? A lover?

"No," the Sergeant answered, "I don't think you can."

"Then I'd appreciate it if you moved on," the man said, adding more authoritatively, "This is private property."

As silly as the taunt sounded, it was all the detective could do to keep from yelling back, in the same childish tone, that the sidewalk belonged to the public. Instead, he stubbed out his cigarette on the well-swept curb and walked away.

There was a delicious irony to it, the idea that *he* was trespassing on *their* territory. Hadn't he felt this same mix of distrust and distaste before, from Eve's friends?

He remembered how they'd spike the most ordinary conversation with pointed references to people and places he'd never heard of; posing questions by way of a reminder that his presence among them was a social fluke, an accident of marriage.

When he thought about them, his polite responses to their less-than-innocent inquiries could still make him cringe.

"No, Dr. Weingarten, actually Eve and I didn't meet at college," Murtaugh heard himself saying, while a voice inside

47

of him raged, No, Weingarten, you bastard. We didn't meet at Duke. I've never been to Duke. *I don't even know where fucking Duke is.*

And yet it was they—these young, attractive, ever-so-upwardly mobile urban professionals—who were clearly the interlopers, sneaking up on him unawares, while he'd been distracted by a beautiful lady. Ambushed by a member of their ranks.

He squelched the thought immediately as it passed through his mind. Eve, after all, had been different.

Different, maybe, but one of them just the same, the detective found himself admitting. Be honest with yourself— wasn't that part of the attraction?

Even to the casual observer it would have been obvious that Eve was in her element at cocktail parties and hospital charity events, at home as a fish in water. A goldfish in a regulated tank. On such occasions, Murtaugh couldn't help being struck by how right the clothes she wore were. Not flashy. Not pretentious. *Right.*

It seemed she'd always read the books others had read, seen the plays they'd seen. There were no fits and starts to a conversation when Eve was around. She understood the lingo. The rhythm of party talk.

For Murtaugh these social outings were like a hitherto uncharted circle of hell. He had the sense of being frozen in time, helplessly clutching a small plate of stuffed mushrooms and a weak drink, while yet another surgeon's wife gushed, "Isn't that fascinating—Did you hear, everybody? Mr. Murtaugh is a *policeman!*"

And then Eve would cut in adroitly, just a beat too fast, telling them that Hunt was a detective, a Sergeant, a hero with citations for bravery and—

But by then the topic of conversation had shifted.

A pity she isn't here to act as a buffer for you during the investigation. He imagined her sitting on Mrs. Rothman's elegant sofa, tactfully interrupting to smooth over something he'd just said. "My husband can be a little abrasive. What he really meant was—"

Forget it, Murtaugh. You're on your own, and, like those ugly old buildings on the end there, you're fast becoming outnumbered. He took a last look at their facades, flattened by the sun so that they appeared to be part of a painting by that guy Edward Hopper Eve liked so much.

No doubt about it. This street was the story of his life. He'd been taught, as were the old-timers, to believe in all the right things. Love of God. Love of country. Love of man, which was justice.

These yuppies, or whatever the hell they thought of themselves as, believed only in what they could see, touch, hold, and keep. What they could collect in their homes. What they could store in their bank accounts.

And they were winning.

But then why should that matter? It was too late in the game to stop identifying with the losing team, Murtaugh decided.

Turning east, the detective caught a glimpse of the old Hoboken. A vendor, his cart filled with fresh vegetables and fruit, was parked on the sidestreet, next to an open tavern door.

"Solve the murder yet, Sergeant?" the man smiled, showing even white teeth.

Murtaugh had questioned him in connection with the Quiles case.

He shook his head. "Not yet. Anything for me?"

The man threw him an apple. "They say Rose Walsh was an old drunk with some bucks in the bank. All I know is she was tight as a crab's ass. Always trying to get something cheaper. Good riddance, eh? But you keep looking for that little boy. There's where you do some good."

"Yeah, sure." Murtaugh rubbed the apple on his trousers. Apples brought good luck. He walked into the shade of the tavern.

The bartender gave him change for the telephone, along with his shot and a beer.

"Lowenstein call, Lou?"

"Late afternoon, he says," Bonelli replied.

"What else?"

"Well, Rose Walsh's money is in her name only. Could be she didn't want the old man to drink it away."

"Keep on it." Murtaugh told him about Jaime and the others. "O'Connell's Spanish is good. Have him check out their story."

Back at the bar, the detective ordered another round. His body felt heavy, on the verge of sleepiness.

And, as he rolled the cellophane in his pocket, he repeated something to himself, over and over.

It isn't pointless . . . it isn't pointless . . .

* * *

Oh, it was no secret, Madie Quinn told Murtaugh. She hadn't cared for Rose Walsh.

Yes, they'd talked, out in the yard, while Daisy and her little Toodles were doing their business, but—and at this point, Madie had lowered her voice discreetly—the Walshes didn't have any *class*.

"Well, you were in there," she said to the Sergeant. "Am I right? Wasn't it a pigsty?" She took Murtaugh's silence as a mark of his professionalism and went on, "Listen, you don't have to tell *me*. Just look at their garden."

They walked among Mrs. Quinn's manicured rosebushes.

At the root of it had been the drinking, she said. About once a week, Rose would raise such a rumpus that poor Madie was kept up till all hours. When the weather was hot like this, she confided to the detective, she'd put on her robe and come out here just to get the whole effect of the goings-on.

That was how she'd met the little artist who lived on the other side, Madie explained. She and her husband came out at night to listen, too. They'd waved and made signals across their fences.

When Murtaugh asked her about the previous evening, she reprimanded him like a forgetful child by saying, "Thursday is Bingo, Sergeant."

She'd gotten home, as usual, at eleven-thirty. It had been quiet then, and the lights were off in Number 518.

Back on the sidewalk, Murtaugh stood for a moment looking at the Walsh house. The front steps were cordoned. His men were still working.

He wondered whether Paddy was in the kitchen with Daisy, or whether he'd thought of an excuse to disappear into the quiet comfort of a neighborhood saloon.

For some reason, his eyes traveled to the top floor of Madie Quinn's building. What he saw at the open window made him shudder.

There, looking down at the street, was surely the face of death. Hair grew from it—it did, he knew, long after all other life signs ceased—hair pressed into geometric shapes of black and gray. On a skull shrouded with pink satin.

He forced himself to blink and look again. The face of death waved at him with a bony hand.

Mrs. Cappricio. The widow who lived upstairs.

He raised his arm in greeting, hoping he wasn't showing the horror he felt.

She smiled, toothlessly, mirthlessly, back at him.

Mrs. Cappricio, ancient and probably senile, must spend

the long days sitting at this window in her babypink housecoat and black hairnet, watching the world go on living.

Murtaugh knew he should see her, but he couldn't face it right now.

* * *

Dana Hall opened the door before he had a chance to ring.

She was wearing a smoke-colored pinafore, the kind of thing girls used to wear over petticoats a hundred years ago. There was a smudge of lavender chalk on her nose. She spoke immediately.

"It's Sergeant Murtaugh, isn't it? Mrs. Libretti was over to ask if you'd been here. She'll be jealous. She only got to talk to your partner," she said, bringing him into the room. "I'm afraid I'll be a disappointment. The truth is, I don't think I can tell you anything that'll be of much help."

Two large Masonite panels were set against the loveseat—the only furniture in the room that looked sturdy enough for his weight—and she moved them quickly. "Please, sit down. Now I'm not supposed to offer you a drink while you're on duty, but I can make tea."

Murtaugh searched her eyes, finding them a clear steel-gray and innocent of any double meaning.

"Nothing," he said.

Whatever he'd expected of Mrs. Hall, the lady who was several years older than the Mister, it hadn't been this.

She and Janis Rothman were probably the same age; and for conventional beauty, Mrs. Rothman was the hands-down winner. Yet Murtaugh found himself captivated by this face, round and pale as a porcelain doll's . . . by the funny-looking pinafore . . . and the inept grosgrain ribbon which let tendrils of amber hair escape onto her neck.

"Would you like to put down your fruit?" she asked, clearing a stack of books off the arm of the loveseat.

The detective looked down at his hands and saw the apple he'd been carrying, like a present taken to a party, all during these afternoon calls.

He surprised himself by saying, "Please. Take it. Maybe you can give it to Mrs. Libretti, with my apologies."

She laughed. Her mouth was crooked when it smiled. "Anything I can do for our men in uniform."

Murtaugh tried to decide the best way to begin. Dana Hall did not wait.

"We've only been here since the end of May, so I can't tell you too much about the neighborhood."

"Did you know Mr. and Mrs. Walsh?"

"We met Paddy on our first day. Oakley and I were trying to move in a big old sofa I'd bought at a thrift shop, but we couldn't get it through the door. Paddy came along and insisted on helping, even though he . . . well, he wasn't too steady on his feet."

Murtaugh nodded.

"I was afraid he was going to have a stroke. His face was purple. He was breathing hard, mumbling about people who were too stupid to measure doors. He actually offered to get a hacksaw and cut the thing in half. We said thank you, no, we were going to take it back. So off he went. But ever since, he ducks his head when he sees us on the street."

"Maybe he's afraid you're going to ask him to move something else," Murtaugh observed, with a half-smile. "What about his wife?"

"I didn't even know her name until this morning. We used to call her Mrs. Paddy. They were both kind of eccentric."

"Mrs. Quinn at 520 said you used to sit in the backyard and listen to their fights," he remarked.

A longhaired, lemon-colored cat brushed up against her legs. Dana picked it up and cradled it.

"This is Lydia," she said, kissing it on the lips. "I hate people who treat their pets like humans, don't you?"

He thought how pretty the cat's fawn fur looked next to her skin.

"Every week or so they'd both get drunk," Dana said, returning naturally to their conversation. "Pretty soon you could hear her screaming about what a bum he was, how the house was a mess, or something didn't work. That was when Paddy got out. We'd see him shuffling along past our window." She pointed to the sidewalk at eye level. "And then she'd really crank up . . . rant, sometimes for hours. At first we thought she was talking to somebody, but after, when we started going out, we realized she was alone."

"You're sure of that? Sure she didn't have visitors after Paddy left?"

Dana considered this. "Pretty sure. Sometimes it's hard to tell where sounds come from in these houses, you know, because they're linked. But Oakley and I sat on the fence one night, and we saw she was in the kitchen, yelling at some imaginary person. When she noticed us, she started screaming that we were spies . . . that she knew what we were up to . . ."

"What do you think she meant by that?"

Dana grinned that crooked grin. "Well, we *were* spying, Sergeant."

"Was that the last time you actually witnessed one of these incidents?"

She shook her head sheepishly. "It was awful of us, I know. But Oakley is going to write a novel someday. And Mrs. Paddy was such a character—she had this wonderful drunken Irish way of—" Dana stopped short. "Oh, I'm sorry. You're Irish, aren't you?"

Murtaugh smiled again. "No offense taken."

A timer went off in the kitchen.

"Do you mind?" She got up and started walking through the apartment. "Please, come on back—"

Murtaugh followed, stopping as he passed the easel. The three-room basement flat was similar to his own. In the front room, where the light wasn't bad, Dana Hall had set up her studio.

A large portfolio was propped against the fireplace, and more panels, some that had already been given a backdrop of paint, were stacked on every available inch of floorspace.

There was a portrait, a work-in-progress, on the easel. He stepped back and squinted to get a better look. The subject was a young woman with closely cropped dark hair and large brown eyes. Murtaugh wondered whether its impact was due to the artist's technique or to the model's arresting face.

"Pastels?" he called to Dana. Eve used to take him to museums in the City on rare Sundays off.

"Payons, actually. They have a greasier base." She appeared at the arch that separated the kitchen from the living room and the small bedroom in between. "It's only a preliminary. The finished portrait will be in acrylics."

"You're very talented."

Dana walked up behind him, the top of her head even with his shoulder.

"Thank you," she said shyly. "I don't get to do these kind very often, though."

Crossing over to the portfolio, she pulled out a pile of large pen and ink drawings. "This is how I pay the rent."

They were expert, detailed renderings of houses: brownstones; spindly Victorians with frontporch swings; cottages; and saltboxes.

"Instead of pictures of loved ones," Dana told him, "people seem to like hanging portraits of their homes over their mantels. I wonder if that says anything about our society."

Murtaugh scanned those gray eyes again, before going back

55

to leaf through the drawings. "They're very . . . individual."

She smiled as though pleased with his comment. "I try to think of them as having faces, you know. Each with some characteristic all their own."

He stopped suddenly at a group of sketches all of the same building.

"Oh, those—" she flushed.

"It's this house, isn't it?"

Dana nodded. "Oakley and I . . . well, it's our first place together—and I thought it might be nice to do a whole set, month by month, with little changes as the leaves turn color, or the doors are decorated one way or another. I'll pick out a dozen or so from these and give them to him as an anniversary gift."

Murtaugh handed them to her. His voice sounded wooden, overly polite. "I'm sure he'll love them."

He followed her into the kitchen, making an effort not to look at the bed, half-made and rumpled, at the shimmery stockings that were draped over the brass footboard. It seemed too personal to be here all of a sudden.

Dana had set out two glasses of lemonade.

"Since you work at home, Mrs. Hall—"

She passed him a napkin, apparently unconcerned that Lydia was sitting on the table. "Dana. Please. Dana Hall. Sounds like something in Princeton that's overgrown with ivy, doesn't it? But I left my old name behind, with my old life, when I married Oakley."

Something caught at the back of Murtaugh's throat. He tried to imagine this Oakley Hall, the guy whose goddamn name could brighten her face.

"Did you notice anything last night? Hear anything from next door?" he asked gruffly.

"Well, Rose was in one of her tirades."

The fight with Paddy. The one that sent him off to Paulie's and to a hard wooden bunk in the park.

"Mr. Walsh said they had some words at about nine o'clock."

She nodded. "Then Paddy left. We even joked about the poor woman. Said we should take bets on how long this one was going to last."

Murtaugh's heart quickened slightly. "You and your husband went into the yard?"

Dana smiled. "Oh, no. Oakley didn't get home until after midnight last night. He was working late."

Murtaugh was puzzled. "But you said 'we' . . ."

"I had a sitting." She met his confused gaze. "For Rebecca's portrait. Rebecca Lincroft. She and her husband Jake own this building."

He thought of the striking face staring out at him from the easel.

"Do you remember when the yelling stopped?"

"Yes," she said, pulling the lemon cat onto her lap. "I think I remember exactly. She let up for a while around ten o'clock. Then she started up again a little after eleven. I remember because that's when Jake came in. Rebecca was annoyed because she'd expected him earlier."

"Was he just getting home?"

"No, he'd been upstairs with a friend." Dana shrugged and crossed to the stove to stir the pot on the burner. "Anyway, when Jake walked in, the yelling started again."

Rose Walsh had been alive at eleven o'clock. Murtaugh took out a cigarette and lit up without asking.

"When did it stop?" he wanted to know.

"Maybe ten or fifteen minutes later. We were having tea." Her voice faltered. "And then it got quiet . . ."

She placed a clean ashtray in front of him. "I laughed about

57

it," she said sadly. "Later, with Oakley. He said he was sorry he'd missed all the excitement."

Dana Hall was sincerely upset. "To think we'll never hear her, ever again."

* * *

When she walked him to the door, he was at a complete loss for what to do with his hands, with his long, clumsy arms.

Dana Hall narrowed her gray eyes. "I'd love to paint you. You have a wonderful head."

The offer was simple, but it had the remarkable effect of transporting him to another time and place—a cubicle in the Emergency Room of the hospital, a private world marked to perfect proportions by paperwhite curtains all around, where an attractive lady doctor was bandaging his hand and telling him he had nice eyes for a cop.

Much later, Eve teased him about his reaction to the compliment. What had registered in his heart as embarrassment had read on his face as outrage.

Dana's remark must have triggered the same response, because she hurried on to explain. "Not for money. It would be for me. For my portfolio."

Murtaugh made a concerted effort to relax his facial muscles. "Why would you want to paint this ugly mug?"

Inwardly, he winced. Mug. Jesus Christ, Murtaugh, she probably thinks you're something out of Damon Runyon.

"I collect faces," she told him. "People in the neighborhood . . . sometimes even strangers on the street, if they're willing to sit for me."

Watching him edge toward the door, Dana smiled. "Of course, I realize you're a busy man. But maybe you and your wife could come for dinner some night, then you could—"

"My . . . my wife was killed. It happened a few months ago," Murtaugh said.

She bit her lower lip. "Oh, I'm so sorry. I guess I've managed to make you feel totally—"

"No, it's all right," he assured her, surprised that it was.

Dana followed him up the three steps leading to the sidewalk. He took in the facade once more, this time marveling at how completely she'd captured it in her sketches, right down to the painted wheelbarrow holding a single rose which some artistic hand had placed outside the upstairs front door.

"If you're serious about the portrait, maybe we can work something out," he said impulsively. Over her shoulder, he watched a man in his early thirties approaching them.

Tall and well built, he looked as though he'd be more at ease climbing the side of a mountain or riding a raft through white waters than sitting behind a desk; but his conservative business suit and sleek attaché suggested a corporate lifestyle.

"Dana!" the man called.

Murtaugh's stomach knotted.

So this was Oakley. He was annoyed at his own disappointment that Dana Hall should be in love with one who so perfectly characterized the opposition.

He watched her spin around. "Jake—you scared me."

Not the husband. The landlord.

He found himself smiling inanely as Jake smiled and dimples creased that bronzed face. His eyes were a white-blue, his tawny hair streaked by sun.

Murtaugh recognized the type—men whose boyish looks were almost pretty, whose innately soft bodies had been toned by repeated exercise. In ten years, Jake Florian would be just another middle-aged man with a tan more florid than brown, and a middle inclined toward a flaccid paunch. But today, he stood before them, an impressive specimen in his prime.

"I came home early," he said, reining in the charming grin. "When I heard the news about Mrs. Walsh, I couldn't seem to do any work."

59

"This is Sergeant Murtaugh," Dana told him.

He shook Murtaugh's hand vigorously. "Listen," he said, his voice dropping into earnest tones, "anything I can do. Really."

The detective didn't feel up to talking to this bright, helpful young man now.

"Maybe tomorrow," he replied. "I'll come by for a few minutes to speak with you and your wife."

Jake looked concerned. "Tomorrow?" Then he relaxed. "Oh, that's right. Tomorrow's Saturday. Becca's at the shop, but I'll be home working on my board."

"Your board?"

"Sailboard," Jake grinned. "I windsurf."

He'd been right about Florian, Murtaugh thought as he walked away. He pictured him standing against a brilliantly colored sail, his hair tousled by the breeze.

The Sergeant was yards away before he heard Dana Hall call his name. She was on the pavement behind him, out of breath from running in floppy, high shoes.

"I thought, since you'll be in the neighborhood anyway, you might like to have dinner with us tomorrow. Oakley can barbecue."

Murtaugh hesitated, until she cut in with a small voice that only partially masked her disappointment. "Of course, if you can't, then we could always do it another time . . ."

"Tomorrow will be fine."

As they fixed the hour, he was again amazed at the things he found himself saying and doing.

CHAPTER

5

MURTAUGH PICKED up the stack of pink message slips and read them one by one, crumpling them into little balls which he tossed onto the floor near the trash.

"That was O'Connell," Bonelli said, hanging up the phone. "He's on his way over. The Sanchez kid's story checked out."

"Surprise, surprise."

"And Lowenstein called. The old lady was strangled. Killer musta dragged her from the kitchen into the living room and put the pins in there."

"What about the time?"

"After ten. Before twelve."

"After *eleven*," Murtaugh corrected him. "The neighbors at 516 heard her arguing until then."

"Lowenstein says she was one drunk broad. He's having the full report sent over." Bonelli looked tired.

Murtaugh, on the other hand, was fresh and alert.

True, he'd stopped in for a quick one before returning to

Headquarters, but there hadn't been that usual surge of anger when the bartender dawdled instead of getting his drink immediately. He'd even made smalltalk with the guy next to him at the bar.

"Davy!" The Sergeant hailed O'Connell as he came into the room. "Come tell us a story."

O'Connell, looking more like a college professor than a detective, sat down on the corner of Murtaugh's desk, his perspiration-soaked corduroy jacket slung over his shoulder.

"Once upon a time," he said, wiping his forehead on a rolled-up sleeve, "there were four kids who were very, very rotten. They took nasty drugs. Killed little animals—besides Fluffy Libretti, three cats and a dog are missing in the neighborhood. I'm talking altogether class acts."

"What about last night?"

"That's where the plot takes a nosedive. Señorita Velasquez says Emil and his pals were playing cards at her place until about eleven when she kicked them out so her baby could sleep. And the bouncer at Zoots distinctly remembers them coming in about eleven. Says they stayed till closing. So I guess these young heroes live happily ever after."

Murtaugh sat up. "Not necessarily. *About* eleven. *About* eleven. Rose Walsh was alive at *about* eleven. Was that long enough for them to leave the sister's, strangle the old woman, and get to the bar to establish an alibi?"

"But how did they get in?" Bonelli asked. "And why? Walsh says nothing is missing from the house."

Murtaugh shrugged. "Maybe just for the fun of it."

"Sounds like our guys," O'Connell put in. "Trouble from the word go. Talk has it that they're into this whole satanic scene."

"You're sure about that?"

O'Connell got up and stretched his lanky arms. "They're supposed to have hiding places all over town for their secret meetings. The locals say that once Jaime tried to get another kid to jump off the battlements at Stevens Tech. Told the little jerk he'd given him the power to fly."

"What happened?"

"Evidently some student and his girlfriend ran to get a security guard. By the time they got back, Jaime and his gang were gone."

O'Connell looked suddenly depressed. "Let's face it. This all amounts to a big fat zero."

Mitchell Bromsky walked in and sat down on the corner of Murtaugh's desk. It protested against his weight.

"Hey, old man," Bromsky drawled. "In case you haven't heard, I'm taking over the Quiles investigation. Rourke gave me the files, but I figured you probably had some notes of your own, scribbled on a coupla barroom napkins. Whadd'ya say, Murtaugh? Got anything for me?"

The Sergeant looked up at the man. "Sorry, Stosh. I'm using this brain. Go ask someone else."

Bromsky reddened, his lips curling maliciously. "So you're on the Walsh case, huh? Guess they figure it'll be hard for you to insult a broad that's already dead." He rose. "But, don't worry—when you manage to do it, I'll be here to pick up the pieces."

Bromsky turned to walk away. Murtaugh noticed he was wearing socks that didn't match.

"Yo, Stosh," the Sergeant called.

Bonelli and O'Connell moved instinctively out of the field of fire. They were both surprised when Murtaugh's voice became gentle.

"Find the kid, okay?" he said. The other man left the room.

"What a turd," O'Connell muttered.

"Forget about him." Murtaugh was dismissive. "Now what do we have from forensics? Any prints?"

"None."

"What about point of entry?"

Bonelli spoke up. "Front and back doors were open. Looks like she let whoever it was in."

"Which seems to rule out our young amigos."

"Maybe," Murtaugh conceded. "But the Walshes weren't in the habit of locking up until they went to bed."

He stood up and walked to the windows. Down below, on Washington Street, people were drifting back from the PATH trains, moving slowly as though stunned by the heat. The digital thermometer on the bank clock read ninety-four degrees.

"Did they find anything in that old carriage house?" he asked.

"A mess," Bonelli told him, referring back to his pad. "Old furniture, trunks, tools. You can't walk for the junk. Except for one thing."

"Shoot."

"There's a space been cleared, with butts on the floorboards. Our guys say somebody's been smoking grass in there—"

"Now who'd be into that?" Murtaugh asked facetiously, lighting up a cigarette.

Bonelli's smile was more like a gritting of his teeth. "You got it. The PRs."

Wonder how long the old boy's had dentures, Murtaugh thought, and why I haven't noticed before.

Maybe it was better Eve wouldn't be forced to witness the humiliating little concessions that a husband fifteen years her senior would have to make to age. Eyeglasses. False teeth. And before you know it you're perking up during those commercials advertising diapers for the elderly.

For crying out loud, Murtaugh, he said to himself, ease up. The booze'll get you before that happens anyway.

Davy took his pensiveness for something else. "Are you

thinking what I'm thinking?" he said, nodding eagerly. "That maybe the carriage house was one of Jaime's little hiding places?"

Murtaugh moved back toward his desk. "I want it torn apart, Lou. First thing tomorrow."

"Will do," Bonelli agreed, scribbling feverishly.

"And now," Murtaugh said, looking from one to the other, "who wants to finish the rest of this discussion over a beer?"

* * *

It had been a momentary setback.

But, Murtaugh cautioned himself, his newly found need for camaraderie might take them some getting used to. He'd seen the surprise on their faces, noticed the way they'd apologetically begged out—Bonelli because the mother-in-law was coming to dinner, and O'Connell because he had a date. And he was touched by the offhand way in which both came over to him before leaving, with a wink and a tap on his shoulder to remind him that they expected a raincheck.

Murtaugh was feeling so good, in fact, he actually considered inviting Bromsky for a drink to shoot the breeze about new developments in the Quiles case. He ruled against it after coming to the conclusion that his optimistic mood was still in too fragile a stage to test so severely. An hour with Bromsky would be pressing his luck. Instead, he stopped off at Rourke's office to tell him about the day's proceedings.

Keep it calm, keep it friendly, he warned himself as he spoke. Wouldn't do to alienate your fearless leader on this one.

Afterward, Murtaugh felt lost and lonely. For him there would be no family dinner, no hot date.

He wondered if Dana and Oakley Hall were sitting down at the kitchen table eating what she'd been stirring on the stove only hours ago. He could picture her animated expression as she told her husband about the detective she'd met who had a good head.

Did Oakley feel a twinge of jealousy, the way he had when Eve spoke of a nice new resident at the hospital?

Walking down Washington Street, he thought of his hot basement apartment. It was only seven o'clock, and that meant the residents of Rose Walsh's neighborhood were just getting home from work.

He turned into a grocery store, and ordered a couple of sandwiches and a carton of milk from the Korean girl behind the counter. Then he cut across town, brown bag in hand, stopping only when he reached Number 518.

Across the street the famous Mrs. Libretti was sitting on her stoop with several other women.

"He's home," she called to him. Murtaugh moved toward them.

"If you're looking for Paddy Walsh, he's still in there," she continued in her shrill voice.

Murtaugh introduced himself.

"Oh, we know who you are." She smiled knowingly.

"I understand you've had some trouble with a few of the neighborhood kids," he said, leaning against the railing.

"The Puerto Ricans, you mean." Mrs. Libretti nodded, her Orange Julius curls dancing. "They killed my cat. I tell you, Hoboken isn't what it used to be."

There was a general murmur of agreement from the others.

"It's terrible," said a spindly woman, as she stubbed out a cigarette with a slippered toe. "I lived here all my life, but we're thinking about getting out. Moving to Lyndhurst."

"She has a sister in Lyndhurst," Mrs. Libretti explained.

Murtaugh attempted to return to his original point. "Why didn't you report these boys in connection with Tomas Quiles' disappearance?"

Mrs. Libretti looked amazed at his lack of incisiveness. "Well, because I never thought they'd do anything to one of their *own,* of course," she said, and then more defensively, "Besides, they only murdered our Fluffy a few days ago, and I did call you people and complained, but nothing was ever done about it."

Murtaugh swore in silence.

With all the men working around the clock to find the boy, it was probably true that no one had bothered to check out the death of a cat—or had thought there could be a connection between the two events. A connection, he felt, was most likely nonexistent anyway.

"If all this isn't straightened out, there'll be a lot of unhappy people giving the politicians what-for," Mrs. Libretti said after he wished them goodnight. "Like I told that reporter, we won't take much more."

He crossed the street, letting her voice trail like a garish ribbon behind him.

The officer on duty opened the door of Number 518 for Murtaugh. He could tell by the only light burning at the rear of the house that Paddy Walsh was still in the kitchen. Murtaugh hoped he hadn't been there, paralyzed by guilt and fear, all through this long day.

"Mr. Walsh?" he called.

The old man appeared at the archway, silhouetted by the light, his skeletal outline thin and angular as a dead tree against the sky.

"What do you want?" he asked hoarsely. "I ain't got nothin' else to tell you. Leave me alone."

Murtaugh advanced toward the kitchen. "I only wanted to bring you this, Paddy," he said, holding out the paper bag. "Some sandwiches and milk. I wasn't sure whether you'd be able to get out yourself."

Paddy backed suspiciously into the far corner of the kitchen. "What do you mean, can't get out? I'm not a prisoner, am I? I can do as I please."

"Of course," Murtaugh assured him in a soothing tone. "I only meant that I knew, upset as you were, you might not have given any thought to food. And you have to keep your strength up."

Paddy circled closer to the bag that Murtaugh had put on the table, nosing it like a hungry animal. His face softened.

"That's nice of you, sir. I guess it's what my Rose would have wanted . . . for me to keep up my strength."

He sat down and allowed Murtaugh to unpack the contents; then, childishly, he looked into the empty sack, as if disappointed there was nothing more.

Beer, Murtaugh thought. I should have brought some beer.

Paddy Walsh, however, was not without his own resources.

"My stomach's weak," he confided to Murtaugh. "It can't take the taste of milk. Over there, in the icebox, if you don't mind—one of your friends went out and got me something from the corner store."

Murtaugh opened the refrigerator and took out two of the three remaining cans.

"Sure, help yourself," Paddy told him. "I was never one for drinking alone."

They sat in silence as the old man ate. Murtaugh finished his beer first. "Will you stay here tonight, Paddy?"

He seemed to shiver. "There isn't anywhere else."

"We could find you a place," Murtaugh offered.

"I don't want nowhere that isn't my own," said Paddy, shaking his head. "There's no need to go into the parlor, after all, so it won't be so bad, now will it?"

Murtaugh lit up a cigarette. "You'll keep the house?"

The old man licked his fingers and went over to the refrigerator for the last beer. He offered to share, but looked relieved when the detective declined.

"No, sir," he said, as he sat down again. "My understanding is that what was my wife's—God rest and the angels keep her—is mine."

Murtaugh nodded and Paddy continued. "So what I thought I'd do would be to sell this place, and the others, and find me one of them nice condominiums somewhere that's warm."

"The others?" Murtaugh asked, trying not to put the man off with a show of curiosity.

"Them buildings the in-laws left poor Rosie when they passed on," Paddy said in a confidential tone. "Put in their wills they's left in her name only." He let out a bitter laugh. "But I reckon they come to me anyway."

Murtaugh leaned forward in his chair. "Which buildings are those, Paddy?"

Paddy smiled, as if mentally calculating the worth of his newly acquired properties. "Well, besides this, there's the two houses near them Puerto Ricans down the end there," he said.

He tipped his can in half salute toward the Sergeant before draining the contents.

When Murtaugh got up to leave, Paddy stood, almost tripping over Daisy, who was lying on her side, like a beached whale.

Walsh grumbled, "Gonna have the old bitch put to sleep. Seems like the best thing to do for her."

A wave of nausea went through Murtaugh. He remembered taking Eve's cat to be put away, after Eve died, after all the tenderness was drained from him. Looking at this dog, as she breathed laboriously on the dirty linoleum, he regretted his harsh act.

Paddy Walsh watched him with cunning, alcoholic eyes.

"You don't look none too good yourself, Sergeant. I'm not the only one's got to keep his strength up, you know."

As he shut the front door, Murtaugh laughed to himself. Paddy was right. He hadn't eaten since those sandwiches at lunch.

"Fellows home?" he asked the young officer at the door.

"Yes, sir."

He walked down to the basement apartment. Although it was after eight, the heat hung in the air thicker than the darkness. He pressed the buzzer, aware of the noisy hum of an air conditioner inside.

The door was opened by a short man wearing a kimono over jeans.

"Come in, Sergeant," the man invited him brightly, after he flashed his badge and introduced himself.

This apartment had none of the messy charm of Dana Hall's studio. It had been decorated with taste, and probably a good deal of money. The living room was sparsely furnished, with chairs and tables very low to the floor, Japanese-style. Rich Oriental hangings and abstract paintings covered the white walls.

Murtaugh thought maybe he should take off his shoes.

"It's after hours," Martin Fellows said, glancing at his watch. "Can I get you a drink?"

"No. Thanks."

Although the track lighting threw dramatic illumination around the room, directing the eye to only its kindest features, Murtaugh could still see that the man was older than he'd first thought. A well-preserved fifty. But the hair must have had some sort of cosmetic assistance to keep it that golden hue.

He'd been searching for the one thing that would definitely label this guy as one of Bonelli's *homosexuals,* and now that he'd found it he felt a little ashamed.

"Turn that down, will you, Richard?" Fellows called into the other room.

A man in his late twenties poked his head around the painted screen separating the rooms and waved.

Martin explained. "We're watching *Grand Hotel* on the VCR. Ever seen it?"

Murtaugh was at a loss. "No, I—"

"Oh, you should. You'd love it."

He wanted to say, How the hell would you know?, but instead he asked, "How long have you lived here, Mr. Fellows?"

The man motioned him to sit. "These cushions take some getting used to," he apologized, lowering himself on crossed ankles.

Murtaugh's knees cracked on the way down. He refused Fellows' offer of a cigarette from a thin case and lit up one of his own.

"Let's see," Fellows said, "it's been five years, I suppose."

"Were you friendly with Mrs. Walsh?"

He hooted with laughter. "Do you mean did we exchange recipes and invite each other over for cocktails?"

Richard, in the other room, guffawed.

"No, Sergeant," Fellows said, more seriously. "Other than living under the same roof, the Walshes and I have very little in common."

"I understand you're quite a successful lighting designer, Mr. Fellows."

"Do I get points off for tooting my own horn?" He smiled, flicking his ash into a mother-of-pearl dish.

"You don't have to. It's obvious, just from seeing this place," Murtaugh replied.

Martin Fellows proved to be quick on the uptake. "Say it, Sergeant," he said, running his hand through yellowy hair. "Why would a guy like me be living in a dump like this?"

71

"Something like that," Murtaugh conceded.

"Well, first of all, the rent's dirt cheap," he said. "And the neighborhood is actually becoming quite the thing."

"Why not get a place of your own?" Murtaugh asked.

"Buy my own little corner of yuppieland?" Fellows smiled, with a raised eyebrow.

"You live here anyway," the detective reminded him.

"Yes, but purchasing property is such a commitment, isn't it?" He was openly mocking Murtaugh now. "And I can never seem to make that final trip down the aisle."

Richard howled.

Fellows became serious again. "Look, my arrangement with the Walshes suits my needs. I've put a certain amount of money into this place because I thought they were here for the duration. Unfortunately, the duration seems to have been shorter than I'd originally projected."

"Are you saying that now Mrs. Walsh is gone, your tenancy is on shaky ground?" Murtaugh asked, leaning to take the proffered ashtray.

Martin Fellows shrugged. "I put it to you, Sergeant Murtaugh—would you bank on anything that concerns Paddy Walsh?"

The Sergeant smiled.

Fellows continued. "Next question." Murtaugh looked surprised. "Well, you *are* going to ask me about 'The Night of the Murder,' aren't you?"

"What can you tell me, Mr. Fellows?"

Martin Fellows sighed. "Well, unfortunately nothing. We were at the opening of a very dull photography exhibit in the Village last night, weren't we, Richard?"

Richard called out, "Deadly."

"The things people say," Martin chuckled. "Believe me, Sergeant, if I'd known there was going to be such excitement, we'd have stayed home with our opera glasses and ordered in Chinese."

"It might have made my job easier if you had, Mr. Fellows," the detective said; and, on impulse, because he guessed it was a game they'd already played, he asked, "Who did it, do you think?"

Fellows was momentarily taken aback, then he broke into a disarming smile. "Why, the *butler*, of course. Or failing that, I'd try the aging tennis star across the street."

Murtaugh sat very straight. "Janis Rothman?" he asked. "Now why would Janis Rothman have done it?"

Fellows' eyes glimmered in those places that the soft spotlights in the ceiling hit.

"Well, have you *met* her? I mean, the girl is absolutely stunned on coke—maybe Rosie was going to report her to the authorities for beating that sniveling brat of hers. Or maybe it has something to do with the skinny husband who fools around." He sounded suddenly impatient. "I really don't know. But then, that's why I'm the designer and you're the cop."

Murtaugh struggled to get to his feet. "Thanks for your time, Mr. Fellows," he said, clutching onto a black lacquered bookcase. A jade knick-knack fell onto the carpet.

"No harm done," Fellows said.

The detective retrieved the figurine, turning it over in his hand.

Martin Fellows came up behind him. "I call her Dorothy. My she-devil from Thailand. Quite a beauty, isn't she?"

"Never thought of the devil in those terms," Murtaugh told him, putting the figure back in its place on the shelf.

"Devils vary, but some can be very beautiful," Fellows said. He watched Murtaugh study the neat rows of books. "They're on the occult mostly."

The Sergeant started toward the door. "Perhaps I'll come back for a crash course."

It didn't take long for the meaning of his words to formulate in Martin's mind. "You mean, you think it might have something to do with Rose being killed?"

Murtaugh called his goodnights into the other room, where Richard, he knew, was no longer watching the VCR.

Then he shook Martin Fellows' hand and noted that, despite the air-conditioning, it was very clammy.

CHAPTER

6

"**H**OW WAS the date?" Murtaugh asked Davy O'Connell outside the Greek coffeeshop on Washington.

O'Connell just winked. "Has promise, Sarge," he said.

He opened the imitation wood door, with its red vinyl underside, and let Murtaugh select a booth.

"We'll have to make this quick," the Sergeant told him. "Places to go, people to see."

O'Connell checked his watch. "Relax. Except for the Librettis and the Hispanics on the corner, there won't be a soul around yet. It's Saturday. Anyone who's anyone is having crumpets and scones at Evelyn's."

Murtaugh looked confused. "You mean that little dive down the street?"

"It's a teashop," O'Connell corrected him. "Just shabby enough to be chic. This time on the weekend, you can't move in there with the crush of our upwardly mobile citizens, reading their copies of the *Times*."

The waitress filled their coffee cups automatically and took the order without writing it down.

"How do you know all about the latest hangouts of the elite?" Murtaugh asked Davy.

"Got to keep on top of it or it'll pass you by, Murtaugh," the young man grinned.

That's the problem, Murtaugh thought. It already has.

"I was by the Walsh place on my way here," O'Connell said. "They haven't started on the carriage house yet."

"Phone Headquarters. And don't let 'em give you any garbage about being understaffed. I want this done," Murtaugh growled.

He usually didn't eat breakfast. The Danish tasted fresh and sweet in his mouth.

"It sort of makes sense that Rose owned those buildings," Davy said when Murtaugh told him about last night's conversation with Paddy.

"Why?"

"Well, you know. They're all of a kind," he explained when he saw the detective wasn't following. "Eyesores."

Murtaugh smiled tolerantly. "Must've already been pretty ramshackle when she inherited them. I bet her folks got them for, oh, maybe two grand apiece."

O'Connell whistled. "And now they'll go for at least two hundred times that."

"Rosie's ma and pa are probably spinning in their graves," Murtaugh said, shaking his head.

"What about the old girl herself?" Davy replied, almost to himself. There was a brief silence. "I can't get it out of my mind," he confessed. "The way she was pinned to that sofa."

"What did it remind you of?" Murtaugh wanted to know.

O'Connell paused. "It sounds crazy," he said, "but somehow it was like being in church, like a kind of crucifixion."

76

The words rang a bell somewhere in Murtaugh's head.

O'Connell kept talking. "I'll check out the local bookstores and the library. See if anyone other than the kids is heavy into the occult."

"I can save you some work right off the bat," the Sergeant said, and he told him about Martin Fellows, his books, and his she-devil, Dorothy.

"A lot of people are involved in it. It's considered—"

"Chic?" Murtaugh asked roughly.

Was that it? Had Rose Walsh been murdered because, like having tea at Evelyn's and jogging by the river, it was the thing to do?

O'Connell was on his way to see the old woman's lawyers in a storefront office a few blocks away. Murtaugh strolled toward the Walsh neighborhood, formulating a gameplan.

As he rounded the corner, his first move was decided for him. David Rothman stood on a ladder, attempting to fix the antique gaslamp hanging over the front door.

"Mr. Rothman?" Murtaugh called from below him on the sidewalk.

"Just a minute," a voice shot back impatiently.

Rothman leaned over to adjust the glass and lost his balance. The delicate globe fell to the pavement, smashing into thousands of pieces.

David Rothman swore for a good two minutes.

When he had spent himself, he spoke defensively to Murtaugh. "It was the original," he said bitterly. "Over a hundred years old. I'll never get another one exactly like it."

Murtaugh could think of nothing to say. His sensibilities stopped short of offering condolences for a piece of glass.

David Rothman, however, was bent on making him understand. "Sure, I could get Eastlake era in some antique shop, but this one belonged to the house. Now the average

77

person, he's not going to know the difference, but me," he went on, "I'll know. I found every single fireplace in there. Six. And believe me, it wasn't easy. Some were walled up, boarded over, mantels in the basement. Christ! It's a sin what people'll do."

Murtaugh introduced himself. Rothman seemed uninterested.

"I figured as much," he said. "Janis mentioned you came by yesterday."

Now that he'd come down to Murtaugh's level, the detective could see that David Rothman was a thin, tall man in his forties. Already the curly black hair was receding, and he wore safety glasses, like the kind athletes use when they're playing a sport. Even in beat-up tennis shoes, he towered over Murtaugh.

"Watch where you sit," Rothman advised him as they moved to the steps. "Iylish'll have to come out and sweep that up."

"Iylish?"

"Our girl," explained the man. "She helps with Melissa a few hours a day. Frees Janis up a bit."

Murtaugh wondered what a freed-up Janis Gillmore would do with herself.

Rothman continued, almost compulsively. "We found her in *The Irish Echo*. They're wonderful people with kids, the Irish. Very trustworthy."

It occurred to Murtaugh that he was saying this by way of a compliment.

Although it was early in the day, Rothman's T-shirt was soaked through. He seemed always to be moving, which might have accounted for the heavy perspiration and for the taut skin that barely covered his bones.

"I guess Janis told you that we didn't have much to do with the Walsh woman. I guess she already said we can't tell you anything about that night," he went on, rubbing his sweaty palms over his blue jeans.

"Yes," Murtaugh nodded, hoping he could calm him. "She told me you only had a passing acquaintance."

"Well, there you are." Rothman shrugged, as if to dismiss the subject.

"I just need you to clear up a few points for me, Mr. Rothman," Murtaugh told him, before the man could protest. "Your wife said you weren't home on Thursday night. Could you tell me where you were?"

Rothman stiffened. "I *was* at home. We watched television until after one." He let out a strained laugh. "Oh, she must have meant I was late getting in from the City. Came back, uh, I guess it was about ten-thirty. Client to dinner, business-related schmooze. You know the sort of thing I'm talking about."

Murtaugh smiled encouragingly, thinking to himself, Both you and I realize, Mr. Rothman, that I know nothing at all about the sort of thing you're talking about. He asked for the client's name.

"Is that necessary?" Rothman asked, with an edge to his voice. Murtaugh had taken out a scrap of paper and sat with his pen poised.

"Well, I trust you'll be discreet," the man muttered.

He gave the client's name as Olivia Marsh and told Murtaugh that her number was in the Manhattan directory.

You've got her number, Murtaugh thought as he wrote down the information; and I've got yours, Mr. Rothman.

He rose. "One more thing," Murtaugh said, folding the paper and putting it into his jacket. "We've got a report that you were seen arguing with Mrs. Walsh last week. Could you tell me what about?"

David Rothman's face might have been stone. Not a muscle

moved. "As far as I can recall, it concerned that dog of hers. Yes, that was it. I told her I didn't want the old mutt near my daughter, and she sort of flew off the handle."

Murtaugh smiled and held out his hand. "Thanks, Mr. Rothman. I'll let you know if there's anything else."

As they shook hands, Rothman looked into Murtaugh's eyes, and the detective thought he could hear real concern in his voice as he asked, "You won't bother my wife unnecessarily, will you, Sergeant? We're trying to make a home for ourselves here, but Janis has had a hard time adjusting. This kind of thing could ruin Hoboken for us."

"I can't promise anything," Murtaugh replied, matching the concern in his voice. "Unless this murder is solved, it won't be a pleasant place to live for any of us."

Then he crossed the street toward Jake Florian's house.

* * *

True to his word, Jake was working on his sailboard when Murtaugh rang the bell.

"Come on in," he grinned, and he led Murtaugh through rooms filled with the most unusual furnishings he'd ever seen.

From the ceiling were suspended an eyecatching assortment of objects: an antique tricycle, a silk kite shaped like a dragon, a clock with no hands. An immense Andy Warholish can opener soared overhead. A leering marionette jester dipped in a welcoming bow. And everywhere were games. Chessboards. Decorative playing cards. Domino sets.

"One of the perks of Becca's shop," Jake told Murtaugh. "She orders something, and it becomes part of the household for a while. Then when we get tired of it, we stick it in the van and take it over to The March Hare."

When they got tired of it, Murtaugh reflected, they got something new. It sounded very simple. Cut-and-dry. As he pictured the endless conveyor belt of replaceable items, he wondered vaguely if anywhere on it were people.

They climbed the staircase, its walls hung with fine old prints, wicker baskets, fraternity paddles. Murtaugh caught a glimpse of a brass bed, heaped with dolls, before they entered the room used as a study.

The tall windows were wide open. Jake switched off the stereo and climbed through one of the windows. He stood on the roof beckoning to the detective.

It was a tight fit, but when Murtaugh emerged, he saw that they'd made a terraced garden on the flat roof. A sailboard lay on its side, propped against a barrel filled with petunias. Out of the corner of his eye, he noticed something move.

"That's Scrabble," Jake told him, gesturing toward a scrawny black cat. "He's ticked off because he didn't get to go to the shop with Becca today."

The pitch on the roof reflected the sun, so Murtaugh found it difficult to really see Jake's face. He just looked like some tanned Adonis, framed by shafts of light.

"Another hot one," Jake commented. He stripped off his shirt and stooped over the board. "I can't wait to take this baby out on the water and feel an honest-to-goodness breeze."

"You're going on vacation?" Murtaugh asked.

"What? No, only taking a short trip over the Fourth," Jake replied.

This was all wrong, thought Murtaugh. They should be inside sitting in the trendy living room. He couldn't remember what it was that he'd wanted to ask.

Ordinarily, he'd have relaxed into the situation, blending into the woodwork, carefully blotting out more and more of himself until the person being interviewed stopped taking him into account altogether. But a curious thing was happening. For the first time in his career, he was consciously trying to make an impression. It embarrassed him it should matter that he be thought of as more than just an ordinary cop. It angered him that he cared.

"Tell me about Mrs. Walsh," he demanded gruffly.

"Rose?" Jake turned around, holding a tin of wax in one hand. "Rose was okay. I mean, she let off steam every once in a while, but otherwise she was a good neighbor."

"Would you say you were friendly?"

He paused. "Yeah. Yes, I guess you could say that."

"Ever in her house?"

Jake rubbed wax into the shell of the board. "I went over once to help patch a leak in the kitchen ceiling. Old Paddy isn't one to do much of that kind of thing, so Becca got me to offer after she heard Rose complaining about it. Oh, and I think we brought them some candy last Christmas. That's all I can remember."

"Bear with me while I try to piece this together," Murtaugh said, fighting against the heat-induced sluggishness that was creeping into his voice.

Jake sat down on a canvas chair next to Murtaugh. "Sure," he said. He was evidently not the kind who needed inducement to talk freely. "I suppose you want to hear about Thursday night, right?"

"We can start there."

"Rebecca and I had dinner at Evelyn's. Know the place?"

"No," Murtaugh lied.

"Over on Washington. Great eggs Benedict in the morning. Dinners aren't anything special, but they're always fresh."

The detective grunted. "I'll have to try it."

"You should," the young man told him, in much the same voice he would have used to encourage the elderly to find a hobby.

"Anyway, afterward, about eight I guess, we walked back

home. Becca had a sitting with Dana Hall for a portrait we've commissioned. Have you seen it?"

"Yes, it's very striking."

Jake smiled even more broadly and said, "We think it is."

Anyone could see he was extremely proud of his wife.

I was married to a beautiful woman once, too, Murtaugh found himself thinking, although you might find that hard to believe.

"Rebecca says Dana's work is going to be worth a lot some-day." The young man shrugged easily. "Struggling artists must hate hearing that. I mean, paintings usually don't go up in value until the artist has croaked or something."

"What time was your wife's sitting?"

"Oh, a little after nine. I was working on the board with a guy from the block. John Deacon."

Murtaugh asked, "When did the couple next door start arguing?"

Without hesitating, Jake replied, "That was also about nine. Right before Rebecca went downstairs."

"You're sure?"

"Yes," Jake told him. "I remember Becca saying she wouldn't be able to keep a straight face while she was posing if it kept up."

"Did you actually see Paddy leave the house?"

Jake nodded. "He was on his way down the street when Becca left."

Murtaugh pressed on. "So you and your friend, Mr. Deacon, worked out here until you went downstairs to bring your wife home?"

"We weren't outside much. We got the board from the shed." He pointed to a small wood-shingled structure down below in the yard. "Brought it up so I could start on it this weekend. John's going with us over the Fourth, so mostly we just sat around talking about the trip."

Murtaugh looked confused. "Let me get this straight. You went into the yard with Deacon—"

"Right," Jake said, fighting impatience.

"Did you see Rose Walsh?"

"See?" Jake repeated. "No, of course not. We didn't see her at all. It was dark in the shed. We just got the board and brought it up."

Murtaugh explained. "Dana Hall told me she and her husband sometimes went out back to listen to Rose. That she'd watched her a few times, in the kitchen."

Jake grinned. "Sorry, Sergeant. I'm not into the voyeur thing myself." He walked to the end of the roof, indicating the wooden steps, pegged to the side of the house. "Besides, we were so wrapped up in getting the sailboard up this darn ladder, I'm afraid we weren't paying attention to anything else."

Murtaugh came over to the edge himself. "You mean you had to climb up this thing?"

Jake laughed. "We don't have stairs like the Walshes do, so it's the only access we have to the yard," he told the detective. "We rent the bottom floor with the understanding that, although our tenants have full use of the patio and garden, Rebecca and I occasionally shimmy down to get to the shed."

The sun beating on his neck as he looked down made Murtaugh feel dizzy.

"Humor an old fella, will you, Mr. Florian?"

"Anything, Sergeant. And the name's Jake."

"This heat is getting to me. Mind if we go in?"

Jake threw a lightweight plastic cover on the board. "Hey, no problem. I think it's clouding up anyway." He led the way back to the window.

Over his shoulder, Murtaugh noticed that no one was working in the carriage house yet.

84

The detective spoke again as they descended the staircase into the living room. "While you were carrying the board and talking to Mr. Deacon about your trip, do you remember whether you could hear Mrs. Walsh?"

Jake sat in a chair that appeared to have been handhewn from thick vines. "That's tough to say. I think I remember her making noise for a while, but then I suppose we just sort of tuned her out."

"When was the last time you recall hearing her when you were with your friend?" Murtaugh asked.

Jake shook his head and said uncertainly, "Maybe ten. Maybe a little after."

"And you went down to the Halls' apartment at what time?"

"Around eleven."

Murtaugh considered this. "I'm not sure I understand your reason for going downstairs to pick up Mrs. Florian."

"Lincroft," Jake corrected him. "Rebecca's name is Lincroft."

"Were you worried she might not be able to make it up the stairs by herself?"

The young man smiled his widest smile, the one that perfectly dimpled his face.

"No, Sergeant, of course I wasn't." He leaned forward, man-to-man. "But the truth is Becca'd told me she wasn't in the mood for John and me, sitting around bullshitting about sailing. So I promised to get her when he left."

"At about eleven," Murtaugh repeated. "And Dana Hall says that's when Mrs. Walsh started yelling again."

"That's right."

"Do you remember when she stopped?" Murtaugh inquired.

He thought for a moment. "Dana made tea, then, well, you know, we stroked her about the portrait. Stayed until almost midnight."

"And by then, Mrs. Walsh was quiet," the detective said, almost to himself.

Jake nodded in agreement. "Yes, I'd say by then, she'd been quiet for quite a while."

* * *

When Murtaugh asked to use the phone, Florian tactfully excused himself and went back upstairs.

He dialed Headquarters and found that two men were being sent over to search the carriage house. They would have begun earlier except that every available man had spent the morning at the river near the old drydocks, where they were dragging the waters in response to an anonymous tip about Tomas Quiles.

So far, they'd found nothing.

It was Bonelli's day off. Murtaugh left word for O'Connell to meet him at a bar across from the PATH at five o'clock.

After hanging up, the Sergeant wandered around the spacious room.

Something about the place reminded him of the Rothmans' sitting room and Martin Fellows' apartment. Each differed in style, but there was a similarity in the very economy of a few dramatic pieces, the liberal use of money to create a complete, hybrid environment. The Rothmans accomplished it by contrasting the gracious old structure with the best contemporary furniture. Fellows had made himself an exotic Oriental hideaway. And here, Jake and Rebecca had capitalized on a talent for marrying the beautiful with the outrageous.

He paused to look at a scale model of a waterfront, painstakingly assembled and expertly painted, which was displayed on a parquet card table.

"One of my dream projects," Jake said, appearing in the doorway.

"You made this?"

The young man shrugged modestly. "They're the fun part of being an architect. You're never in as much control of a project after it passes the cardboard and paste stages."

"How'd you manage to get such detail?" The detective was honestly impressed.

"Patience," Jake told him simply. "Nothing worthwhile happens overnight."

Murtaugh heard the unmistakable condescension in his words. He felt a sudden urge to overturn the table, to see this cool young man scramble after his creation.

Instead he said, "It's pretty amazing what some of you new people have done with these old places."

Jake beamed. "Bet you didn't think Hoboken had it in her, huh?" he quipped.

"Had what in her?" Murtaugh asked without blinking an eye.

Jake replied patiently. "I guess it's my trade, Sergeant. I'm talking potential. In a few years this place is going to be like living in a little piece of New York."

Murtaugh laughed out loud.

"I'm serious," Jake told him.

"Oh, I know you are," the detective said. "It's just that the old-timers moved here just to get out of New York. Wonder how they're going to adjust."

Murtaugh opened the front door, almost knocking over the wheelbarrow with that single bud, unfurled to the brink of extinction.

Tomorrow, he thought as he set it in place, or maybe even this afternoon, this flower will die.

Jake smiled good-naturedly. "One of Rebecca's decorating statements. I'll tell you something, Sergeant. They look real pretty, but every once in a while I wish I wasn't always knocking into one of her arrangements—"

Murtaugh laughed again, this time appreciatively. As he

closed the iron gate, he decided to go to Evelyn's for a sandwich.

From the Halls' basement apartment came the sound of classical music. Dana was probably painting, in her smoke-colored pinafore.

CHAPTER

1

AT EVELYN'S, two sulky teen-aged girls, aprons over their shorts, were getting ready to close.

He was told that *of course* Evelyn's didn't serve lunch, but that they'd reopen at five-thirty for dinner. He wondered why such a small, uncomfortable place—a place that, even without close inspection, appeared none too clean—should be where Hoboken's beautiful people came to be fed.

Murtaugh went across the street for a burger.

The March Hare had been next on his agenda, but he decided to put some distance between himself and that segment of the block's population.

Instead, he walked to Jaime Sanchez's building. Kids were playing out front again today, this time watched over by a few hip-looking adolescents, lounging around a big radio. The music was so loud he could feel the beat throbbing through his leg muscles as he went up the steps.

The door was open. He checked the mailboxes and found a listing for Sanchez.

Four flights, Murtaugh, so buck up.

On the dark stairwell, between the third and fourth floors, he saw a crude drawing of the symbol Jaime wore on his jacket, the same symbol that Mrs. Libretti said was left in her garden near the hacked-up body of her pet.

It was an oddly shaped star with seven points, its middle refracted like broken glass by a bolt of lightning.

The hall smelled of cooking that had been built upon and layered like spices in one of those Oriental woks. The smell did wonders for his heavy, burger-laden stomach.

He was about to knock when the door opened.

Jaime's father was a slight man, graying at the temples and wearing a pale blue dress shirt and polyester slacks.

"Yes, sir," he said, with a trace of an accent, when Murtaugh showed him his badge. "He is here."

The man looked apologetic. "All day he sits inside, all night he's out on the street."

In the corner, an old woman sat looking at a soundless television.

"My wife's mother. She does not hear, but she likes the pictures." He smiled. "It's not so bad. If she does hear, she still does not understand, you see."

Murtaugh nodded and the man continued. "Now, Sergeant, you will tell me what I can do for my son."

"Do you mean you feel he's in some kind of trouble, Señor Sanchez?" Murtaugh gently asked.

The man was surprised. "I have four children. This is the first the police come for."

Murtaugh explained he was questioning people about the Walsh murder. Sanchez shook his head so vehemently that the old woman called to him in Spanish.

Ignoring her, he told the detective, "I worry about the bad friends. The drugs. But not this. Not from my son."

Murtaugh had heard it all before. But he liked this man. There was no point in giving him any more pain until he was sure about Jaime and those dead-eyed kids his father naïvely called his "bad friends."

"May I see him?"

"Sí," Sanchez answered. "I must take over at the shop so my wife can come home to make dinner."

Murtaugh was directed toward a hallway on the other side of the kitchen. He knocked on the first door, then entered.

Jaime Sanchez lay on the narrow bed. In the dim light of a candle, his skin seemed even more lusterless than yesterday, not pale so much as completely lacking in pigment. Jaime Sanchez looked dead.

"Hello," Murtaugh said.

The boy didn't answer. He swung his leg over the side of the mattress and leaned against the wall.

Murtaugh continued in a friendly voice. "Your father let me in. He says you usually stay in bed late."

The room had been painted a phosphorescent shade of orange. There was another bed on the adjacent wall. Everywhere were posters of rock musicians, their faces permanently frozen in somnambulistic anger.

He'd never heard of any of them before.

Surely they were on the fringe of popular music, Murtaugh thought. Maybe O'Connell would know. But he doubted he'd be able to remember these bizarre names.

There was something religious about the whole layout. The candles. The narrow pallet. These icons of violence on the walls. And that brought a discomforting thought to mind. What was it Davy had said about a crucifixion?

Murtaugh turned to the boy. "You should come home earlier. Then you'd get a good night's sleep."

Jaime Sanchez sounded enraged, but his expression remained the same. "That ain't none of your business, man," he said, spitting the words into the detective's face. "You gonna arrest me, man? If not, get the fuck outta my room, *comprendez?*"

Murtaugh sat at the edge of the bed, opposite. "Tell you what we'll do, Jaime. First, I'm going to wash your filthy little mouth out with soap like somebody should have done years ago, and then we'll take a stroll over to *my* room. At Headquarters."

Jaime said nothing.

"Good." Murtaugh smiled. He wanted a cigarette, but there wasn't an ashtray in sight. Just the beds, the posters, and the candle; a lamp that had been spray-painted gold; and a statue of the Virgin.

"Why do you meet in the Walshes' carriage house?"

The boy looked up sharply. "What's a carriage house?"

Murtaugh was undaunted. "Call it what you want, kid. Shed. Garage. We know you've been there. We know you use places like it all over the neighborhood."

Jaime seemed to relish this line of inquiry. "Yeah? Well, if you know so much, how come you don't tell *me* why we meet there?"

Murtaugh considered for a moment. "Okay, I will. I think you and your compadres buy your dope in the park next to the elementary school. Then I think you find a nice quiet place, a place like Mrs. Walsh's carriage house, to get high. And that's when I think the trouble starts. A little bragging. Some chanting from one of them happy-time albums you listen to, over that class artwork you leave in the dirt. Then, before you know it, somebody's cat gets sliced up. Then somebody's dog, and then somebody's wife. Is that how it happened, Jaime? Is that how it got out of hand?"

"You're nuts, man," he protested. "Nothin' I say's gonna make you believe me anyway."

Murtaugh took the offensive. "How do you get in, Jaime? The only access to those yards is through the back doors. How do you get back there? From the roofs?"

Without a word, Jaime stretched out on the mattress again.

"We'll find out, Jaime," Murtaugh promised him. "And we'll find out what the symbol you wear means, and what kind of power you think you've got, and where you really were on Thursday night."

The boy sat bolt upright. "I told you where I was, cop," he shouted.

Murtaugh walked to the bed and looked into the nothingness of those black eyes.

"Sure," he said.

As he went through the kitchen he heard the sound of something being hurled against the bedroom wall.

He wondered, in passing, whether it had been the lamp, the candle, or the Virgin.

* * *

Murtaugh found The March Hare on a stretch of Washington Street that was predominantly Hispanic. On one side was a launderette, with huge stainless steel drums which allowed you to see the clothes being tumbled dry, as in the old commercials. On the other was a novelty store that sold religious statues and decorative lamps with dolls in wide Spanish tulle skirts at their bases.

Sandwiched in between, the neatly painted ironwork of Rebecca Lincroft's shop looked a bit lost and out of place. Still, Murtaugh noticed, if you crossed the street, two Victorian buildings were being gutted. A large billboard advertised that only two of the new townhouses remained.

The door tinkled pleasantly when opened. Inside was another world.

The March Hare was a two-floor affair with an old-fashioned metal stairway leading to the gallery above.

Customers milled casually through the clever displays of books, games, and oddities. It was as though Rebecca's home was simply one of her husband's scale models for a project, a project that Jake might concede had gotten out of his control, had run rampant.

Murtaugh made his way past two lavish, life-size puppets. He skirted an oak table where a chess game was in progress. The set was obviously handmade, with each piece a caricature representing well-known politicians and public figures. The likenesses were funny, in a cruel sort of way.

Several people stood around waiting for the next move. Others browsed through the stacks or sat at small tables in the rear of the shop, listening to jazzy harp music piped over the sound system.

They don't just come to buy things, Murtaugh thought, they come to see each other.

His attention drifted upward.

Rebecca Lincroft sat on a tall stool far above his head. She was framed to advantage by a grouping of gameboards—Checkers, Monopoly, Trivial Pursuit, Scrabble—hanging from invisible thread.

Murtaugh wasn't sure, if he'd met her on the street, that he would have recognized her from Dana's portrait; and yet, it surely looked like her. What Dana had done was to make the most of an interesting face, without flattering it.

Rebecca's eyes were large, doelike. They almost overwhelmed the tiny visage, and would have done so totally, if her hair wasn't shorn so that it fit like a cap. She wore a white blouse pressed so its collar stood up around her neck as stiff and glossy as an eggshell, and a pleated navy jumper. On Dana Hall the effect would have been awkwardly charming. On Rebecca it was almost unnerving in its starched perfection.

He thrust his hands behind his back, suddenly aware of the telltale gray bracketing his shirt cuffs.

Rebecca hopped off the stool, revealing how small she stood. Murtaugh tried to imagine her with Jake Florian, that tall, handsome guy who looked as if he'd just stepped out of a Pepsi commercial. He couldn't.

"You're Sergeant Murtaugh, aren't you?" she asked.

He smiled. "Am I that obvious?"

"No," she assured him, her voice pleasing and musical. "But Jake called and said you might be by. Would you like some coffee or tea?"

Murtaugh declined, then indicating the customers, "I can come back when you aren't so busy."

"Oh, no one makes major purchases on Saturday. It's more a social outing today. They'll be back during the week to pick up whatever they've staked out." Rebecca laughed.

She motioned to a small room behind one of the display counters. "We can be private here."

Inside, he was uncomfortable. The air-conditioning didn't reach this cramped space; and his frame seemed too large, something which needed to be folded or bent. Rebecca's size suited it perfectly.

"I won't take much of your time," the detective began. "Your husband told me the events of Thursday evening as he remembered them. I'd just like to hear it again in your words."

The large eyes widened in mock terror. "Checking for inconsistencies, Sergeant?"

"Nothing so dramatic, Ms. Lincroft," Murtaugh assured her.

Rebecca sat on the edge of the desk. "I suppose you've

heard all about Paddy and Rose's quarrel," she said in a more businesslike voice.

He nodded, and she went on. "Paddy left around nine, and Rose went on a rampage."

"Did you catch any of what she was saying?"

Rebecca shook her head. "I think it was pretty much the usual. What a bum he was, that kind of thing."

"And this went on while you sat for Dana Hall?"

"Yes," she told him. "We even joked about it."

He was already edging out of the room. "You didn't go out? Go near the back window maybe?"

"Sorry."

Together, they began the descent down the ironwork stairs. On the way, Murtaugh stopped to look at a handsomely framed poster.

He read it out loud. " 'HE WHO HAS THE MOST TOYS WHEN HE DIES, WINS.' " The detective said dryly, "That's a new one on me."

Rebecca tilted the close-cropped head and smiled. "Really? They're real movers. We can't keep them in stock."

A breathless young woman rushed up to them, thrusting a receipt into Rebecca's hand. "It's a return. You never taught me returns."

"In a minute." She walked past her employee to the door, saying, "I wish I could have been more help, Sergeant."

And then he was out in the heat again.

"He who has the most toys when he dies, wins." The phrase kept running through his mind.

That's their problem. All of them.

Murtaugh continued toward the river thinking about David Rothman with his hundred-year-old lamps and Martin Fellows' bizarre collection of demonic art. He remembered the tidy little streets and miniature houses on Jake's scale model

. . . a thousand-dollar chess set . . . and a trimmed coloring book picture—the only sign of a child—hanging in an otherwise barren house.

Toys. Nothing more than toys.

He tried to decide whether what he was feeling was moral indignation or merely the sour grapes frustration of somebody who could never hope to play.

* * *

Davy O'Connell had stopped by the river before keeping his appointment with Murtaugh. The prevailing mood among the men was relief. There had been no sign of the boy.

He told the Sergeant that Bromsky was leaning toward the theory that Tomas had been picked up by someone in a car and spirited away, probably to Manhattan. They were enlisting the help of city runaway services. A poster had been issued.

Murtaugh could see it as he looked past his companion's head. Tomas Quiles' third-grade picture, showing a somber, darkly handsome little boy.

"How's Maria?" he asked O'Connell.

"She's downstairs, living with her folks while we monitor the phone," he answered. "Still clinging to the chance that the kid's alive."

Murtaugh said, "Let's hope she's right." But he said it without conviction.

Murtaugh set down his beer, the first of the day. "So. How about Rose?"

The transition from one case to the other seemed chillingly natural. "She was alive at eleven. And that lets a lot of people off the hook."

"Like the Hall woman. Rebecca and Jake Florian. The Rothmans—if you believe the wife isn't protecting him."

97

Murtaugh interrupted. "Which reminds me. Find out what you can about Mrs. Rothman when she was Janis Gillmore. How she met her husband. Why she quit tennis."

O'Connell seemed on the verge of remembering something.

"Damn," he muttered. "There *was* some kind of scandal, I think. Just escapes me what kind."

"Fellows seems to think she's a doper," Murtaugh offered. "And check into Florian's friend, Deacon, and this Olivia Marsh dame who's supposed to have been with Rothman."

"By the way, Jaime and the boys are pretty well known in the local record shops and bookstores," O'Connell said. "They're into one of the quainter fringes of the heavy metal scene."

Murtaugh raised his eyebrows and Davy explained. "You know, a lot of noise and deep lyrics like, '. . . this world sucks, let's go dig up some graves.' Real quality stuff."

The Sergeant laughed. "Gotta keep up with it, O'Connell, or it'll pass you by."

"Yeah, well, to each his own," the young detective said. "Only these kids ain't just connoisseurs of music, Sarge. They've got a taste for a good high, too. Hallucinogens, mostly."

"PCP?"

Davy nodded. "They may be a part of that ring dealing at the elementary school. It's gonna be tough to prove, especially now, with every manjack aboard otherwise engaged."

They both finished their beers in silence. Then Murtaugh asked, "So who killed Rose, Davy boy?"

He loves these games, O'Connell thought. And he had to admit, they were a helluva lot more interesting than feeding tidbits into some computer.

Out loud he replied, "I want to say the kids—"

"But?"

The young detective shrugged. "Too many alibis. We're

fuckin' up to our necks in 'em. Besides, what if it *is* some psychopath driving through town who picked the Walsh house at random, same as the Quiles kid?"

"Same as the Quiles kid," Murtaugh echoed aimlessly. "How did this psychopath get in the house?"

"You said the doors were open. Or maybe he looked like someone she could trust and she let him in herself," O'Connell suggested.

It was a possibility, Murtaugh thought. Maybe one of the neighbors had seen whoever it was and wasn't telling.

There was something about the whole situation that didn't feel right. At the moment it was like a grain of sand in an open cut—annoying, nothing more. Murtaugh knew he should wait, wait for it to fester, to infect.

Then why did he feel an urgency, an intuition that time was of the essence?

"Another date?" he asked O'Connell as they left the bar.

When the young man grinned, Murtaugh winked at him and said, "Me, too."

He walked down the street, back toward his apartment, leaving O'Connell to ponder whether he'd discovered the reason for the Sergeant's new frame of mind.

* * *

The place got sun only until noon, so he had to switch on the lights before entering. The neat rows of large flies were there, like fat crows on telephone wire, hunched and immutable.

He swung his arm so that those closest buzzed into a crazy Chinese fire drill of flight, returning complacently to their original spots after he moved away.

There was no time to make the appointed rounds with a newspaper. He changed into a clean shirt and the trousers he'd attempted to press with the steam of this morning's shower. Then Murtaugh closed the door, leaving the filthy insects to their silent watch.

* * *

He'd actually thought of bringing flowers.

For crying out loud, Murtaugh, he'd chided himself, it's a barbecue, not the junior prom.

In the local liquor store, he stood for fifteen minutes among the wine racks. It was the first time he'd ever been indecisive about booze. Not an Italian vintage. That would remind him of Eve. And not German. He instinctively knew she'd find them too sweet.

He picked up a bottle of Mouton Cadet and brought it to the register.

"Slumming tonight, Sergeant?" the man at the counter teased. "We have some lovely little Canadian beers which might be more up your alley."

When Murtaugh got out into the evening air, he realized he was blushing.

CHAPTER

8

JAKE FLORIAN was right when he'd predicted a change in the weather. The heat was still unbearable, but now there was an element of electricity in the air, in the hot breeze rustling the leaves upward, and in the blueblack portions of the sky that had not been scudded over by clouds.

Paddy Walsh weaved unevenly down the sidewalk, on his way back from Paulie's. Keeping out of sight, Murtaugh studied the way the old man hoisted himself up the stairs of 518, using the rail to drag his useless legs toward the door.

He fumbled with the keys, and the detective felt sure he'd tumble backward; yet Walsh was surprisingly facile with the lock. The pattern of Paddy Walsh's existence was well-entrenched, if precariously executed, the detective decided. Here was a man who, if he fell, would land on his feet.

Murtaugh must have walked past the Walsh house pondering these things, because he found himself standing in front of Madie Quinn's. Without looking, he knew that Mrs. Cappricio was in her perch at the window.

He felt guilty about forgetting to visit the old woman. Her fleshless skin, in the light of the approaching squall, appeared violet, like the inside of a shell.

Again, she waved. He forced himself to smile up at her before hurrying down the pavement to the Halls' apartment.

* * *

Dana answered the door. Little beads of perspiration on her curling upper lip and shiny stuff she'd put on her eyelids gave the impression she'd been dusted in silvered talc.

She took the bottle from him, exclaiming with pleasure, "French is my favorite! Oakley always buys German, but this is more to my taste."

Murtaugh smiled. He had made the right choice.

She insisted on taking his jacket, saying it was too warm to be formal. On the easel, he noticed Rebecca still took precedence, although Dana had obviously tried to organize the other panels.

Oakley Hall entered from the kitchen and crossed to shake his hand.

"Glad you could make it," he said. "I've been back at the grill. Looks like we might have a race with Mother Nature out there."

So this was the guy, Murtaugh thought, as they sized each other up discreetly.

A polo shirt showed off his trim, athletic build. Mrs. Libretti had called it. Oakley was younger than his wife—perhaps only in his mid-twenties—with those classic, all-American good looks which magnify youth.

Next to him, Murtaugh felt overdressed and old. Next to him, Dana herself appeared more ragamuffin plain than yesterday.

She made the introductions too quickly, as if nervous that they should immediately like each other.

"Dinner companions can drop the 'Sergeant,' " Murtaugh told them.

"Oh, but then what do we call you?" Dana wanted to know. "Not Hunter. That sounds more like an occupation than a name. And Hunt doesn't do you justice." She paused thoughtfully. "Actually, I like plain old Murtaugh, if it's okay with you."

He said it was. But he didn't tell her it was what his wife used to call him.

Murtaugh and Oakley went into the garden, leaving her to uncork the bottle.

As he turned the chicken on the grill, Oakley said, "I figured you might want to ask me a few questions—and I didn't want you to feel funny about bringing it up."

He began brushing the chicken with a tangy-smelling sauce. "Dana's probably already mentioned how fascinated I was by Mrs. Walsh. I even put one of her tantrums on tape, thinking I could use it as material for a novel I'm working on."

"You see, Sergeant," he said easily, "I'm from the South. A town with three hundred people and a blinking light. Living so close to your neighbors like we do here, well, it's been an adjustment. The first time I heard Rose screaming, I didn't know where it was coming from or who was doing it. But I couldn't get over that whoever it was didn't care a fig about who was listening."

Murtaugh laughed sympathetically. "I can understand how it must be for somebody from another part of the country."

"We're *all* from another part of the country," Oakley said, and seeing Murtaugh's confused expression, he explained. "I mean, Jake's originally from Minnesota, and I think Rebecca's people are in New England. Across the street, the Rothmans are Floridians. Of course, most of them lived in Manhattan first, but heck, it's strange to think how everybody ended up here, isn't it?"

There was something in Oakley's friendly voice, with only the silky edge of a drawl to it, that was relaxing. But his eyes were a little too anxious, almost shrewd. Murtaugh wondered how much of a hometown boy Oakley Hall really was.

Rain was beginning to fall in big, unsteady drops, as though some unseen hand were milking the clouds of it. Murtaugh helped pile the chicken parts on a platter, and they had just enough time to grab the utensils when it started in earnest.

Dana was where they had left her, still wrestling with the corkscrew.

"I'm not very good at this," she apologized.

Oakley groaned affectionately. "Did you notice who's doing the cooking tonight?" he asked the detective. "We didn't want to scare you off."

Murtaugh recalled Dana's nervous spooning of that nameless concoction yesterday. She's trying to be something she's not, he thought. For him.

The oak table was set with heavy earthenware dishes. The detective suddenly imagined Janis Rothman in her formal dining room. She would put out some handpainted china in a dramatic motif. She would light long candles. And then, she would wait for her husband to come home.

Dana's voice startled him. "There's a light in the Walshes' yard," she said anxiously, looking out the window.

He'd noticed earlier that the men were going through the carriage house.

"I didn't sleep last night." Dana shuddered. "I couldn't stop thinking about it."

Murtaugh saw a flicker of acknowledgment pass from Oakley's eyes to his wife.

They sat down to dinner. Dana steered the conversation this way and that, seeming to know intuitively when to in-

troduce a new subject and how to prompt the two men to
talk.

Each seemed resolved not to bring up the murder again,
until the end of the meal when Dana said apologetically, "I've
been trying to be good, Murtaugh. But my curiosity is getting
the upper hand."

She leaned toward him. "Is it true," she asked, "that the
murder was ritualistic?"

"Dana," Oakley reproved her.

Murtaugh nodded noncommittally and busied himself with
cutting his chicken to avoid saying more.

"See, I told you," she said to her husband. "Oakley's done
a lot of research on the occult."

The young man cut in, "Don't make it sound like a hobby."
He explained to the detective, "I work for a Christian publication. I'm writing an article about this new preoccupation
with satanism we're seeing among kids today."

A Christian publication. What the hell does that mean?,
wondered Murtaugh. It triggered a chain reaction of images:
soapbox evangelists and healers; people who spoke in tongues
and handled snakes; Jesus freaks and right-wing fanatics. Is
that what Oakley Hall was into? For the second time today
he was suddenly reminded of O'Connell's description of the
murder. A crucifixion.

And what about Dana? He noticed that she'd become unusually quiet. If only he could get past those gray eyes, see
into her thoughts, her beliefs. He didn't know why, but he
felt they were different from her husband's.

Not that it would prove a thing. He'd married a Jew, and
for a Catholic that was a three-hundred-and-sixty-degree turn
on a treacherous highway. But she had taught him tolerance.
She had made him to be humble and unselfish in love—which
was more than twelve years of parochial education had been
able to do.

Oakley was still talking, telling him that he'd been working late on an article the night of Rose's death.

"Unfortunately, Sergeant, everyone else at the magazine had already finished," Oakley said, smiling brightly. "So technically, I'm without an alibi, as they say in the movies."

Murtaugh made light of the information. One thing's for sure, he thought as he watched Dana touch Oakley's sandy hair when she cleared his place. She doesn't believe her husband could harm a fly.

That reminded him of what was waiting in his own apartment. He readily assented to Dana's suggestion that they have coffee in the studio so that she might make a few sketches while they talked.

She worked in charcoal, very unobtrusively. Murtaugh lost his self-consciousness after only a few minutes and moved without inhibition.

He found himself talking about Eve, answering Dana's kind, sensitive questions. This time it wasn't like probing the wound. He was telling this young woman stories about his work, stories about his marriage. He wanted her to like Eve, and she did, he could tell. She stopped him only once.

"How did she stand you, Murtaugh?" Dana laughed. "All that Truth, Justice, and the American Way idealism, mixed up with Irish guilt! How'd she put up with all of it?"

He laughed with her, thinking, if you only knew. If you only knew what happens when all that baggage gets lost along the way and you're left with nothing.

Oakley was quiet, seeming to be more intent on the music playing on the stereo than anything else. It occurred to Murtaugh that he might be bored at the prospect of another evening of posing. Did he appreciate his wife's talent?, the detective wondered, without bothering to ask himself why he cared.

It was after twelve when Dana deposited a pad, filled with

tens of small drawings onto his lap—Murtaugh smoking, Murtaugh laughing, Murtaugh preoccupied.

"Now, if you'll really pose," she told him, "I have an idea of how I'd like to capture you."

Oakley went into the kitchen to bring out the coffeepot.

"I don't know," Murtaugh said uncertainly.

"Take a look at my credentials," Dana smiled, handing him a sketchbook. "You'll see I only do fascinating people."

He turned page after page, pleased to see some of the locals.

"I want to ask the woman who sits at the window a few houses down, know who I mean? But I'm a little scared of her. Maybe someday I'll just plant myself across the street and—"

She stopped to acknowledge Murtaugh's cry of recognition.

Behind the pad, on a separate panel, was a more finished study of a face he knew very well.

Dana continued. "Oh, I'm almost ready to begin painting him. Incredible eyes, don't you think?"

Murtaugh nodded without speaking, without being able to look up from Jaime Sanchez's face.

* * *

A dish crashed somewhere in the kitchen, and the lemon cat came bounding into the room, sliding on the hardwood floors.

"Dana!" Oakley bellowed.

She rolled her eyes. "Lydia and Oakley aren't used to each other yet." The cat rubbed against her possessively.

"You've got to teach that cat not to go up on the table," Oakley said, storming into the room. "I just found her eating out of the sugar bowl."

"How well do you know this boy, Dana?" Murtaugh asked, failing at an attempt to sound casual.

She sat down next to him, with a look at her husband that said this is not the time to discuss the cat.

107

"His name is Jaime Sanchez. I met him in the park." She went on enthusiastically. "Such sadness in that face. So young, and so much sadness."

Murtaugh turned to her. "Are you sure it's sadness? He looks angry to me."

"I told you, Dana," Oakley said, his voice still filled with resentment about the spoiled animal.

He appealed to the detective. "She's too trusting, Sergeant. Do you believe she actually gave this little hoodlum a key to our apartment?"

"You gave him a key?"

Dana seemed unconcerned. "Jaime's harmless. Sometimes he picks up my groceries for me before he comes to sit. I think he needs the money. A couple of times, when I had an appointment at a gallery, I dropped off our key, so in case I was late, he wouldn't have to sit outside with the bags."

Murtaugh was silent for a moment, his head swimming with hazy thoughts.

Oakley tried to enlist his support. "Tell her, Sergeant, it wouldn't take him five minutes to have that key duplicated."

"You're being Southern again, Oakley," she said firmly. "They breed 'em suspicious of foreigners down there, Murtaugh. You're either white or you're black. But you were born and raised in Hoboken. What's your excuse?"

"I'm afraid it's classified at the moment," he replied. "Let's just say I wouldn't give Sanchez your key again. And I'd be careful of letting him in when you're by yourself."

"That's silly."

The detective sighed. "I don't think so. The kid's trouble. He's messing with drugs. Probably selling them to small children. And at least one person on this block believes he's dangerous, that he and his friends tortured and killed a cat."

Murtaugh watched as she instinctively pulled Lydia onto her lap.

"I don't believe it," she said. "Jaime's rebellious, but he isn't *bad*."

Oakley was impatient. "Dana, you can't blindly put your faith in someone because he has sad eyes."

"Why not?" she demanded. "I'm an artist. I see things you don't see, and I tell you Jaime's okay."

"He's a policeman," Oakley reminded her, "and he says that maybe he's not okay."

Murtaugh interrupted. "When was the last time you gave Jaime the key?"

"Just a couple of days ago. On Thursday. That's when he usually comes to pose," Dana told him.

"And before that?"

She shrugged. "I guess it was the Thursday before."

Even with a clear head, Murtaugh wasn't sure what it meant. All he knew was that Thursday evening, only hours after Jaime had let himself into the Halls' apartment, Rose Walsh was murdered. And a week prior, on the day that Sanchez had first used Dana's key, a little neighborhood boy disappeared.

He forced himself not to concentrate on it now, not to think about whether there might be other connections, about the low metal fence that separated the two yards, about sheds and carriage houses.

"Humor an old fella," Murtaugh said. "Promise me you won't take any chances until this is settled."

She looked him straight in the eyes, hugging the cat to her chest. "All right, old fella. But I won't cancel our sitting."

At the door, Dana asked, "And what about you? Will you come back to pose?" Under the shelter of Oakley's draped arm, she looked so hopeful, so sweetly serious, that he agreed to call early in the week to set up a time.

It was still raining. As he mounted the steps to the sidewalk, he heard a small voice at the screen door calling, "Be careful, Murtaugh."

CHAPTER

9

THE WINE had made him drowsy. Instead of bothering with the flies, he fell immediately into a deep sleep.

When the telephone rang at three o'clock, he felt so refreshed he thought at first it was morning.

O'Connell's voice was on the line. "We found the Quiles boy," he told Murtaugh.

"Alive?" Murtaugh asked, knowing the answer.

"A blow to the back of the head. I think you'd better get over here," O'Connell said. There was noise in the background.

Murtaugh could picture him cupping his slim professor's hands over the receiver. He was about to ask why he'd been called, but the young detective spoke again, this time more loudly. "He was in the carriage house, Hunt. Wrapped up in an old carpet and stuck in a trunk."

The Sergeant knew O'Connell wanted him to say something comforting. He knew it by the way he'd called him by his given name, by the slow, deliberate manner in which he'd pronounced each word.

"I'll be right over," Murtaugh told him.

He dressed quickly and in the dark so as not to have to face the silent colony of flies, like mourners in black coats.

It would have been easier if the news about the boy hadn't been expected. The thing that happened to his heart or his stomach when Davy O'Connell whispered Tomas had been found—the way it dipped and came back again to his throat—all of it would have been better if it had been only shock taking hold of his body.

Only it wasn't shock. It was the sure, sickening jolt of certainty.

Yes, Murtaugh told himself as he walked through rainy streets, he knew the child was dead. Most of the guys on the case probably had.

But Murtaugh alone had known the boy was in that carriage house. Known it, the way you sometimes know after glimpsing a stranger's face only once that within him is something bad, something rotten.

Turning the corner of that street was like rounding the bend where a dream becomes a nightmare. All the elements, which on Friday morning had seemed so easy to grasp and catalogue, had suddenly gone haywire.

The lights from police cars, and those from windows, were reflected by puddles of rain, so they became multiplied, fragmented into shining prisms of yellow, blue, white, and red.

Again a barricade held back the crowd of onlookers, only they too had been transformed by the storm and night. Dampness made hair stand on end. The sheen from Acrilan and nylon sleepwear gave the crowd a weirdly uniform appearance. Mrs. Libretti stood in front in a short housecoat and furry slippers.

111

They make those legs of hers look like Q-tip swabs, the detective thought, laughing to himself irreverently.

Bonelli had also just arrived. They nodded to each other and went into the house.

Paddy Walsh, still dressed, was literally cowering in the front hall. He wavered, a moth between two flames—the living room, where he had found his wife; and the kitchen, where you could see those bright floodlights which shone over a dead little boy.

Murtaugh would have liked to be able to give him a five and send him off to a bar but the bars were closed, and Paddy Walsh was too terrified to make it down the street anyway.

Davy O'Connell met them at the back door, where men were climbing up and down the cement steps which gave access to the backyard. Murtaugh could see the outline of the body.

"It was locked. The storm held them up most of the night, and they didn't get around to breaking it open until an hour ago." O'Connell's face blanched. "They said they wouldn't have rolled out the rug except Grover smelled something. Christ."

Bromsky was talking to Lowenstein, near the remains. Murtaugh walked toward them, keeping his head at eye level. He had to prepare himself for the sight.

The Halls' apartment looked dark. Could they really be sleeping, he wondered, through all of this? Then he craned his neck. Someone stood on the roof watching the scene, but he couldn't tell whether it was Jake or Rebecca, or both.

"We've got to stop meeting this way," Lowenstein said. The flippancy tipped him off. Lowenstein was shaken.

Tomas' decomposed body was curled up in a fetal position on the threadbare carpet.

"You've told Maria?" Murtaugh asked Bromsky, his voice catching.

Bromsky nodded. "The whole family's camped out down-stairs. 'S like a scene from one of them operas, with people throwing themselves on the floor and ripping their clothes."

Murtaugh moved to hit him, almost losing his balance. He dipped and swayed over the child's corpse. This sudden aerial view of the remains made him feel like a vulture. And wasn't that really what they were? Scavengers picking for goodies, searching for tidbits?

I could have fallen and crushed the boy, he screamed silently to himself, I could have broken all that was left. He put his fist to his mouth, hard against his teeth, and began walking in the other direction.

Lowenstein followed breathlessly. ". . . approximately a week or so, I'd say. There's a good possibility he was killed the day he disappeared."

Murtaugh looked at his lips, thinking it might help him to make sense of the words. "Has he been . . . tortured . . . in any way?" he asked softly.

Lowenstein shrugged. His eyes were completely obscured by the glare of the lights on his thick glasses. The detective tried to remember how old his son was. They'd gone to his bar mitzvah years ago.

None of the preliminary evidence suggested that the boy had been tortured or sexually assaulted, Lowenstein said. The two needles, which he was sure Murtaugh must have noticed protruding from Tomas' bound hands, were put in after death as they had been in the Walsh murder. The killer left a signature.

Murtaugh listened. They strolled to the fence which separated the Walshes' yard from the patio where Oakley Hall had grilled chicken. Stooping over, the detective saw that, although the rain had washed away all prints, there was a worn path on both sides of the metal doweling. The fence had been scaled, and often.

He stood abruptly, catching Lowenstein wiping his glasses in the same old way, but when he met the doctor's myopic eyes, he saw anguish in them.

Murtaugh heard a commotion on the back stairs. Maria's father, the grandfather of the child, was struggling to enter the yard.

"Sergeant!" the old man called. "I want to see my grandson. I want to see my boy."

"It's better to wait, Señor," Murtaugh coaxed him.

The man's face was a maze of pain and anger. "Why? So they lay him out nice on a slab? So they make him pretty?" He hurled out the word as though it offended his dignity.

Maria Quiles was an unwed mother. A sweet, obedient daughter who felt her lifelong duty was to repay her parents for her only trespass against their authority.

Murtaugh knew Señor Quiles regarded Tomas as not simply a grandchild but the son he had never had. How could he deny him his right to see the boy, not only in death, but in murder?

He let Quiles pass. Bonelli and O'Connell fell into step behind the man. They watched his back stiffen as he looked down, and his knees buckle and drop until he was next to the child, touching. They heard his long, swelling moan. It was the sound an animal makes when it wants to commune with others of its kind, a desperate attempt to merge his vital presence with the lifeless form on the ground.

Murtaugh helped him to his feet.

Quiles grasped the detective's hand. "Thank you, Sergeant. I must always remember his suffering so I will remember how to hate. Thank you." He moved back toward the house, like a sleepwalker.

"See he gets home, Davy," Murtaugh said. O'Connell took off, glad to be going somewhere, anywhere.

"I'd like to see Fellows, if he's around," Murtaugh told Bonelli.

"No one answers. The place is locked up tight," Lou replied.

They were putting the body on the stretcher.

"Let's get out of here," Murtaugh muttered. Bonelli looked relieved. They skirted past men and climbed the stairs, moved through the kitchen and down the hall.

Paddy Walsh stumbled out, seemingly from nowhere.

"Got no respect for the dead," he shouted, slurring his words. "Get outta here, all of you, and leave me be!"

He confronted Murtaugh. "I know what you're thinking— but at least I got respect." The old man swayed, pulling away when the detective tried to steady him. "I got respect for the dead."

Bonelli shook his head in disgust.

Murtaugh said, "Come on, Paddy, let's go up to bed."

Surprisingly enough, Walsh offered no resistance. With a look over his shoulder directing Bonelli to wait, he took the man's arm and guided him upstairs.

"Can't sleep," Paddy confessed, his body a leaden weight against Murtaugh. "It'll be different after she's in the ground, I think, don't you?"

They reached the landing. To the right was a darkened room with a double bed, covered with a rose-colored chenille bedspread. The shiny veneered headboard was in the shape of a fan, a style popular in the forties.

Paddy tugged on his arm. "Here," he said, motioning toward a door in the opposite direction, "I can't think to stay in *her* bed, you know."

Murtaugh snapped on the light.

The room where Paddy Walsh had slept, probably for most of the years of his marriage, was no more than a rectangular cell.

At one time, it had probably been the wardrobe for the master bedroom. The walls were makeshift, and in several places large holes showed their consistency to be no sturdier than cardboard. The only furnishings were a twin bed, a small table with a night-light, and a crucifix on the wall. Instead of a closet, a wire coatrack stood, sparsely hung with the old man's clothes.

Paddy lowered himself onto the mattress. As thin as he was, Murtaugh noticed that there was barely room for him to turn over.

Had the poor bastard been exiled from his bedroom across the hall because he was a drunken bum?, Murtaugh wondered. Or was he a drunken bum because he had been exiled?

In the final analysis, he decided it was a case of two people who'd grown to hate each other so passionately that their hate inexplicably became the tie which bound them together. Paddy missed Rose. Missed her as surely as he himself missed Eve. She was the driving force that kept him living. And yet he'd despised her.

Paddy cried, making sniveling sounds. His nose and open mouth ran into rivulets of water on the hard pillow.

"When will the funeral be?" Murtaugh asked.

"Tuesday."

The detective nodded. "You won't be alone tonight," he said. "There'll be men downstairs, again."

Walsh tried to sit up on bony elbows, resting his head against the cardboard wall which had been painted an insistent hue of pink. Rose's favorite color had been the shade of her name.

"And tomorrow the priest'll be by," he said, his voice angry again.

Murtaugh turned to leave.

At the door, he stopped. "You know what happened tonight, Paddy. You know the boy was found out back. Now listen," he urged the man. "This is very, very important. Why would anyone want to put that kid's body in a trunk in your yard?"

"They hate us."

"Who?" Murtaugh asked. "Who hates you?"

Paddy glowered, his rheumy eyes suddenly flashing. "All of 'em. The Spics. The other ones. They hate us because we were here first."

Murtaugh knew this was all he would get. They were here first.

"One more thing. About the trunks. Where did you keep the keys to them?"

"In the locks, I suppose," Paddy said disinterestedly.

"They weren't in the house somewhere?"

He scoffed. "It was only junk herself could never throw out. Those that had keys must've been in the shed."

Murtaugh turned off the light. "If you need anything," he whispered, "or if you want to talk about something, tell the men downstairs to call the Sergeant."

Paddy Walsh was nodding already. "Sure," he said sleepily. "That's kind of you, sir."

The detective knew by morning Paddy would no longer remember their conversation.

* * *

The reporters outside the Walsh home had been insistent this time. They passed Bromsky on the front walk issuing a statement, admitting it appeared there was a connection between the two murders.

Instead of going directly back home, Murtaugh asked Lou to drop him off at Castle Point.

He couldn't sleep. Not yet. A walk in the park overlooking the river would do him good.

Here there was always the smell of coffee in the air, pungent and disturbing, because unlike homey kitchen brews, it radiated from a factory which advertised the superiority of its beans to all the people on the other side of the Hudson.

It was still dark, although almost five o'clock, and the clouds were only now beginning to disperse. Continuing down the street toward the battery at Stevens Tech, he felt smothered by the thick morning air, the smell of mass-produced coffee mingling with the overly sweet honeysuckles which grew along the path.

The campus was deserted. Even the guard at the gate was gone.

Murtaugh passed a tall glass-fronted building and walked out onto the ramparts. It was perhaps the best view of the New York skyline—totally unobstructed, spanning from above the Empire State Building all the way to the Twin Towers.

He was curiously unmoved. Those buildings that, even on this cloudy morning, looked permanently etched against the sky, truly scraping it, seemed to have nothing to do with him. He could scarcely imagine such a place to be inhabited.

Tourists and residents of the surrounding areas came out here all year long, on clear days and evenings. It was one picture that must have been photographed a million times. From these heights Jaime Sanchez tried to get a kid to jump because he'd given him the power to fly.

Maybe the view had infused him with false confidence, carelessness. This in mind, the detective tore his gaze away and looked downward to the river. The sight of the abandoned drydocks, the roofs of the dilapidated warehouses, and skeletal pier saddened him.

If Hoboken had the better view, New York's seaport had the better deal. For all the renovation, Hoboken was no better than a ghost town, a glimmer of its former self.

The harbor mocked him, so he turned his back on it and faced the mansions on Castle Point. Most of them were now fraternity houses or multi-family dwellings.

Ever since he was a kid, the sight of their copper-topped turrets and ivy-covered walls, the leaded and stained-glass windows, and the formidable carved doors fascinated him, more than the silent backdrop of that city across the water.

He knew the architecture like the back of his hand, knew the year each was built and the names of the original owners. His feeling toward them was almost proprietary.

One of his favorites, a stone Gothic monstrosity with a rounded observatory turret, had been on the market for weeks. This morning, for the first time, he noticed the sign out front was marked "SOLD." It annoyed him to think of the childless but successful couple who would move in and begin cheerfully remodeling its gloomy expanse.

They were all dead, he knew, the men and women who built and lived in these houses. If he believed in the occult, like Martin Fellows, he would have fancied them gliding down the grand old staircases, sending thrills of terror through the crowds of co-eds partying with beer and marijuana; or disturbing the silkflower arrangements in a young professional's apartment, leaving a trail of crumpled leaves along the Oriental rugs.

Murtaugh was roused from his thoughts gradually by the dull thud of something that was being rhythmically smacked. He looked down to his right, onto a terraced court, almost completely shrouded by bushes.

Janis Gillmore Rothman, all alone, in a short white skirt and sweater, was hitting tennis balls against a wall. She took them from a bucket and served so hard that her breath was expelled in perfect time with the ball's crashing off the concrete surface. She hit them, one after another, with a vengeance.

* * *

119

Murtaugh walked home quickly. He took off all of his clothes and picked up a newspaper. Then he went from the living room to the bedroom to the kitchen, killing the flies with the same force that Janis had hit her tennis balls.

He fell into an exhausted, restless sleep.

CHAPTER

10

I⊤ was almost funny. Headquarters looked like a military stronghold under siege. The men had been working around the clock for over a week now and they were tired. In their eyes you could see it. The bewilderment. Their eyes said, What do these killings have to do with this place?

Sure, Hoboken had its share of violence. Dope-related, mostly, the odd crime of passion. The outer edges of town were a repository for corpses, courtesy of those wackos over in New York. But mostly, these cops were watchdogs. They watched the street. The crowds during parades and religious festivals. They watched for drugs and burglaries and accidents. Not for this kind of thing. This kind of thing was out of their league.

Murtaugh instinctively knew what they were feeling. He saw it as he passed Bonelli's desk, noticing the small patch of whiskers on the underside of his chin. He knew it, and he saw it, but he couldn't feel it. For the first time in as long as he could remember, Hunter Murtaugh was in his element.

He felt proud of himself for sitting down, letting the urge for a drink overtake yet not overpower him. He felt the righteousness of the abstemious.

Even the memo on his desk from Alison Randall detailing a plan to cut down on paper usage didn't bother him. He read, half amused, about the collection of recyclable paper that would be picked up from every man's desk each afternoon. About the points given to the one who recycled the most.

What about the guy who does the least?, Murtaugh laughed cynically to himself. What are you gonna do about me, Ms. Alison? Shoot me, and then gather my remains so you can recycle my hide?

Lowenstein's report was different. He read that slowly, his chair swiveled away from the others.

The M.E.'s office was being pressured into issuing statements catch-as-catch-can, before all the tests were completed. So far, it appeared Tomas' death was the result of several blows delivered to the back of his head by a blunt instrument. He had been bound afterward so the killer could insert needles into his tiny wrists. There were no other marks on his body. He had not been sexually assaulted.

Forensics found nothing in the way of fingerprints on the trunk or anywhere else. The murderer may have used gloves. A yard-to-yard had been conducted, but no weapon turned up.

Murtaugh looked out onto Washington Street. In a little while, he would walk over to the Quiles home. The church bells which rang all through town were silent now. Soon the family would be back and he would pay his respects.

Davy O'Connell, talking softly on the telephone, turned to

the Sergeant. "Pick up. It's Lowenstein. He says he found traces of PCP in Tomas Quiles' body."

*   *   *

The Quiles family lived in an immaculate unrenovated rowhouse. Maria's father ran a prosperous fruit and vegetable stand near the PATH. As a result, unlike some of the Hispanic families who settled in Hoboken, the Quiles had been able to buy their home and the apartment building next door. Their quarters were on the first two floors of the brownstone, which they shared with Señora Quiles' widowed sister. Three of their daughters were married and had moved to neighboring communities.

Maria and her illegitimate son lived in the apartment upstairs. Five days a week, Maria went off to her job as a beautician in an upscale unisex salon, leaving Tomas to be taken care of, and fussed over, by his grandmother and great-aunt. They did everything for him, even walking him down the block to the elementary school when he was old enough to attend.

And now he was dead, and the rooms of the lower residence were crammed with relatives, friends, people from the neighborhood. They brought cakes and covered dishes filled with food.

When Murtaugh entered, the conversation stopped.

Señor Quiles came over to him to shake his hand solemnly. The crevices of his nut-brown face were moist, but it was difficult to tell whether from tears or perspiration. The room was sweltering.

In the corner sat Maria Quiles, slightly removed from everyone else. Her mother was surrounded by women whispering in Spanish, which to Murtaugh's ear sounded very beautiful; women who constantly touched hands, hair, faces.

The detective felt sorry for Maria. Something told him that

she was isolated in her grief, the natural mother, but somehow less important than the adoptive mother, Señora Quiles.

He'd seen it before with women who had babies out of wedlock. If they lived with parents, the children grew up treating their own mothers as sisters, more often turning to the grandparents for discipline, for love.

Murtaugh moved toward her.

She was impeccably dressed, as usual, in a well-cut dark suit. This morning she wore no makeup, but her eyes and coloring needed none to emphasize their natural fineness. Her hair, a mélange of shades from deep red to black, was pulled back tightly.

"Maria," he said, extending his hand tentatively.

She averted her face. "You come now, Sergeant Murtaugh," she told him. "But before, you leave us for the other man to take care of, and see what happens to my baby."

He sat down. "Maria. Look at me," he said softly. "It wasn't Bromsky's fault. Tomas was beyond help, long before he came on the scene. Maybe even before you realized he was missing. There was nothing anyone could have done."

She hit her knee with a fist that clutched a lace handkerchief.

"Can we go somewhere for a minute?" he asked, putting his hand beneath her elbow. "It's important."

The room became quiet again as they walked to the stairs.

"Maria—," Señor Quiles said, his voice alarmed.

"I'm all right, Papa. I will do what I can to help them get this man." She led Murtaugh up the steps to the third floor.

On the wall next to the light switch was a framed photograph of the little boy. It was the same one that had been used for the posters. Maria sat on a vinyl kitchen chair and began crying loudly.

After a moment Murtaugh spoke. "We've talked about Tomas before, Maria. About his friends. How he did in school. Today, I'm going to ask you something, and I want you to think carefully before you answer me."

She looked at him. Her eyes promised nothing.

The Sergeant began to pace. "The doctor who examined Tomas found traces of PCP in his body. On the street it's called angel dust—"

Maria stood and lunged at him in one liquid movement. "No!" she screamed. "My Tomas was not a boy like that!"

Murtaugh tried to calm her. "There was no indication of habitual use. He may not even have known what it was. Someone could have given it to him. Someone he trusted, Maria." Her shoulders relaxed. "Now think. Did Tomas know anyone who might have access to something like that?"

The young woman shook her head, but he could tell she was considering his question.

"There's a kid next door named Jaime Sanchez. He has friends—Ricky Rodriguez, Emil Velasquez, Miguel Herrara. Any of those names sound familiar to you?" he asked.

She looked up at him. "Maybe Emil. Maybe Tomas mentioned a boy called Emil."

"Good, Maria," Murtaugh told her in a soothing voice. "You think some more about it. Ask some of Tomas' friends. Talk to your parents."

Maria was frightened. "My father would kill me if he knew about the drugs. He would blame me for working, I know it!"

"Don't tell him then," the detective advised. "Just ask them about the names of those boys."

Maria grabbed his arm. "They are the ones?"

"They know where to get the dust," he told her. "Maybe they'll be able to tell us how it ended up in your son."

"You will not leave it to Bromsky," Maria demanded.

"We'll both be working on it."

Before leaving, he looked around the room. Against the front wall there was a bureau with a framed picture of the Virgin and a plaster statue on it.

Many small candles burned in glass holders.

Murtaugh wondered if Maria would blow them out now that her vigil was over or whether they would extinguish themselves.

* * *

Dana Hall was on her way home from the bakery when she spotted Mrs. Cappricio. The old woman stood on the porch outside her front door, hanging onto the railing as if measuring the distance of the eight steps against her own strength.

For the first time, Dana saw the body attached to the skull at the window, small, emaciated, dressed in the traditional old-world widow's weeds. Black dress, black stockings, black shoes, black babushka.

She called for Mrs. Cappricio to wait, but the old woman obviously couldn't hear; so she hurried to Number 520 and called again.

"Do you need some help?"

The woman squinted, then smiled a gummy smile, which broke her face into a thousand wedges of wrinkles.

"If you know how old I am, you say, how she stand at all," she said in a surprisingly firm voice.

Dana left her box of sweet rolls on the stoop and came up beside her. "How old are you?"

"Ninety-t'ree," Mrs. Cappricio answered. She placed her paper hand over Dana's arm. "November itsa make ninety-four."

"Well, I hope I'm as good at your age," Dana Hall said.

The woman laughed, as if, however she might appreciate the kindness, she was too old to be fooled by flattery.

Her veiny arms felt no more substantial than a dry breeze

against Dana's skin. They took shuffling babysteps down the steps, pausing often.

Murtaugh watched them as he came out of the Quiles home.

A few doors down, Jake Florian, who was sweeping the sidewalk, also noticed the improbable pair—their heads bent over in concentration—one ancient and one copperpenny bright.

By the time the women reached the pavement, both men had come over to meet them.

"Where are you off to, Mrs. Cappricio?" Jake asked, with a teasing grin.

She put up her free hand to shield her eyes from the sun, but said nothing.

"Are you okay, Murtaugh?" Dana asked the Sergeant.

Jake became serious. "I can't believe that such horrible things can happen to innocent people, but I guess this proves they do."

Murtaugh introduced himself to Mrs. Cappricio, taking her hand politely.

"He's a policeman, Mrs. C," Jake told her, with a wink, "but you don't have to go with him unless you've been naughty."

"I done nothing," Mrs. Cappricio said, her voice trembling.

The detective could imagine the effect these murders had on a helpless shut-in. He wondered whether she'd heard the news from Madie Quinn or had seen it on television.

"Of course you haven't," Dana was cooing. "Now where was it that you wanted to go?"

The lady looked confused.

"We can help you," Jake offered. "We can take you there."

"I'ma go to bank," Mrs. Cappricio said hoarsely. "I'ma want to go to the bank."

Dana bit her lower lip, a habit Murtaugh found appealing.

"Oh, Mrs. Cappricio, I'm sorry," she said. "Today is Sunday. All the banks are closed."

"They close?" the woman echoed. "They all close?"

Jake took a wallet from his hip pocket and peeled off a few bills. "Look, if you need something to tide you over or you want me to get you some groceries, here."

"No, grazie," she declined, holding up her ghost of a hand. The movement was jerky, the gesture of a marionette.

"I wait," she told them. She turned, grabbing onto Dana. "I go home now."

Considering her frail condition, Murtaugh knew it was a long, long journey.

He made a sign to Dana, then said, "Let me help you, Mrs. Cappricio. I'd like to talk to you for a few minutes."

"I'm ver' tired, mister," she insisted. "I'm need lay down."

Murtaugh took her arm and patiently steered her toward the door. "It won't take long. We can chat on the way."

Dana picked up her bakery goods.

"I guess we'll all get funny when we get that old," Jake said as they went through the gate of Number 516 together.

Dana left him sweeping. She wanted to make tea in case Murtaugh stopped by after his conversation with the old woman.

* * *

They didn't chat on their way to her apartment. Mrs. Cappricio's body labored simply to breathe. Murtaugh felt it wheeze and sputter like broken bellows in his hands.

She lived in one large room, the kind advertised in the papers as a flexible studio.

Murtaugh had seen places like it before. He knew the kind of old people who inhabited them. Widows and widowers living on fixed incomes, ordering their meager grocery lists over the telephone, seldom going out, even for fresh air.

A day came when they laid everything on the kitchen table—wills, deeds for burial plots, telephone numbers of relatives and friends, rosaries. Then they crawled into bed and waited.

A neighbor or the landlady found them, sometimes not until days later, and the police were notified. It was a routine, orderly death. Clean and neat like the contents of their rooms.

The summer sun had baked this top floor so steadily that it was oppressively hot. The detective helped Mrs. Cappricio into an old morris chair next to the bed. Her bloodless hands were cool.

She's probably lucky she doesn't feel the heat, Murtaugh thought, noticing the thick pile of blankets on the bed.

"Can I get you something to drink, ma'am?" he asked. "Some water?"

She closed diaphanous lids, gauze over yellowed marbles. "No," she said weakly, "I rest now."

Murtaugh sat on the chair opposite her.

"Mrs. Cappricio," he said, hating himself for continuing, "I'm sorry to bother you, but this is very important."

Mrs. Cappricio looked frightened. "I'ma know none of these important things," she protested. "What you want with me?"

"I've seen you at the window, ma'am," he smiled.

They both looked at the small wooden chair in front of the window facing the street.

"Yes. I see you sometime." The words seemed to come from far away.

He put his hand over hers, very, very gently. "Terrible things are happening on this street, Mrs. Cappricio. A little boy is dead. Your neighbor, Mrs. Walsh, was murdered in her own home." She stiffened.

"We're asking the people who live here whether they saw anything recently—anything at all—that might help us find the person who's doing these things."

Mrs. Cappricio withdrew her hand, and for a moment her

cloudy eyes focused, pinpoints of shrewdness. "What make you think an old woman like me know something you don't?"

Murtaugh was patient. "Because you watch at the window, Mrs. Cappricio. Because maybe you saw someone go into a neighbor's house on Thursday night."

White fists hit the air helplessly. "I'ma not see!" she panted. "Tella you friends I'ma not see nothing!"

For the first time color pumped into the bony face, but it was unhealthy, purplish.

Murtaugh tried to soothe her. "I'm sorry, Mrs. Cappricio. It's my job to ask. Don't worry. No one will bother you about this again."

Mrs. Cappricio relaxed. Once more he asked her if she wanted anything before he left.

"Maybe glass brandy, please," she said shyly. "Doctor Zott, he says itsa good for me."

She gestured toward a low shelf beside the sink, asking, "You knew my Doctor Zott?"

"I think I know the name," Murtaugh called as he took out the bottle and poured the syrupy liquid into a glass.

"Yes, the doctor, he'sa die in nineteen seventy-two," Mrs. Cappricio said, her voice stronger than before. "I'm outlive the Doc, what you say to that?"

Murtaugh turned. She had taken off the babushka and folded it neatly on her lap. The hairnet underneath made her look bald, backlit as she was by the sun. But he could have sworn the expression on her face was triumphant.

"Pretty good," he told her. "Hope you outlive us all."

It was when he went to pick up the glass that he noticed it.

On the other side of the hot plate was a window overlooking the backyard. Another small chair had been placed in front of it, turned to face the Walsh's carriage house.

Murtaugh carried the brandy over on a tin tray. He placed

it within reach of the old woman and took her sliver of a hand in his big one.

Then, before going to the door, he left a card with his name and number on it, where she would find it later, on the end table.

It touched him to see that, by the time he got downstairs, Mrs. Cappricio had come over to the window just to wave good-bye.

* * *

The uniform on duty was sitting on Paddy Walsh's steps. "He went off with the priest," he called to Murtaugh.

"What about Fellows?"

"Still not home," the officer replied, winking. "Must be one hell of a weekend date."

Everyone, even the indomitable Mrs. Libretti, was opting for sitting behind closed, and presumably locked, doors today. The block looked deserted.

As Murtaugh passed Number 516, he heard Dana Hall call his name. She came out, wiping her hands on a cotton skirt which fell in loose folds to her ankles.

"Cup of tea?" she asked. Her face was anxious.

"I can only stay a minute," he warned.

They sat together at the table. The lemon cat was perched on the window ledge, greedily eyeing a plate of pastries.

"That young boy . . . it's so awful," Dana said. Again, the bitten lip.

"Did you know him?"

"Not really." She picked up tiny specks of confectioner's sugar off the oak table with the tip of a nervous finger. "I saw him at the park a few times. You know, looking at all the older kids. He seemed very shy—" Her voice broke.

Murtaugh leaned toward her. "Ever see him with Jaime and his friends?"

131

Dana got up and took the kettle off the stove. "No," she said, then wavering, "at least . . . not *with* them . . ."

"Around them?"

"A lot of people were around them," she protested. "It wasn't what you're thinking."

Murtaugh abruptly changed the subject. "I enjoyed last night. A shame it turned out the way it did."

"We watched you from the window," she told him. "Until I couldn't stand it anymore."

The detective sipped his tea. "I wanted to apologize for talking so much about Eve. You probably found it morbid." He felt his face reddening.

"Stop it, Murtaugh," Dana said very simply. "I know how it is."

Some new quality in her voice made him look up from his plate. Those gray eyes were so open he almost looked away again; but he didn't, and in the end, it was she who broke the gaze.

"That's how I met Oakley actually. I was ready to open up to someone about something . . . painful. And he was willing to listen."

Murtaugh said nothing. He was thinking about the painful thing in Dana's past. He hoped it no longer hurt her. Why did he feel so protective of this young thing who spooned altogether too many teaspoons of sugar into her cup and dressed as if she shopped at church rummage sales?

"Do you know Janis and David Rothman?" he said aloud.

She bit into a crumb bun. "They're not a particularly outgoing couple. In fact, Oakley and I haven't made too many friends in Hoboken yet."

"What about Jake and Rebecca?" he suggested. The front door opened, and he watched her face light up with anticipation.

Dana said casually, "I don't know. Rebecca's been very supportive of my work, but—"

"But they don't like me," Oakley said, stepping into the kitchen. He was in tennis whites, his hair soaked with sweat. Lydia scurried out of the room.

His wife rose, putting her arms around him. "You don't know that for sure, Oakley."

"Once they found out about the kind of magazine I work for, they cooled off," he explained to Murtaugh. "Probably think I'm some kind of religious fanatic." Oakley smiled. His teeth were perfect. "And maybe I am."

"You're not," she said too quickly, like Eve at a cocktail party qualifying his assertion that he was just a cop. Dana looked at her husband and added loyally, "You married me, didn't you?"

Murtaugh wondered what she meant. Oakley kissed her on the lips, keeping his eyes open and looking at the detective all the while.

* * *

He promised to sit for her on the next evening.

Oakley walked him to the door. "I'm glad you'll be here," he said. "I'm working late and I don't like leaving her alone."

Murtaugh stepped over the tennis gear in the middle of the foyer. "Ever play with your neighbor across the street?"

"I wish. But I don't think she takes to the courts anymore," he replied.

Murtaugh looked as if he was trying to remember something. "There was some talk when she left the game, wasn't there?"

Oakley sighed. "It was a shame. She was really good."

"I recall reading something—"

"Drugs," Oakley put in. "Her coach said she had to withdraw because of ill health, but according to the tabloids she was doing so much cocaine she'd actually become violent. Started carrying around a gun. Threatening other players."

He stopped, as though sorry he'd repeated gossip. "I suppose that's why she doesn't play anymore. It probably brings back all those ugly times."

Murtaugh nodded. "Could be. Although I doubt you ever get something like that out of your blood."

Oakley watched him go, wondering to what, exactly, the Sergeant had been referring.

* * *

He was late. There was a lot of paperwork to be done before the meeting with Rourke tomorrow morning.

He wouldn't have stopped at all except for those voices from behind a tall hedge at the edge of the park. Young angry boys talking in Spanish. Murtaugh tried to catch what they were saying, but they were speaking too quickly for him.

Then Emil Velasquez ran out of the park.

My God, he's only a baby, Murtaugh realized, seeing him for the first time without the company of his friends. Emil paused between two parked cars, looking unsure of whether or not to go back to the others. From his position behind the boy, Murtaugh could almost believe that he was crying. His head was bent and his skinny frame shook visibly.

"Emil!" Murtaugh called.

When the boy saw who it was, he ran down the street, the awkward hodgepodge scramble of someone not at ease with his body.

Maybe kids his own age make fun of him, the detective thought. Maybe that's why he's trying to establish an identity with a faster crowd.

Emil gave up trying to evade him and collapsed on the front stoop of the prewar. For once there were no kids playing

134

outside. Murtaugh knew their parents were too frightened to allow them on the streets.

What about Emil's family? Weren't they concerned—or did they know something the others did not?

"Where's the fire?" he asked, coming up to the boy.

Emil struggled to compose himself. He looked at the Sergeant with his usual sullen stare. "I don't have to talk to you," he said.

"Your friends tell you that?" Murtaugh inquired. "Because if they did, they're very wrong. Did it ever occur to you, Emil, they might tell you a lot of wrong things? A lot of lies?"

"You don't know nothin'."

Murtaugh laughed. "Is that what they said?"

The boy's knees started to jiggle in compulsive little starts. "I know you knew him, Emil. Tomas mentioned your name to his mother."

"So I knew him," Emil scoffed. "That a crime?"

"No," Murtaugh said solemnly. "But giving him the dust was."

The black eyes widened. "I didn't give him no dust."

"Who did, Emil?" Murtaugh pressed. "Was it Jaime? Or maybe Miguel?"

At the sound of their names, Emil toughened, as though they could be incanted, could be summoned supernaturally to protect him.

He stood. "It was no one. And you got no right to bother me. You got no right."

Murtaugh's eyes narrowed dangerously. "What are you going to do, Emil? Call the cops?"

Then he shook his head as though the quivering kid disgusted him. "You watch too much television, sonny."

Emil turned and ran up the steps, but Murtaugh, with only a slight effort to control his breath, made it there before him.

He put out a big hand and clapped the frightened youth

135

against the door. "Do you know what happened to him, Emil?" he said, letting the boy feel hot breath on his face.

"Somebody came up behind him and they bashed in the back of his head. Then they trussed him like a pig and took two long, pointed needles." Murtaugh grabbed his wrists. "Oh, I'd say about as long as this, and they shoved them in through the skin, past the bones as far as they could, so they didn't break off, till they came out all the way on the other side."

The boy gulped. Murtaugh watched him blink away tears. He released his grasp, came even closer, so that their heads touched.

"You're the weak link, Emil," he whispered. "They don't really consider you one of them."

He started down the stairs. At the bottom, he turned. "Know what they say about weak links? They're easy to break. And if I know that, they know it, too."

Murtaugh only made it past Paulie's, and its promise of liquid comfort inside, because he knew Emil Velasquez was watching him as he walked up the street.

CHAPTER
11

THE MEETING was worse than Murtaugh had expected, and he'd expected it to be pretty bad. If the experience of Rourke and Bromsky in the same room wasn't enough, there was Alison Randall, sitting in the corner and occasionally raising her hand to give an opinion, like a precocious child.

For one thing, they were convinced he was wasting time, dragging things out with old-fashioned methods of interviewing, by his purposeless loitering in the neighborhood.

"Granted, it's a lovely way for the Sergeant to make friends, which are a commodity he has sorely been lacking," Bromsky roared. "But he's pussyfooting around the solid leads we've got like an old lady in a manure heap."

Rourke cut in, "You're speaking of these young Puerto Ricans, Bromsky, right?"

The Captain was secure in the knowledge that the Hispanics were responsible for all of Hoboken's problems, and it griped him that even now Murtaugh, who'd lost a wife to the bastards for Chrissakes, couldn't be counted on to agree. He was fed up with the fair-haired Sergeant sticking his holier-than-thou attitude right in their faces.

Patience, he said to himself, just feed him a little more rope.

Bromsky explained that they were on the trail of Jaime's drug connection, who hadn't been seen around town for days. And, he said, the bouncer at Zoots admitted that the boys may have come into the disco later than he'd first thought, eleven-thirty or eleven-forty-five.

Kids on the block were talking, and so were concerned members of the Hispanic community. The death of Tomas Quiles had shaken everybody up, and there was suddenly a wealth of information about these boys who sold drugs, dyed the long ends of their hair, and wore strange clothing.

"Has anyone mentioned specifically that they're violent?" Murtaugh wanted to know. "Said anything about them belonging to a cult?"

Bromsky was impatient. "I'd say that was obvious, wouldn't you?"

"I hope you're talking evidence, Bromsky," said the other detective. "Remember, intuition doesn't count."

"Except for the intuition I got about you—"

Now Rourke was angry. "While you two are jumping on each other's backs, you may not have noticed our phones ringing off the hooks. City Hall. Chamber of Commerce. Those pain-in-the-ass reporters."

He leaned forward. "It's a bad time for all of this to happen." Murtaugh wondered vaguely when a good time would be. "The City Council's got the hots for those developers that did Baltimore over. Could mean a lot of money, with them people here. They want us to look like a fuckin' virgin when they come calling."

Alison Randall raised her hand, caught herself, and ended smoothing her perfect hair. "This is a political issue, gentlemen," she reminded Bromsky and Murtaugh. "Certain people think a seaport here would give South Street in Manhattan too much competition. If we don't get this killer in hand, it could tip the scales."

"We're talking low profile," Rourke interrupted. "Not a lotta hysterical residents putting their property up for sale, a lotta fucking bad press."

He stood up by way of announcing the meeting's end. "We didn't let a few rotten Puerto Ricans ruin us in the sixties," he said, "and we're not going to let them do it now."

*   *   *

Murtaugh hadn't had a drink since Saturday. Even the meeting didn't make him lose control. Feeling cocky, he suggested that O'Connell and Bonelli join him for a good German lunch at his favorite restaurant.

It was dark and cool there. Everything calmed him—the rows of steins around the bar, the plaster draft horses pulling a keg advertising his favorite beer, the wooden booths, and the bartender, who wore a lariat instead of a tie.

He ordered a Weiss beer, telling the two detectives, unselfconsciously, "My limit, boys."

The waitress brought their beers in balloon-stemmed glasses, with raspberry cream on top.

O'Connell talked about Janis Rothman, repeating in greater detail what Oakley Hall had told Murtaugh yesterday.

"Where'd she hook up with Rothman?" he asked.

"They met at a party. He was a friend of one of the other players," O'Connell told him. "Pretty soon he was part of her entourage. This was before Rothman's job with the bank. I got hold of a back issue of *People* magazine, right around the time when they announced their engagement. They described Rothman as 'the son of a successful New York retailer.' I think papa was giving him pocket change."

He continued. "Then she left tennis. They got married and moved to Manhattan."

Bonelli couldn't sit still any longer. "You really think they did it, Hunt? People like that?" Meaning, people who weren't Puerto Rican.

Murtaugh was noncommittal. "I don't know, Lou. Something there isn't right. I'd like to find out just how violent Janis Gillmore was back in those days. And whether she developed her drug problem before or after she met her husband."

"It was about the same time," O'Connell said. "And as for Rothman's alibi, this Olivia Marsh woman told me—maybe too eagerly, if you know what I mean—that they had dinner on Thursday. Just out of curiosity, I called his firm. He may have eaten with the lady, but she's no client they ever heard of."

Bonelli was still not satisfied. "Why would a guy like Rothman want to kill a kid?"

Murtaugh realized Tomas' murder had made their work a whole new ball game. There were those who considered the death of poor old Rose as just deserts. But a child—now that was something totally different.

"Why would Jaime and his friends want to kill a kid?" he countered.

"These young dopeheads . . . ," Bonelli began, looking to O'Connell for support.

"Power," Davy offered. "For the thrill of it."

Murtaugh took a bite out of his knockwurst. "You may be right," he conceded. "What we need to find out is why the boy got high before he was killed."

He eyed Bonelli's beer, contenting himself with water.

The trouble was that everyone they'd questioned could produce alibis as if they were going out of style.

He thought about the day Tomas died. As far as they could
determine, the last time he'd been seen was at noon. The
child had gone to a local shop to pick up a newspaper for his
grandfather, as he did once a week, on Thursdays. Ironically,
it was probably one of the few times he was allowed on the
street alone.

Assuming he was killed sometime during the afternoon, as
Lowenstein maintained, then there were only a few candidates. Janis Rothman. Jaime Sanchez, for the period before
his three-thirty sitting. And Rebecca Lincroft, who said she
was supposed to appraise an antique doll, and when the client
wasn't in, had gone to a shopping mall, leaving her assistant
alone in the shop until after three.

O'Connell read his mind. "The bitch of it is that where
some people have an alibi for one of the murders, they don't
for the other."

"Except for Mrs. Rothman and the kids," Murtaugh sighed.

"And listen to this," O'Connell told him. "For the hell of
it, I checked out that photography opening Martin Fellows
and his boyfriend were supposed to have been attending on
the night Rose was killed."

"And?"

"It wasn't on Thursday. It was on Wednesday."

He asked himself why Fellows would tell such a blatant lie.
Then it occurred to him that he had believed him, not even
feeling it was worthwhile to verify. Maybe he really was too
trusting of his own impressions. Perhaps Davy O'Connell,
with his logical mind and knowledge of computers, and even
the slow, methodical Lou Bonelli had the right idea.

As if on cue, O'Connell nudged the older man. "Tell him
what you found, Lou."

Bonelli cleared his throat. "Concerning that same evening,

141

Hunt," he said stiffly, "Oakley Hall couldn't have been in his office working all night. He'd called in to say he wouldn't be in at all. That he was out on the road, doing some kind of research on witchcraft."

* * *

The restaurant, which had seemed a cool haven when they entered, became more noisy and crowded as their meal progressed. Murtaugh was relieved when they were out on the sidewalk. The heat anesthetized the gnawing feeling he had in the pit of his stomach.

Washington Street was festival-loud. They dodged mothers with strollers and teen-agers carrying cranked-up radios.

"Isn't there such a thing as a summer job anymore?" Bonelli complained.

But they all knew there was. Adolescents in white paper hats and dirty uniforms served burgers, or donuts, in the fastfood places which dotted the street, their shiny faces soaking up the grease. There was still such a thing as a summer job. For those lucky enough to find one.

Was that where Jaime and his gang had gone wrong?, Murtaugh wondered. Too much idleness? A lack of money leading to drugs, and finally murder?

A few blocks down the New York bus was holding up traffic as usual. They could see the early commuters disembarking.

Martin Fellows, in a crisp linen suit, stepped off gingerly.

"Excuse me, boys," Murtaugh told his companions. "I have to see a man about an opening. See you when I see you."

He took off at a jog, reaching the man by the time he turned onto his own block.

"Hello, stranger," the detective said, trying not to wheeze from the exertion.

Martin Fellows jumped. Then he smiled broadly. "Why, Sergeant, how kind of you to walk me to my door."

"I have an ulterior motive," Murtaugh said.

The little man chuckled. "So do they all, Sergeant. So do they all."

Dana Hall was sitting on the curb across the street, sketching her building. She waved to them.

"Pretty, in a Little Nellish way, isn't she?" Martin commented. "And her work is quite good. I've been thinking about asking her to do my portrait. But I have the sinking feeling that it would be accurate."

"Accuracy doesn't concern you much, does it, Mr. Fellows?" Murtaugh asked, while Martin fumbled with the key.

They walked into the apartment, not as dark as his own, but with an air of neglect about it that made it different from the exotic refuge the detective remembered.

Martin Fellows was coy. "Ah, accuracy is much overrated. Like a heroine from one of the plays of Mr. Tennessee Williams, I prefer illusion, any day."

Murtaugh was having another look at the booklined shelves. He turned. "Writers can afford to deal in fiction. Unfortunately, I can't."

Fellows sighed. "You're referring to the fib I told about the evening that Rose was done in, I suppose."

Murtaugh said nothing.

"Oh, I might as well have it out. Come into the bedroom, will you?" The detective hesitated.

"I won't bite, Sergeant," the man said impatiently. "It's just I'm trying to catch the next bus, and I have to pack."

"Where are you off to now?"

Fellows took out a suitcase, stamped with fleurs-de-lys, from the closet and threw it down on the Japanese mat bed.

"To Richard's," he said, as he fished into his wallet and tossed something to Murtaugh. "His number and address, in case you miss me."

"Why did you lie?"

143

Martin Fellows suddenly looked tired. "The cards warned that I was entering a hostile period."

The detective watched the man, sitting forlornly on the mattress, a pile of expensive shirts on his lap.

"Cards?"

"The Tarot." It occurred to Murtaugh that he was not being flippant, but rather, deadly earnest.

"For the record, I didn't kill anyone." He offered the detective a cigarette and kept on talking. "I don't know why I decided to lie. In a way, since I hadn't hurt anyone, I didn't really consider it a lie."

"Where were you?" Murtaugh asked.

"During the time the boy was killed, I'm not sure. The papers weren't clear about when it happened," Fellows said simply. "But I was here watching *The Petrified Forest* with Richard on the night they cooled Rose."

"Dammit, Fellows," Murtaugh scowled. "Why didn't you say so in the first place?"

"Did you know when you're angry you look like a young Spencer Tracy? Of course, one seldom saw him angry in films." He was gazing at their images in the mirror on the wall. "I, on the other hand, favor Claude Rains when I smile. Although he wasn't much of a smiler."

"Stop it," Murtaugh ordered.

"You should have seen your face when you first walked in here, Sergeant," Fellows told him. "I could see you chalking up the points . . . Homosexual—or did you simply use the phrase 'old queen'?" He gave a scornful little laugh. "Access to the backyard. Admits to have dabbled in the occult for years. Am I on track?"

Murtaugh was cold. "It didn't occur to me to make a list until I found out you lied."

"Perhaps I underestimated you. But try to look at things from my point of view. The boy had been missing for a week.

144

It wasn't only my sense of the dramatic that told me there was a connection somewhere. A lot of people would consider me suspect, simply because of who I am."

"You just told me you didn't kill anyone."

"So did Henry Fonda in *The Wrong Man*," he retorted.

Murtaugh's anger surfaced. "Forget the movie shit and talk sense."

Martin began packing. "Do you know what frightens me? Being the subject for some young shrink's thesis—'homosexual abducts young boy, kills woman he identifies as own overbearing mother.' We've both heard the scenario before."

When the detective began to protest, he continued. "Surely you're aware there's been a backlash against those of my proclivities. It doesn't matter if the truth eventually outs. Once something like that gets into the papers, you're finished. Look at that girl across the street."

"But you had an alibi," Murtaugh argued.

Martin replied bitterly, "And how long do you think that would hold water after they find out who pays for Richard's little East Side flat?"

"All right, Fellows," Murtaugh said wearily. "Say I buy it. What else? You're a perceptive guy. What went on that night?"

Martin began zipping up his bag. "I wish I could tell you, Sergeant. I mean, it would be in my own best interests, wouldn't it? But really, we sat here eating popcorn, drinking a bottle of Pouilly Fuissé, and watching the goddamn movie."

"You saw nothing outside or at the window?"

He shook his head.

"Hear anything? The slam of a door out in the yard? Rose's back door?" Murtaugh tried hard not to sound desperate.

Martin thought for a moment. "I may have heard something from outside, I'm not sure," he said. "I probably just attributed it to that hunk next door fooling around with his surfboard again."

Something about Martin Fellows made the detective believe what he was saying. He had to remind himself that he'd believed him last time, too.

"How long will you be gone?" Murtaugh asked as they walked to the door, Martin lugging his suitcase.

He winked. "Perhaps indefinitely. I just may make that final commitment." The detective looked uncomfortable. "Have I, at long last, managed to shock you, Sergeant?" Fellows sounded almost gleeful. "You're a married man, aren't you?"

"My wife was killed. Last year."

Martin continued, his tone more kindly. "You should understand, then. There comes a point when you don't want to be alone anymore."

Murtaugh felt like telling him that murder shouldn't be the precipitous event in establishing any sort of permanent relationship.

Yeah, he reminded himself, just remember that.

He said, "Tell me something, as an expert in the occult. What is the significance of long, thin needles used in a ritualistic way?" He held the door for the man.

"Why, voodoo, of course," Martin replied, without further prompting.

"And what exactly is voodoo's purpose?"

"To drive out evil spirits," he told Murtaugh. Then he went off on his short legs to catch the bus.

*　　*　　*

Dana was still sketching. On his way over to the Rothmans, Murtaugh stopped to say hello.

"The anniversary present?"

She smiled. Out in the sun, he saw for the first time the dark smudges under her eyes.

He wondered why she was losing sleep. Could it be she

knew her husband had lied about his whereabouts on the night of the Walsh murder?

He stooped to take a closer look. "This one's different, isn't it?"

Dana agreed. "I try to take a new perspective with each, so I'll be able to choose contrasting views of the house."

Over the wrought-iron railing someone had slung a pair of shoes and forgotten about them. In Dana's drawing they became the focal point, haunting and visually fascinating. And yet, he could see from here that they were just a perfectly ordinary pair of old-fashioned, lace-topped black shoes, the kind he'd seen suspended from the rafters in Rebecca's shop.

He admired the artist for her eye. Maybe she was right after all when she insisted that Jaime Sanchez didn't have the face of a murderer.

Stop it, Murtaugh, he warned himself. That kind of thinking can get you in trouble. You, of all people, should know you can't tell a murderer by his expression.

"Are we still on for tonight?" she asked, grabbing her charcoal and pad, and preparing to go.

"Sure." He watched her cross the street and disappear into her apartment before heading for the Rothmans'.

The detective was halfway up the stairs when he saw Janis Rothman and her wailing daughter through the shutters of the large bay windows. Something about the woman's face, about those telltale crimson patches on her cheeks, disquieted him. He wondered suddenly if she physically abused the child.

Had the paranoia and violence of her youth really subsided? Or was Janis' aloof exterior only masking a darker, more dangerous side?

He rang the bell. It was a full minute before Mrs. Rothman answered the door. She seemed about to object; then, with an apathetic shrug, she invited him into the house.

Melissa was still crying, but the noise came from above, probably within her bedroom, which Murtaugh pictured as all lace and pink, with uncomfortable wicker furniture.

"I don't know why you want to question me about the boy," she said with a put-upon sigh. "I never met him, and neither did my husband."

The Sergeant sat down, unasked. "It's not about Tomas Quiles, Mrs. Rothman. It's about some of your neighbors."

"I don't see—" she began.

Murtaugh smiled. "By the way, I caught your practice session the other morning at the college. You certainly haven't lost your touch."

The remark completely disoriented her. "How did you—?"

"I like to go up there early myself. I find it's a good time for working out things that are bothering me," he said.

Janis Rothman began to cry.

Her reaction shocked him, the ice maiden scrunching her face up until it was splotched and ugly. Her tears were embarrassing because they were deeply private.

Dana Hall would have looked natural, wiping her nose on a paint-smeared smock, picking up her skirts and holding them to her eyes. There was nothing handy to wipe away Janis' tears. Her beautifully tailored khakis, her expensive cotton sweater with the collar turned up rakishly—these lines were too clean, too perfect, for emotional outbursts.

"I'm sorry," he heard himself say. "Is there anything I can do?"

She shook her head.

Melissa ran into the room, holding a pair of socks.

"These, Mommy?" she sniffed. Janis composed herself, even managing a smile.

The child recited, "Pink goes with this outfit. Red doesn't."

"That's right," Janis said, and she hugged her, this time

148

with real feeling. "I don't know why we always have problems on Iylish's day off." Then, suddenly, as though just remembering his presence, she turned to the detective. "You . . . you want to know about our neighbors?"

Murtaugh offhandedly began by asking about Mrs. Libretti.

Mrs. Rothman wrinkled her nose in distaste. "She's a busybody. David can't stand her."

"Why not?"

"Well," she said softly, made uncomfortable by her daughter's presence, "the Librettis just aren't our kind."

She kissed the little girl. "Go get a granola bar, Melissa. I'll be in soon." Melissa ran into the kitchen.

"Wash your hands before you eat," Janis called.

Murtaugh automatically looked down at his own. "What about Jake Florian and his wife?"

Her endorsement was unenthusiastic. "Oh, they're all right."

"Have you ever gone out together socially?"

"Yeah, sure," she told him. "David sees them occasionally."

"But you don't?"

She was dismissive. "I'm not into party games. Frankly, Rebecca and her precious shop merchandise get on my nerves. I've never seen the attraction in playing cards or Trivia or whatever they do." A weak smile. "It bores me."

"And you don't care that your husband goes without you?" Murtaugh asked.

Janis stared hard at him. "You might as well know, Sergeant. I don't get along with many people. Restoring the houses, partying with friends—that's what makes David tick. It's got nothing to do with me."

Murtaugh couldn't remember ever meeting anyone so miserable. Present company excepted, he thought wryly to himself. But that's different. Janis Rothman was young and talented. She had everything going for her.

He let a little laugh escape. It echoed in the high-ceilinged room, somewhat wistfully. He'd meant it to be a cue, but the woman sat silently.

"I was just thinking that you must love your husband very much to stay here where you're so unhappy," Murtaugh said finally.

When Mrs. Rothman spoke, her voice was devoid of emotion. "I'd be unhappy anywhere. David understands that."

What had been the attraction? Young Janis Gillmore could have had any man, yet she married one she was obviously incapable of loving. His mind raced, trying to decide the best way to bring up the matter of the drugs.

Janis did it for him. "You've probably heard the rumors. The cocaine. The fights off court. David stuck with me through all that."

Murtaugh said gently, "Sounds like an understanding guy."

Janis gave one of her bitter half-smiles. "We both got what we wanted, I guess."

"Oakley Hall, across the street, is fond of tennis." Murtaugh tried to change the subject. "Have you hit with him?"

She shook her head. "He asked me once, but like I said, I'm not one for mixing."

"He's an attractive young man," Murtaugh suggested.

Janis was unimpressed. "I suppose. He looks like all the rest of them."

"The rest?"

"Those whitebread boys who were on the circuit with me," Janis explained.

Whatever passion drove her, Murtaugh decided, it wasn't sexual.

"Will you want to talk to David again?" she asked as she opened the front door. "Because we're going away for the Fourth of July weekend."

"Sailing?"

Janis was confused. "No," she said, "to the mountains."

"Oh," Murtaugh smiled. "Jake and Rebecca mentioned they were going sailing. I thought you might be going along."

She gave him a look that he knew was meant to make him realize how out of touch he was.

Of course, *everybody* went away for the Fourth, he was learning.

And, they never went to *lunch* at Evelyn's.

CHAPTER

12

DANA DECIDED to paint him standing, hands in pockets, in what she called a three-quarter.

Murtaugh laughed. "So I don't get to see my face the size of your canvas, after all. It was good enough for Rebecca Lincroft, but a frightening proposition when it comes to me."

"On the contrary," she admonished him. "This will be my masterpiece. My one chance to do something very John Singer Sargent."

In response to his raised eyebrows, she picked a large book from one of the piles on the floor. Murtaugh leafed through the pages. Each featured another subject, sitting, standing, reclining, in great Edwardian rooms.

"This one's in the Metropolitan, isn't it?" he asked, pointing to a group of women, narrow-nosed and white-shouldered, sitting on tuffets of taffeta.

"That's right," Dana nodded, impressed. It had been what

he was trying to do. Impress her. "Do you go there often?"

"Not really." He didn't want to play that game, pretending he was someone he wasn't, and yet he felt reluctant to tell the whole truth. That he'd gone often with Eve, and never since.

He kept his eyes on the book. "I probably wouldn't know a really great painting if it fell on me."

"You underestimate yourself."

"No, really," he insisted. "I found out that the one I like the most in the museum is probably a fake. I can't even tell the genuine article."

Dana sat next to him. "I have an unorthodox view on that subject."

"Oh yeah?"

"Yeah." All at once she sounded very serious. "When you look at that painting, does it draw you in . . . stir up something inside of you that you didn't even know was there?"

Those gray eyes unsettled him. "I guess it does."

"Then it's the genuine article," she said simply.

He closed the book with a clap. "The guy was pretty good."

Dana stood up quickly. "Every important person of his time sat for him. It was a status symbol, you know, having a Sargent in your collection." She sighed. "Not the same for artists today, I'm afraid."

"We take Polaroids instead," he joked.

"And they fade," she said. "One day you go to look at Uncle Harry and he's all gone."

Dana positioned him in front of the easel. "Don't worry, Murtaugh. This one'll be for keeps. You can leave it to Head-quarters in your will, so they can have a Sergeant in *their* collection. Then when anyone asks, they'll tell them, that was the famous detective, Hunter Murtaugh. It's an original Dana Hall, you know."

He laughed. "I might not even wait till I croak. I know several people who'd enjoy hanging me over their desks right now."

Murtaugh was surprised to find that posing wasn't half as bad as he'd expected. Once he discovered he could move his head and talk, he didn't mind at all. It was sort of like standing in a crowded PATH train.

Dana seemed to know the exact moment his limbs were becoming stiff. She let him light a cigarette while she worked on, poking around for a rag and some new colors.

Noticing her sketch of this afternoon, the Sergeant commented once again on its originality.

"Oh, would you stick that back in the portfolio?" she requested. "I don't want Oakley to see it."

As he did, Murtaugh caught a glimpse of several more versions, each view of the old house slightly different, the way a suspect is with each new interview. He looked at Dana. The way a woman is every time she wears a new dress.

"I'm glad I worked on one today," she was saying. "Originally, I'd gone out to see if Mrs. Cappricio was at her window, but when she wasn't, I sat down and sketched the house instead."

The detective stubbed out his cigarette, and she ordered, "Let's get to work."

Murtaugh couldn't remember how he'd been positioned. Dana Hall expertly moved his face, cupping her hand underneath his chin so she could adjust it to exactly the right angle. Her fingers were cool, and they smelled like those funny crayons.

"Any deep symbolic meaning in how you've got me standing?" he asked.

Her wrists were already making furious motions with the chalk. "Certainly. We can't see you full face, because we don't know what you're thinking. And because you always make us believe you're not looking directly at *us*."

"Touché," he said, in a mock tone of surrender.

"Hands are in the pockets, the way you usually have them, suggesting you've got secret messages inside."

Murtaugh laughed. "Only cigarettes. Honest."

She picked up another crayon. "Posing you this way, I get to use a lot of dark colors, which is how I see you. And the shape of your back is hulking. Sad, somehow, too."

"Always got to get that sadness in," Murtaugh teased.

"I'll admit I'm drawn to it," Dana told him.

"Oakley never looks sad," Murtaugh observed, immediately regretting his spiteful tone.

Dana only flicked black lashes over her gray eyes. "He's different," she said.

Lydia let them know when the session was over. She rubbed against the artist's legs and yowled.

"Time for a snack," Dana announced, scooping the cat up in her arms. "Lydia's brazen when it comes to food."

Murtaugh walked over to the easel. It was incredible how quickly she'd worked. Almost as if she was being timed.

He regarded the image critically, feeling a little like he did when he heard himself on tape; as though, at first, it seemed to be someone else, and then, suddenly, it became apparent it was more truthful than the picture of himself he had in his head.

"Well?" Dana asked, biting her lip.

He scanned the face, which, in contrast to the sweeping lines of the shoulders and back, was polished, detailed. With her crayons, Dana had captured the texture of real skin, craggy and lined. His own eyes shone back at him. Knowing. Cynical. Sad.

"Poor bastard," Murtaugh mumbled.

Dana smiled. "Does that mean you like it?"

He nodded, feeling a lump of emotion in his throat, though he couldn't have said why.

She offered him wine, but seemed displeased when he accepted. After pouring it, she put the bottle out of sight.

They're all nervous, he thought. Even this girl who hardly knows me. They don't realize I've got it under control. It disturbed him that his problem should have been so obvious in the first place.

"So that's Murtaugh," he said, trying to get her to talk again.

"I think so. Have you ever wanted to be anyone else?"

He shrugged. "Eve used to say I'd be good as a lawyer. Intimidating the hell out of some jury in a three-piece suit."

"Rumpled, but expensive," she suggested. "Why didn't you do it?"

"I could have taken classes at night, but—"

Dana shook her head. "Know why I think you didn't? Because you're good at being a detective. Because this is what you're supposed to be."

He was to remember the remark in the days to come.

* * *

Murtaugh woke in the middle of the night, blanketed in sweat. He reached a shaky arm over to turn on the light and get a cigarette.

He'd dreamed he was standing in front of the brownstones on Rose Walsh's block. The long windows in every house were shuttered, and at intervals, Rose's pop-eyed face appeared, first at one, then another.

Murtaugh attempted to enter, but the front doors were locked. In frustration, he sat in the middle of the street to watch.

The faces of all the neighbors, and little Tomas Quiles, too, began playing a grotesque game of hide-and-seek, sometimes within their own homes; and then, just as suddenly, disorienting him by being somewhere else.

Dana Hall came out to ask him to tea. As he followed her, he realized she was not Dana at all, but Eve. He entered the basement apartment and flies swarmed toward him. With nightmarish certainty, he knew they were trying to feed on his brain.

It was four-thirty. Murtaugh got up and fixed himself a cup of instant coffee. The milk was sour, so he took it with a small glass of whiskey instead.

* * *

Rose's funeral service was in the church where Murtaugh went as a kid, where he occasionally retreated now when he was sure he'd be alone. It was old-world dank and gray, even on this bright, hot morning.

The detective met Bonelli and O'Connell outside. They climbed the steps together; and once inside, each man automatically dipped his fingers in holy water and crossed himself.

Eve had been fascinated by the life-size wooden statues of saints and martyrs. She'd stared at their bleeding hands, at the agony on their faces.

"Weren't you afraid of them," she'd whispered, "when you were little?"

Murtaugh hadn't really understood the question. For him, their richly painted figures evoked comfortable and safe childhood memories.

He'd been an altar boy here. He'd walked through these stone arches holding his mother's hand. Even the hazy picture of his father's casket at the altar was somehow precious, reassuring.

Today, however, Eve's words were thrown into new light. He was reminded of Rose on her couch. Of a bound little boy. And he shuddered.

The detectives sat discreetly at the back of the church. Paddy Walsh was in the front row. Mrs. Libretti, with a group of neighbors, perched in the pew behind him. She turned around and waved at the men as if they were old friends.

It was a short, emotionless service. The priest made a limp reference to the circumstances of Rose Walsh's death; otherwise, Murtaugh thought, he might just as well have phoned it in. Tomas Quiles' mass would be a different matter. He wasn't looking forward to the raw display of grief he'd see on Thursday morning.

The Sergeant crossed himself and rose while the men from the funeral parlor carried the white casket into the sunlight.

Bonelli was going to the cemetery in Jersey City where Rose would be buried, next to her mother and father. They watched Paddy Walsh, his staggering controlled only by the firm hand of the priest, bend his head and disappear into the black limousine.

O'Connell winked disrespectfully. "You know what they say about Irish wakes," he said to Murtaugh.

Bonelli was waiting for the meager party of mourners to pass, lagging behind in his beat-up Buick, looking sincerely sad.

Try as he might, Murtaugh couldn't shake the malaise left by his dream. He walked back to Headquarters with the young detective, hands in pockets, barely covering the dangerous edge that was creeping back into his voice.

O'Connell stopped to talk to someone outside the building, and Murtaugh signaled he was going inside. Before he got to his desk Bromsky hailed him.

"We had your amigos in here this morning, Murtaugh,"

the man said, relishing each word, "and guess who they brought with them?"

Murtaugh sat down, crumpling the latest Randall edict and shooting it into the basket. "I give up."

The redfaced detective told him. "The Spics found themselves a lawyer. Seems some self-appointed representative of this department, who shall remain nameless, roughed up one Emil Velasquez, and the little bastard ran home to sister, who called up her social worker, no doubt. So they turned up with a fuckin' bleeding heart lawyer."

Murtaugh began rolling the cellophane in his pocket again, making loud, crinkly noises. He'd have to content himself with these childish ways of annoying people. They might be the only pleasures left for him soon.

"For crying out loud, Murtaugh." Bromsky was at the end of his rope. "Whose side are you on, anyway? You think it's funny these snotnosed junkies are getting away with killing a defenseless old woman and a kid?"

A defenseless old woman. Murtaugh wondered what Paddy Walsh would think of that description.

Bromsky wasn't finished. "Let's hope you find it just as funny when you're out directing traffic in front of the Lincoln Tunnel."

Murtaugh got up and walked past him. It was hot. There was really no reason he should be here. He considered leaving O'Connell a note, but somehow the act of writing on a piece of recycled paper was symbolic of all the bullshit in the place.

He put his shoulders to the swinging doors.

In the small recess of the yellow ochre wall, where the water fountain was, Murtaugh saw Davy O'Connell and Alison Randall.

He watched as she stooped to drink, saw the young detective press up against her. He didn't have the time to avert his eyes as Randall turned, and they kissed with the ease of lovers.

Murtaugh froze. It was impossible to retreat or advance without disturbing them. From down, way under, where his feet were rooted, he felt a surge of emotions—embarrassment, anger, envy, loss.

Alison squirmed away, whispering, "David. Not here."

They saw Murtaugh.

He nodded stiffly and continued down the hall, praying that he could get away quickly, without having to be subjected to the explanations Davy was offering with his eyes.

In the bar across the street, he told himself he was being silly.

Betrayal is a melodramatic word. A word for kings and statesmen. It has nothing to do with a burnt-out cop who, misinterpreting the deference of a younger colleague, comes face-to-face with his own foolishness when the truth rears its ugly head.

He'd almost believed O'Connell liked, even admired, him. Now he understood that the detective had reasons of his own for not being as vocal against him as the rest.

Yes, Davy and Ms. Alison must have spent some great evenings together, recounting their Murtaugh stories before tumbling into bed.

And which part bothers you most, old boy?, he thought, downing his shot in one gulp. The bed or the betrayal part? Why shouldn't a handsome kid like that, with those degrees of his, and those college professor hands, take up with a girl who wore narrow, soft leather slippers?

Face it, he decided, while ordering another. You're pissed off because you're washed up both ways—you ain't worth squat as a detective, and there'll be no more women with pretty shoes in your future, either.

From here on out, it'll be a lone fight until the bastards

win and have you helping the kiddies at a crossing somewhere, or worse yet, collecting bins of recycled paper every afternoon. Even Lou Bonelli, good old reliable Lou, will probably breathe a sigh of relief when you're gone.

It was lunchtime, but Murtaugh wasn't hungry. There was too much to do before they kicked him off the case. He'd have plenty of time to eat later.

When he hit the pavement, the sun unfocused his eyes, reducing everything into shapes and colors, compatible, in a way, with the buzz in his head. Murtaugh walked along, counting each pace as though that would hasten his progress.

He didn't see Dana when he passed her, and by the time he heard her call his name, he could safely pretend he hadn't.

Dana was not so easily snubbed.

"Are you all right?" she asked, panting slightly as she ran up to him.

"Oh, hello," he said.

"You looked like you were in another world." Dana frowned, biting her lip.

The detective realized that it really was an annoying habit.

"I'm busy," he said.

His reply took its toll on her face. She stammered, "I'm sorry. I . . . I won't keep you. I'm on my way to the doctor's—"

Look at her, Murtaugh thought. She thinks I'm drunk, and she's hanging around like I owe her an explanation.

Out loud he said, "Nothing serious, I hope."

Dana flushed. "Oh, no. Just routine."

They were holding up the flow of people who were looking through a bargain rack of shirts and dresses on the street.

"Well," she smiled, "I hope you'll come over soon . . . to pose."

Murtaugh moved to let a Spanish woman with a baby carriage by, putting distance between himself and Dana.

"I'll see you when I see you," he promised noncommittally.

As he continued down the street, Murtaugh wondered what it was he'd first found so special about her.

Cut the crap, he thought, you know what you found special. She paid attention to you, and you're so pathetic you lapped it right up.

You don't see Rebecca Lincroft or Janis Rothman showering you with any dinner invitations. Dana Hall isn't like them. Dana Hall isn't like Eve.

When it came right to it, she was rather pushy—expecting him to have time to talk to her, treating her little drawings as though they were more important than his investigation.

Seen here, in the harsh glare of midday, he decided she was a misfit, out of place among the attractive Hispanic women and smart young professionals who passed her. She looked washed out, her hair going limp in the humid air, wearing that ridiculously overlarge jacket over her skirt.

Dana Hall was a waif who'd married a guy better suited to some country club princess. That was the only reason she was trying to latch onto a loser like himself.

But I won't let her weigh me down, Murtaugh vowed. It's enough to keep myself afloat without her on my back.

He stopped at The March Hare, opening the door slowly to muffle the cheerful jangle of bells. It appeared to be deserted, and there was no music coming over the speakers.

A woman, who had been kneeling behind the counter, stood up suddenly.

"Can I help you?" she asked.

She was so blonde and pale that she appeared almost albino. Like Rebecca Lincroft, she was small, but Murtaugh could see she had an extraordinary figure, barely sheathed by a short, nubby sort of dress. When she moved away from the display case the light traced perfect outlines of her legs against the material.

"Sergeant Murtaugh," he said roughly. "Has Ms. Lincroft gone out to lunch?"

She shook her head slowly. There was something bovine about her. A purewhite cow's face atop a flawless body.

"Rebecca doesn't always come in early during the week, because no one's around until after work." She paused, giving him time to think of them, those attractive customers of Saturday afternoon, installed behind desks all over Manhattan.

Murtaugh smiled. "And you're—?"

"The assistant," she told him. Then she added, as an afterthought, "Lindsay. Lindsay Bartholomew."

The name sounded familiar. She must have guessed it, because she added, "I live on Rebecca and Jake's block. One of your men, an old Italian guy, was over to talk to me a few days ago."

Old Italian guy, Murtaugh laughed to himself. She probably thinks I'm ancient, too.

"Would you like to wait?"

Murtaugh wasn't sure why he'd come in the first place. "No," he said. "Tell her I'll catch up with her at home."

He walked past the chess set and the boardgames to the door. As it clanged, Lindsay Bartholomew called vapidly, "Have a nice day."

Murtaugh took a last look at those unbelievable legs and her pale, lashless eyes before heading out into the street.

* * *

It was a wasted afternoon. Murtaugh ended up having another drink; and then, simply because he was walking aimlessly when he saw the open door, he sat for a full half hour in an empty church of some Protestant denomination—Baptist or Lutheran, he wasn't sure.

Marveling at the clean lines of the place, the simple cross over the spare altar, he was reminded of something important.

163

But he couldn't put it into cohesive thought, so it lapsed into just another gnawing feeling.

A young man, his face pitted with acne, hurried down the aisle and began practicing the organ. The sounds of the unfamiliar hymn made him keenly aware that he didn't belong here, that there were other places he should be.

CHAPTER

13

MURTAUGH HAD FORGOTTEN about the press conference. By the time he reached Headquarters a few reporters from local papers still skulked around, but the television crews were gone, leaving a dejected, after-the-party atmosphere in their wake.

Bromsky stood in the hall talking to one of the journalists. Murtaugh pretended not to notice his attempt to flag him down. With blinders on, the Sergeant walked to his desk, hoping not to be bothered by anyone, wanting simply to sit.

Lou Bonelli was in his chair.

"Hunt," he said, sounding relieved. "I was just leaving you a note."

"I know, I know. The press conference," Murtaugh growled. "Looks like they managed without me."

Bonelli shook his head. "No, Davy and me, we've been trying to find you for over an hour."

"So? Now you found me."

Ah, Hunt, Bonelli said to himself, why'dya have to pick today to start screwing yourself up again?

He told Murtaugh, "That old lady at Number 520. Mrs. Cappricio? The downstairs neighbor found her a little while ago."

"Same as the others?"

"No." The other detective shook his head. "Looks like natural causes, but with all the things going down, we thought you'd want to check it yourself. Davy's there now."

They took Bonelli's car. Murtaugh, close to vomiting, kept his head halfway out the window, wishing hopelessly for a cool breeze.

The body was being carried into the ambulance, but today no crowds of gaping onlookers pressed against the barricades. A few teen-agers eating icecream cones watched the proceedings.

Has death become commonplace here?, Murtaugh wondered. Maybe its regularity had made the neighbors lose their sense of occasion. Or maybe they were frightened, shaken to their bones. Maybe they stayed away as a superstitious gesture meant not to tempt fate.

Madie Quinn's door was open. She stood in the hall talking to O'Connell. An ugly, snootfaced white poodle, rusted at the feet and mouth where the fur had turned orange, darted about, nipping at the heels of anyone who passed.

"Poor thing," Madie said. "Like I was saying to this young man—Toodles, don't bother the nice detective—I think these killings happening right next to us was too much for her."

"Looks like a heart attack," O'Connell told Murtaugh.

"Where's Lowenstein?"

O'Connell looked grim. "Out with the flu. We got Hasaad."

Murtaugh swore, excusing himself in front of Mrs. Quinn. The others knew what he was thinking. Changing horses in midstream was unlucky. But he knew Lowenstein must be pretty sick not to show up at a time like this.

"It's had me so upset that I went to my daughter's right after church. Stayed the night and didn't come back till yesterday," Madie said.

"What time did you find her?"

Madie caught him inadvertently kicking the dog, which had seemed about to mistake his leg for something else. She picked up Toodles protectively, and he detected a slight coolness in her voice.

"When I didn't see her at the window, I should have checked right away, I guess," she told them, "but I thought she was just napping. It wasn't until after lunch that I decided to go up and say hello. I do that every so often in case she needs anything. Then when I knocked, and there was no answer, I had a *feeling*, you know?"

"The door was open," O'Connell whispered to Murtaugh.

Madie cut in, "Well, that's not unusual. She didn't hear so good, so she left it unlocked during the day, so's I could walk right in if she didn't know I was at the door."

Murtaugh was anxious to get upstairs. He thanked Mrs. Quinn and watched her carry Toodles into her tidy apartment.

"Hasaad around?" he asked O'Connell as they climbed the stairs.

The young detective looked displeased. "In. Out. Said it looked like natural causes and that the old woman had been dead for at least a day."

"Time?"

"Late Sunday was all he'd say," Davy answered. He led the way into the room. "She was found over there," he said, pointing to the morris chair.

"Anyone else screwing around here?" Murtaugh wanted to know.

167

O'Connell appeared anxious to impress with his efficiency. "I had them dust for prints. Do the whole tap dance. We thought that's what you'd want."

Murtaugh, not in a gracious frame of mind, said nothing.

"Seems pretty routine, Hunt," Bonelli piped up, just to break the silence. "Her time to go, was all. A miracle the old lady lived this long."

Murtaugh went over to the shelf in the kitchenette. The brandy and the tray were back in place, and the glass had been rinsed.

He paced around, his footsteps echoing hollowly. Mrs. Cappricio was gone. Her presence had been diminutive, but her absence was already felt in the small room. It seemed to have been uninhabited for a long time.

"Did anyone turn up my card?"

The two men hesitated, unsure of the Sergeant's reference and unwilling to tangle with him when he was in this mood.

"My card," he repeated impatiently. "One with my name and number on it. Except for the murderer, I was probably the last person to see her alive."

Bonelli laughed uneasily, as though Murtaugh was joking. "You don't think somebody murdered the old woman, do you?"

The Sergeant, standing next to the bed that hadn't been slept in, he was sure, since Saturday night, said simply, "I saw her at about noon. She was terrified."

O'Connell offered a meek explanation. "Hey, living alone at that age, with some nut preying on your neighbors, who wouldn't be?"

Murtaugh rubbed his eyes with the back of his hand. "It was more than that," he said. "I think she saw someone, when she was looking out the window."

Davy O'Connell crossed toward the little chair facing the

street. "If that's the case, chances are somebody else saw whoever it was, too," he said. But he didn't sound convinced.

Murtaugh scowled. "She didn't see him come through the front," he muttered, indicating the rear window with his hand. "When I was here, that chair was facing the yard." It had been moved so it now faced inward, its ladder back against the kitchen wall.

The detective picked up a tin of hard candles on the end table. He ran his finger over the unbroken seal.

"Find out where these came from," he barked.

O'Connell was skeptical. "I bet you'd find those in the apartments of just about every senior citizen in town. My grandmother always kept them around in a little dish."

"It wasn't here on Sunday," Murtaugh snapped. "Check out the local stores, see which ones carry this particular brand. Then see if anyone remembers selling a tin anytime in the last few days."

Bonelli brightened. "Like to a Puerto Rican, maybe, eh, Hunt?"

The Sergeant only moved over to the nightstand next to the bed. He searched through its one drawer, taking out a yellowing stack of photographs and a pile of greeting cards tied with a faded ribbon.

"Her husband." O'Connell pointed out a gaunt young man with deep-socketed eyes.

Tubercular, Murtaugh guessed. Mrs. Cappricio had probably been a widow most of her life.

Davy went on. "And that's the son, in the uniform. Both deceased, Mrs. Quinn says."

The old woman had nothing—no family, no friends, no money—nothing at all to connect her with this world, except for those shadowy images she saw from her perch high overlooking the block.

Those and, Murtaugh knew, a canny will to survive. He recalled her gleaming eyes as she spoke of dead Doctor Zott. She'd outlasted all of them, and he let her down.

The other detectives watched expectantly while Murtaugh retraced his steps in the room again and again. Finally, after leafing through the Bible and opening each drawer in the old bureau, he walked, like a man asleep, over to the telephone.

For some seconds the Sergeant only stared, then he picked up the dusty black thing, the same model he'd had when he first joined the Force. Underneath its felt bottom was a small white rectangle with his name embossed in navy letters.

Murtaugh turned the card over several times, as if he might find the answer to Mrs. Cappricio's death recorded on it somewhere.

"Think she was planning to call you when she heard someone enter the apartment?" O'Connell asked.

Uncharacteristically, Bonelli interrupted. "But she was found in the chair," he reminded them. "And the Pakkie doctor says it was her heart got her in the end."

Murtaugh put the card back under the telephone. It would remain their secret, his and Mrs. Cappricio's.

"Let's go," he said. "There's nothing else we can do here."

O'Connell stopped him. "If you're sure it was murder," he challenged, "how do you explain the absence of the needles?"

Davy O'Connell had a way of hitting the nail on the head.

When the Sergeant spoke his voice was almost friendly. "That's what we've got to figure out."

He opened the door and peered down the empty stairway. "Did the killer hear someone coming?"

He walked to the window. "Did he see something outside that made him nervous?"

O'Connell was interested. "A Sunday afternoon. Hot," he said. "People out in the street."

"A guy would have to be nuts to take a chance like that, in broad daylight," Bonelli told them.

"Nuts or desperate," Murtaugh agreed.

O'Connell nodded. "Or else someone nobody would suspect."

They were falling into the old pattern again, and the Sergeant cautioned himself not to be seduced into it. For whatever reason O'Connell was playing along, it wasn't because they were on the same wavelength.

Alison Randall proved that.

"Don't forget," he said, "it wasn't a typical Sunday. Mrs. Quinn was at her daughter's. Walsh was with the priest. And in case you haven't noticed, parents are keeping their kids close to home. I bet the pavement had been just about rolled up."

O'Connell persisted. "There's still such a thing as looking out windows."

Murtaugh turned and walked out.

"I'll check it out with the neighbors, Hunt," Bonelli said, following him.

They left the apartment to be sealed by another uniform.

Murtaugh refused their offer for a ride back to Headquarters. He watched them walk to the curb—O'Connell uneasily, Bonelli shooting a backward glance over the curve of his shoulders—before tapping Madie Quinn's door.

The Sergeant heard Toodles' manicured paws frenetically attempting to get traction on the expanse of floor and throwrugs inside. Its bark was sharp and metallic, like a car door catching.

Madie had been on the telephone.

"My son-in-law is coming to pick me up," she told Murtaugh, "so I don't have much time."

His eyes traveled to the flowered canvas overnight bag and the bright pink pet carrier.

171

"This won't take long."

They sat. Madie offered him a candy dish, and when he refused, she began unwrapping a miniature Reese's cup. The smell of peanut butter wafted between them.

"I like my chocolate," she said, smacking her lips.

"Mrs. Quinn," the detective began uncomfortably, "on Sunday, the day she died, Mrs. Cappricio tried to get to the bank. Do you have any idea why?"

"The bank?" Madie shook her head. "No need for her to go there. Her social security gets automatically deposited."

Something didn't add up, Murtaugh thought. "You're saying it was unusual behavior for her?"

"Plenty unusual," Madie agreed. "She never went out at all since, oh, summer before last when she had that nasty fall."

"How did she get her groceries?"

Madie let Toodles lick the melted candy off her fingers, without missing a beat in the conversation.

"It was delivered, same as what she needed from the pharmacy." She winked confidentially. "When she started with her glass of brandy, I got it once a month from the place on the corner of Washington."

Murtaugh leaned toward her. "We didn't find more than five dollars in the apartment, Mrs. Quinn. How did she pay for things?"

"Oh, I took care of what little expenses there were." Madie smiled, then she explained. "Instead of paying regular rent."

The Sergeant was momentarily taken aback. The old lady in the garret had owned Number 520.

"Then you were her tenant," he reasoned slowly, "not her landlady."

She wiped her hands on some small Christmas napkins that were on the coffee table. "Heavens, yes. I only came three years back when my husband passed on."

"And you were close?" Murtaugh questioned. "You and Mrs. Cappricio?"

Madie rolled her eyes indulgently. "She was a good old girl. The old ones are easy, Sergeant. It's the young ones that are hard to handle."

She picked up a triptych frame with the photographs of three pimply adolescents.

"Like I tell my daughter, you've got to sit on them when they're young," she said. "If I hadn'ta sat on her when she was at that age, who knows how she would have turned out?"

Murtaugh kept respectfully silent for a moment, as though to consider the possible directions, the dangerous paths avoided, by the sat-upon daughter of Madie Quinn. Then he went on, gently, "I suppose you'll be staying with your family for a while."

"I like my Bingo, and my privacy, Sergeant," Madie sighed, "so's it won't be for long. But we'll never find another place like this one, will we, Toodles?" The dog drooled.

"Do you know who will get the house?"

"Only one she had was a nephew. Lawyer. Never come around at all, but he always sent a card at Christmas," she replied.

Murtaugh remembered the beribboned stack, mentally calculating that for twenty bucks of Hallmarks, the nephew was getting a return in property worth considerably more.

"Maybe he'll decide to keep it," the detective suggested. "Then you . . . ," he stopped short of including the poodle, "you can stay."

Madie Quinn clucked her tongue. "Oh, he'll sell, all right. He's a *lawyer*." She repeated the word as though it didn't belong in Hoboken.

But it did belong in Hoboken, Murtaugh thought. All around them, lawyers and architects, bankers and doctors, were moving in. They were young, however, part of the massive baby

173

boom, a set never sat upon. Maybe, in Madie's mind, they didn't count in the way that Mrs. Cappricio's lawyer-nephew, probably somewhere in his sixties, did.

He got up to leave. Toodles followed him, pirouetting to the door.

"Sergeant," Madie said, with sudden alarm, "these questions—you don't think poor Anna was . . . ?"

Murtaugh pressed her hand. "We're not taking anything for granted, Mrs. Quinn. Have a nice stay at your daughter's."

The name Anna kept going through his head as he walked, like the line of a song.

Anna. It seemed even more pitiable that he could have prevented Anna's death, than old Mrs. Cappricio's. Murtaugh had been certain, at the time, that her fear wasn't groundless, yet he'd continued on his way, tossing her a card as though it were some kind of protective shield.

The woman was trying to get to the bank. She'd summoned her reserves of energy in order to make the arduous climb downstairs. Besides money, what would be at a bank?

He made a mental list. A notary public. A copy machine. A safety deposit box. There were several small keys in one of the bureau drawers. Could it be that Mrs. Cappricio had been anxious to open a deposit box? And, if so, was it to take something out or put something in? Murtaugh paused in front of a bar. It was almost five o'clock, too late for the bank, and the whitehot haze of this summer day would make it an eternity until nightfall.

Wait, he bargained with himself, have something to eat instead.

Across the street was a small candy store. Eve often stopped here to buy homemade sweets. Like Madie Quinn, Eve liked her chocolate.

Today a shade was pulled down in the window in an effort to save the wares from the sun.

Murtaugh entered and immediately felt ridiculous, seeing himself magnified in the glass cases of freshly dipped strawberries and pecan rolls. The smell made him sickish. He wanted a drink so desperately that he found himself snarling at the kid behind the counter when he went over the quarter of a pound mark.

Turtles, Murtaugh laughed bitterly. Is that what I've come to? Wandering the streets and eating cashew and caramel turtles out of a dainty white bag?

In only a few minutes, the candy melted and was over his fingers in sticky clumps.

He circled back to the bar, stopping in the men's room to wash his hands. Then, because he knew it was senseless to fight the inevitable, Murtaugh ordered a shot and a beer.

CHAPTER

14

THERE WAS something wrong with a place where old ladies
will wave at you and yet not speak. Where couples were
mismatched. Where everybody has a personal toy, a private
secret.

Murtaugh thought of Dana Hall, so open and vulnerable.
Even she had something in her past which could only be
alluded to by cryptic remarks and shared looks with her husband.

Oakley was another enigma. If he was really a wholesome
Bible-bearing boy from the South, then why had he lied about
the night of Rose's murder? Why was Murtaugh left with the
feeling that he was not so backwoods as he represented himself
to be?

The Sergeant ran down the roster of people—people he'd
known for less than a week, and who had since been scarcely
out of his mind. Maybe Bromsky was right. The interviews
hadn't turned up a lick of hard evidence.

176

Incongruously, his mind returned to an embarrassing memory.

When he was sixteen, and in the throes of a painful crush on his English teacher, Murtaugh once impulsively raised his hand to interpret some lines of poetry she'd been discussing in class.

The poem, real and immediate to him as he'd read it to himself, suddenly evaporated into nothingness. He was unable to say anything about it, even guess at its meaning.

Miss Rickwood prompted, but when he only stammered, she shook her head with the put-upon expression reserved for slower students and told him that those who would be quick on the draw ought first to make sure their guns were loaded.

He never liked her after that day.

Murtaugh had known what the poetry meant. Known it so intimately, so implicitly, it rendered him impotent, at a loss for words.

Later, when he became a detective, he got that same feeling during a case. He began to believe that investigations were like poems: if you paid enough attention to images, emotions, a few telling phrases, then you'd know in your heart what it added up to, even before you could articulate it.

For the first time, he began to doubt what had been, for him, a personal philosophy. Maybe it was all garbage, he thought. Maybe what mattered was simply to let people know your gun was loaded.

Murtaugh paid for his drinks.

Tonight he'd forget the inhabitants of Rose Walsh's neighborhood, and the friends and family of little Tomas Quiles. Before the brass pulled him, Sergeant Hunter Murtaugh would show them he could play their game as well as his own.

The boy had been found in the carriage house, and whoever killed Rose probably entered from her back door. If he discovered the point of entry to the yard, he might also discover who had entered.

Murtaugh walked the southern end of the street looking for a passageway. A passageway would have enabled someone to scale the fences until they reached the Walsh property.

There was none.

In a little while, people would be coming home from work, but now it was quiet. The shades were drawn in the Halls' apartment. No one was home.

He was almost to Paulie's when he noticed an alley. It was so narrow no light penetrated, although Murtaugh could see vague outlines of some aluminum trashcans at the rear. He edged toward them.

At eye level, in back of the refuse pile, was a concrete wall.

Unsteadily, he pulled himself up, using the cans as a foothold. He sat on the wall, judging the height of the jump necessary to land him in the first of the backyards.

This could be it, he told himself. From here, someone with a certain amount of agility could make it over the walls and fences to Number 518. There would be no danger of being seen by anyone in the houses on the next block because of those high limestone partitions separating the adjoining lawns. And in the dark—

Murtaugh stopped at the first fence, rusted metal like Rose's and only about four feet high. He scanned the lay of the land from the alley to where he stood. The rain had washed away whatever footprints might have been there before Saturday. Still, the sparse grass was flattened in spots and the ground was choppy.

With one of the new residences, it would have been easy to tell how traveled the path really was. They landscaped and tended their gardens, making any disturbance simple to spot.

The people who lived here used their yard as a repository for old bikes and tools. A handmower lay on its side, uselessly, almost covered by long blades of grass. Grayish underwear flapped soundlessly on the clothesline. In the adjacent yard, things looked much the same.

Murtaugh grasped the doweling and hoisted himself up on it. His pocket caught a piece of wire. He heard it rip as he fell with a thud on the other side.

Immediately, the barking began. It wasn't until he reached the middle of the yard that he actually saw the German shepherd, crouched in a doghouse only a few feet from him.

The dog was old, but big. His teeth, caked with tartar, were still alarmingly numerous; and bared as they were against his grizzled leatherish lips, the detective decided it would be best to make a run for the next fence.

The wire on this one was smaller. He was trying to find a toehold when the dog caught his leg.

Murtaugh hurled himself forward, falling into the neighboring garden with his weight on one arm.

Christ, he winced through gritted teeth, I've broken something.

He sat on the ground until the roaring in his head subsided, only partially aware of the dog's persistent barking and the sound of voices.

"I'm calling the police," said a large woman in a limegreen mu-mu.

Murtaugh looked up and saw that she was talking to him.

On the other side, an old man was bobbing up and down. Murtaugh forced himself to get up, to focus his eyes. He realized the man wasn't really bobbing, he was holding the collar of the German shepherd which jerked his arms in the direction of its prey.

"He *is* the police," the old man told the woman. "Aren't you?"

Murtaugh nodded. He knew he should show them his shield, but he couldn't move his arm.

"See? I told you," the man said smugly. "I seen him coming out of Paddy Walsh's that day."

The woman was not impressed. "What are you doing in my yard?" she demanded.

"I . . . uh, we're trying to . . . discover if it's possible to get from one end of the block to the other by—"

She came closer.

"You're drunk," the woman howled. "Can you beat that? A drunk cop breaking into my own backyard?"

This is a nightmare, Murtaugh thought, as he flexed his elbow and wrist, and he had a feeling it was going to get worse.

"Is that dog out here all night?" he asked the old man. The dog growled.

He listened to the man's longwinded discourse of his pet's schedule. From here, he could see the Halls' patio, and beyond it, the Walsh's carriage house. If the killer had managed to make his way through this obstacle course, he must have been someone younger and more fit than himself.

Murtaugh asked the woman if he might go through her house to get to the street. He would have requested to use the telephone, vaguely believing that act might lend him credence in her eyes, but it hit him with a jolt that there was really no one to call.

* * *

Paddy Walsh sat on a barstool in the black suit he'd worn in church.

At first, Murtaugh considered pretending he hadn't seen him. There was time to walk out of Paulie's as devil-may-care as he'd walked into it.

So what if the mu-mu'd woman still kept watch on her front stoop?

He caught a glimpse of himself in the bar mirror, and the

absurdity of the situation made him smile. His red face, the torn jacket, the pain shooting from his wrist to his elbow—why shouldn't he sit down next to Paddy, just two pathetic old codgers seeking solace from a flowing bottle?

The television set was tuned to the news. Paddy watched the press coverage of the funeral, his tears rolling into his glass.

Murtaugh walked up to Dominick and ordered. He could have sworn Paddy looked happy to see him before he had time to become suspicious.

"Will you quit your following me, sir," he said, "and leave me in peace?"

Murtaugh took a sip of beer to quench his real thirst. "No business tonight, Mr. Walsh," he assured the man. "Just pure relaxation."

Walsh sagged. "It's easy for you," he whispered, "but there's no relaxing from your sorrows, is there, Dom?"

Dominick, in the way of all good bartenders, nodded sympathetically.

They sat in silence for a long while, drinking. Two musicians, male and female, came in with large cases of sound equipment and a guitar.

Paddy and the Sergeant half-swiveled around on their stools so they could listen to the couple argue as they set up their microphones and speakers.

"I've got this round," Murtaugh said, sliding his money across the bar with his good hand.

Paddy was wary, but obviously unable to turn down a free beer. "That's kind, sir."

"It's Murtaugh."

"Irish on both sides, are you?" Paddy asked, and when the detective nodded, he went on enthusiastically, "That's grand. I thought there was something about you the first time we met."

The memory of that occasion, only days ago, sobered them both.

When Murtaugh spoke again, it was to Dominick.

"You usually have entertainment?"

"Monday through Thursday. The owner thinks it'll draw a crowd." Dominick shrugged, looking around the empty room.

"Doesn't seem like they have much of a following."

The bartender leaned forward confidentially. "Nothing's gonna help," he said sadly. "Truth is, our regulars ain't enough to keep us going. There's talk of puttin' some kind of fancy exercise club in here."

Paddy shook his head. "It's changing, boys. I'm glad to be getting out."

"Where you off to, Paddy?" the bartender asked, saving Murtaugh the trouble.

"Somewhere tropical," the man winked. "Florida, or Atlantic City, maybe."

There was a pause. Finally, Murtaugh said, as casually as he could manage, "Think you'll have much trouble getting rid of the houses?"

"Naa," Walsh replied. "Had a few offers already."

Murtaugh whistled low. "Already? Looks like somebody was pretty anxious."

Paddy became wary again. "Well, I'd better be close about that," he said, putting a finger to his lips. "Not wise to talk until it's signed and all."

The detective was curious. Already, he repeated to himself. Then he remembered the brownstone without Eve. Those bright, attractive Sunday drivers standing in the foyer where he cowered in his loneliness, impatient to get back to his drink. He shouldn't be surprised that Paddy wasn't staying without Rose.

He considered probing further, but decided neither of them

was drunk enough to speak without inhibition. There would be plenty of time, and other ways to find out who was so interested in Walsh's property.

Three young men and a woman entered the bar. They greeted the musicians and sat at one of the tables near the makeshift stage.

"Rose loved her music," Paddy said, his voice maudlin.

Murtaugh signaled to Dominick for a refill. He kept his own cold glass against his arm, hoping it would keep down the swelling.

"Were you childhood sweethearts, Paddy," he asked softly, "here in Hoboken?"

Paddy laughed. "Me and Rosie? Naa. I was a sailor boy when I met her. What about yourself? Ever wear a uniform?"

"Viet Nam, early on."

Paddy became chatty again. "Served time in a real war myself." He laughed mischievously. "They said I was too old, but they took me anyway. Ahh, wasn't Rose wild when I re-enlisted after we tied the knot? Her ma always said I did it just to get out of the house."

Murtaugh let him talk. "They never took to me. Rosie's ma and pa. Thought I was out for her money, on account of me being younger and all."

The detective smiled. "I guess that's a pretty common thing these days. Older woman, younger man."

"You mean, like the ones next door?" Paddy said, blinking his glassy owl eyes.

An edge of bitterness crept into his voice. "But it's still the same, isn't it? Her playing the tune and him jumping through the hoop."

Murtaugh was puzzled. It was hardly how he would have described Oakley and Dana's relationship. Was it possible that this old man had seen otherwise?

The singer welcomed them to Paulie's. There was applause from the table of friends. She spoke into the mike with rehearsed, breathy tones, as though the amplification was actually necessary.

Dominick whispered, "They write their own songs." He shook his head. "I dunno. All sounds the same to me."

Murtaugh watched them, the skinny singer with her mannish shirt and wildly streaked wisps of hair; and the skinny guitar player, as colorless as a piece of paper.

Recycled, he thought. Recycled from somewhere back in the sixties.

The woman attacked the opening number voraciously, seeming at times to bite the microphone.

Paddy piped up loudly, "What a load of shit, eh, Dom?"

The bartender walked over to his table of customers.

"How about something sweet," the old man roared, "like 'My Wild Irish Rose'?"

They played on while he repeated the title of his request, again and again.

Murtaugh left a few bills on the bar. Looking over his shoulder before he walked out to the street, he saw Paddy Walsh crying into his beer.

*　*　*

Nights like this never seem to want to give in to darkness, Murtaugh thought as he crossed the road. It was still hot and muggy. He flexed his arm.

Well, at least it isn't broken, he comforted himself, though it's probably sprained. He tried to remember where the Ace bandages were.

There must be a few around. You were married to a doctor, remember?

He remembered.

Something about going to Headquarters in the morning

with his wrist wrapped appealed to him. He was a ridiculous bastard, so why not look the part? Davy and Ms. Alison would have a field day with it.

The bricks of the elementary school glowed bonewhite in the dusk. Murtaugh was almost past the steps before he noticed Jaime Sanchez sitting within the shelter of the front door. The boy had been watching him.

He climbed up the steps and lowered himself onto the concrete. For a split second, catching the youth's granite profile, Murtaugh imagined Dana was right. He looked sad, like a lost little boy.

"Waiting for someone?"

Nothing.

The detective tried again. "Who's the mastermind, Jaime?" The boy averted his head.

"See, before all this hoopla in the neighborhood, we got a few complaints from some of the local clergymen. Seems somebody was vandalizing their churches. Desecrating the altars."

Sanchez got up, but he made sure his voice reached him. "You want to tell me, Jaime? You want to let me know who's feeding your sick, little twisted mind?"

"Talk to my lawyer, man."

"You do that very well," the Sergeant called. "What else have you been coached into saying?"

He caught up with the boy, his voice becoming more conversational. "Why didn't you tell me you knew Mrs. Hall?"

"You didn't ask," Jaime answered. "So now I got to tell you everybody in this town I know?"

They were walking in step. "She says she's given you a key to her apartment several times."

"So what of it?"

"The first just happened to be the day Tomas Quiles was

killed. A few hours after the second, Mrs. Walsh was murdered."

Jaime yelled, "I went to have my fucking picture painted,
man. Nothing else."

"When was the last time you saw Tomas Quiles?"

"Who says there was a first time?" Jaime demanded.

"I know there was a first time," Murtaugh told him. "And
I believe the last was on the day he died. I think you gave
him the dope the medical examiner found in him."

Jaime whirled around, the shadows on his face making it
masklike. "Tomorrow me and my lawyer see your pal Bromsky. I don't have to say shit to you tonight."

From the other end of the street, Murtaugh saw two figures
approaching. Ricky and Miguel. He wondered why Emil hadn't
been included in this rendezvous.

Murtaugh threw an offering into the last light of this longest
of days. "Dana Hall thinks you're innocent."

Jaime stopped moving.

"She says you're rebellious, but not bad," he called softly.
"Is that true?"

It was impossible to see the boy clearly.

Jaime said, "People like you ain't gonna listen to people
like her and me anyway."

He sauntered toward his friends, leaving Murtaugh to ponder what kind of people Sanchez and Mrs. Hall were.

CHAPTER

15

MURTAUGH ARRIVED late, but sober. On his way down the hall he met Alison Randall who looked stunning in a jade-colored suit. She avoided his eyes, and when he raised his bandaged hand to say good morning, she only nodded, apparently flustered.

Compared to other desks, his own was bare. It was not a working space. It was the desk of someone being phased out.

But not yet, he thought, as he removed his jacket and threw it over the back of the chair. First, I'm going to piece together what I know.

"Bromsky had the kids in?" the Sergeant asked Bonelli.

"They just got here. Lawyer and all."

Murtaugh shook his head. "What does he think he's going to hold them on?"

O'Connell walked over to them.

"Can I talk to you for a minute, Hunt?" he asked; then dropping his voice, "It's personal."

"Not now, Davy," the detective answered. "There are a few things I want to go over with you and Lou, first."

Bonelli reached for his pad. O'Connell sat.

"The time has come—" Murtaugh stopped and laughed quietly. "The time has come, the walrus said, to speak of many things . . ."

"The walrus?" Lou asked, thinking maybe Hunt wasn't as sober as he looked.

"Lewis Carroll," Murtaugh said.

The name sounded familiar to Bonelli. He leafed through his notes.

"I want to talk it all out," Murtaugh continued, "so when they put me out to pasture, you'll know every angle I've worked."

The men looked uncomfortable, but said nothing.

He told them about his experience of the previous evening.

"Sure that arm isn't broke?" Bonelli was concerned.

The Sergeant ignored him. "The point is, it would take some doing to get into the Walshes' yard by climbing the fences. Especially if you were carrying anything heavy."

"You mean, like the kid," O'Connell said.

"Nothing points to him being killed in the carriage house," Murtaugh agreed. "The body was probably put there later."

Bonelli scanned his pad.

"The old man said the carpet the boy was rolled up in didn't look familiar," he told them, "but he couldn't say for sure it hadn't belonged to them. Rose had all her folks' stuff out there."

"If the killer moved the body, then we might have the motive for Mrs. Walsh's death," O'Connell said.

"She saw him." Lou sounded excited. "So he bumped her off, same as the widow next door."

Murtaugh rubbed his wrist. It didn't really hurt, but he

was aware that something wasn't right with it. Same as these theories.

"I see two problems," O'Connell said thoughtfully.

"Good."

"First, assuming the dog was either not in the yard or tied up," he reasoned, "a few athletic teen-agers might have been able to make it over those fences carrying a body."

Murtaugh recalled little Emil Velasquez running down the street. Maybe the others were more coordinated.

"And disregarding that possibility for a moment," the young detective continued, "how the hell could anyone *else* get into the carriage house?"

"Two possibilities," Murtaugh replied. "The front door. Or the back."

"And you think it was the back?" O'Connell was skeptical. "Then who did it?"

"One of them with adjoining yards," Bonelli offered weakly, "except they all got some sort of alibi."

"Unless they're all lying."

"No," Murtaugh said, surprised at how uncomfortable he felt whenever faced with the possibility that Dana Hall was anything other than what she appeared to be. "Not necessarily. Rose was alive at eleven. Florian and the two women heard her."

No one spoke, so he went on. "The upper part of the house was empty. Now I've been on the roof, and there's a pegged ladder leading into the garden."

"You think somebody got in while Florian and his wife were downstairs, and that he used their ladder to get into the Walshes' backyard?" O'Connell asked. "Then how would the killer have known the house was empty? And how did he get in?"

Bromsky came in without a word. He went to his desk and began pounding on the typewriter.

189

Murtaugh seemed unaware of his presence. "Either he had a way of knowing or the door was unlocked. Let's hear more about this guy Deacon. I'll ask Florian if he left the house open."

O'Connell snapped his fingers. "We're forgetting someone," he said. "Oakley Hall could have come home, seen his wife inside with the Florians, and run upstairs."

"What about the boy's body?"

"Maybe it was already in the trunk," O'Connell suggested.

"Maybe," Murtaugh repeated.

The telephone rang. The Sergeant acknowledged the caller with a grunt. He placed the receiver neatly back into place and picked up his jacket.

"An invitation from the top," he told the detectives through clenched teeth.

"The little bastards got away this time," Bromsky called to Murtaugh. "But I'm gonna nail 'em. I'm gonna follow their slimy Puerto Rican butts around town till they screw up."

As the Sergeant pushed through the doors, he heard Bromsky shout, "And one fucking less bleeding heart around here is gonna make my job all the easier."

* * *

"You're not going to make me do this by the numbers, Hunt," Rourke said affably.

"You bet your ass I am," Murtaugh replied.

"We both know what the end will be." The Captain drummed his fingers on a manila folder.

Yeah, it'll be the round file for me and that stack of papers with my name on it.

"What's the point?" Rourke asked.

The point was time. Red tape meant more time for him.

He could be suspended from the investigation, of course,

but he wouldn't be transferred to the rubber-gun squad. He wouldn't be assigned to traffic duty because some lady in a mu-mu had been the straw that broke the back of his career. Not yet.

They talked procedures, Murtaugh half tuned out, listening only for the words that meant he was off the case. Rourke danced around them. They remained unsaid.

For the moment, Murtaugh reminded himself bitterly.

No wonder Randall wouldn't look me in the eye, he thought, on his way out of the building. She'll have to find another fish to fry now.

O'Connell caught up with him.

"Buy you lunch?" he asked.

Murtaugh declined politely. "Not today, fella."

They walked together down Washington Street. The humidity had gone down overnight. This morning it was almost cool.

"You all right?"

"Fine," Murtaugh said, closing the subject.

He stopped on the next corner, indicating he wished to take a different route. Any different route.

"Look," O'Connell began, "I feel like I should explain about the other day—"

"No need to explain to me," Murtaugh replied. He was ashamed of his petulant tone.

Davy smiled. "I know. That's what I keep telling myself. But somehow, since you saw us . . . I've felt guilty."

When Murtaugh said nothing, he hurried on. "Stupid, isn't it? I mean, why shouldn't I be able to like two people who don't much like each other?"

The Sergeant said, "This is unnecessary."

"Sure. But you haven't been entirely right about her, you know. She isn't really the way she appears to be."

"Who is?" Murtaugh dug his hands deep into his pockets, taking comfort in the throbbing from his wrist, the way he'd often taken comfort in his grief.

What a nut case, he said to himself. You really like being hurt.

O'Connell stood there helplessly. "If you'd give Alison a chance, I think you'd find her attitude toward you would be a lot different in the future."

"Listen, kid." The Sergeant took out a cigarette and lit up with his good hand. "I don't have a future. Here, anyway."

Davy looked stunned. "Those shits," he muttered.

"Stop worrying. It's a lousy life anyway."

But the young man persisted. "Know why I became a cop in the first place, Murtaugh? Because I thought we needed a change from people like you."

He grinned. "So buck up. You won."

"Yeah? You think so?" O'Connell asked him. "Well, now I'm not so sure."

"See you when I see you." Murtaugh winked, leaving O'Connell looking depressed. He himself felt as if a weight had been lifted from his shoulders.

* * *

Murtaugh hadn't expected to find Maria Quiles in the hair salon, but she was there, leaning on the Formica surface of the front desk, holding a Styrofoam cup in both hands.

He'd been to the shop before so the sight of the Mylar wallpaper in its bright jungle design was not as distracting. There was something about all these metallic surfaces—the mirrors, the chrome, the shiny walls—glittering semaphores that signaled what went on inside this place was artificial, unnatural.

192

They sat on a cushioned bench.

She said, "At first I think it would be better to keep busy. It's not."

Murtaugh wanted to say something comforting, but his own experience with bereavement made him tongue-tied.

"You hurt your hand," Maria noticed.

He dismissed it. "Listen. We've questioned those boys. Have you heard anything else? Remembered anything?"

Maria nodded slowly. "Maybe, I think. I look through . . . through the toy chest. And I find a record." She grimaced when she said the word. "These players are strange. Their faces are like devils, you know?"

"Tomas bought the record himself?"

"It's possible," she admitted. "Papa gives him money every week."

Murtaugh put his hand on hers. "Kids nowadays go in for that kind of thing. Even young kids. Nice kids."

"I know," she said. "Because of this I call his teacher."

The detective forced himself not to hurry her. "I think maybe last year she has seen Tomas as much as me."

Maria played with the Styrofoam cup. "She tells me Tomas is very smart. Very, very smart. But she thinks he is also lonely," she told him, beginning to cry.

"The teacher says maybe he spends too much time with grown-ups. That he looks for friends, older friends." The cup splintered in her grasp. "She says Tomas was a good boy, though. He was so good."

"I know he was, Maria."

A customer walked into the shop. As Maria wiped her eyes, Murtaugh told her he would be at the church in the morning.

Outside, he let this new picture of Tomas Quiles carry his thoughts. Tomas—a child born out of wedlock, bright, pampered, surrounded by adults—taking his first steps toward autonomy. Buying records the older boys played. Hanging around the park.

His grandmother and aunt walked him to and from school every day. They made his favorite food for each meal. They encouraged his precocious nature. But they hadn't been able to provide the kind of companionship he needed.

Was it in his unlucky choice of friends that his fate had been sealed?

Murtaugh remembered how someone else had put it. Mr. Sanchez said bad friends were Jaime's downfall.

* * *

It was long after dinner when Murtaugh went to see Oakley Hall. Dana would have had time to clear the dishes and curl up with her lemon cat, or perhaps do some work on one of her paintings.

The break in the heat spell seemed to bring darkness earlier. He knew by the way the leaves turned upward and rustled there would be rain again tonight, but he preferred to imagine it as the sounds of approaching autumn.

With a start, he realized it would be the first September without Eve. The first fall without the job that had consumed his life for so long.

He pushed these ideas from his mind.

Number 516 was lit up, each window looking burnished gold, the way it does only during those few moments after sunset.

"Murtaugh," Dana said, when she opened the door, "I was just thinking about you."

The memory of their last meeting nagged at him, and he replied too gruffly, "Actually, I'm here to see your husband."

They were inside by now, and he noticed that Dana was wearing an old chenille bathrobe.

"He's not here," she told him in an anxious voice. "It's going to be another late night."

Murtaugh would have liked to touch her arm, tell her everything was going to be all right, that his visit was only routine. Instead, he went over to the easel, where the studies for two portraits—Hunter Murtaugh and Jaime Sanchez—were propped up, side by side.

"An unlikely couple?" she said, trying to read his thoughts.

The detective turned to her. "Will Jaime come to pose tomorrow?"

"No," she told him. Her eyes flickered, then she added, "Yes."

She believed in the boy that much. Another Thursday. Would anyone be dead as a result?

He said, "Maybe we can get together afterward."

"I'd like that." She smiled. "Oakley won't be home, though. He's finishing a big article. But if you need to see him I'm sure he could—"

"No, it's nothing important," Murtaugh told her. "Just say I'll be in touch."

They made arrangements for the following evening. Dinner again, and then a sitting. She would work in acrylics this time.

On the pavement, Murtaugh felt vaguely guilty. He told himself there was really no reason. He'd talk to Oakley Hall at a time of his own choosing, and without Dana's gentle eyes to inhibit him.

* * *

A couple passed him, mounting the stairs to ring Jake and Rebecca's bell. The door opened, and lights from within spilled in a yellow crack toward the street. For a moment Murtaugh wavered there, like an insect drawn toward the brightness. Then he heard someone call his name.

Rebecca Lincroft stood in the doorway. "Sergeant? Is something wrong?"

"No," he assured her, "only a housecall in the neighborhood. Good night."

She stopped him. "We're having a few friends in. Why don't you join us?" He hesitated. "It's very informal."

He followed her into the living room. From behind, Rebecca looked cut all of a piece—dazzling white dress, nipped around boyish hips; pale stockings melting into pumps, not of leather, but of richly textured material. Even the back of her neck and arms was creamy, untouched by sun.

She introduced him with a gentle admonition. "As much as I know we're all dying to ask Sergeant Murtaugh about the murders, I've promised him a relaxing drink—so I know you'll all abide by the ground rules."

There was a smattering of laughter.

His first impression of the five people blatantly giving him the once-over was how well their toned bodies meshed with the contours of the furniture.

"Michael Grace," said a man in a candy-colored striped shirt, casually rolled to the elbow. "And this is Deirdre."

Deirdre had deep brown hair, cut in a perfectly straight line against her cheek.

"You've met David." Rebecca nodded toward Rothman, who was nervously shifting his weight from one foot to another.

"I know you," Lindsay Bartholomew interrupted inanely.

Murtaugh decided that women who looked like Lindsay were secure in the knowledge their impact was not necessarily verbal.

"And John Deacon," Rebecca concluded.

Deacon extended his hand.

"Haven't had the pleasure," he said, "although I've met

your man O'Connell." He made Davy sound like some sort of domestic help.

Murtaugh took a stab at a congenial smile, remembering what his man O'Connell had told him on the telephone this afternoon.

John Deacon hadn't gone directly home on the night of Rose's death. After he left Jake's, he walked to a trendy new restaurant—Murtaugh didn't tell Davy he was familiar with it—where he met Ms. Bartholomew. They had seafood salads and white wine before strolling back to Lindsay's brownstone. He stayed until morning. An odd coupling, the detective thought. Deacon was a stud in sheep's clothing, affecting an ease that wasn't inbred. He had a feeling this guy was outclassed and trying hard not to show it.

Murtaugh was trying to picture them as lovers, when Jake entered, carrying a tray of crystal glasses and a pitcher.

"Sergeant," he said, putting them down and clasping his hand, "what a fabulous surprise."

At the sight of Murtaugh's bandage, he was solicitous. "An accident?"

Murtaugh shook his head. "Just realizing the limitations of age."

"Ah, I bet you're not much older than me," Jake said, with the confidence of a younger man. He pulled his wife to his side.

"Becca," he said, "we'll have to get the Sergeant out on the board. Make him feel like a kid again."

Rebecca appeared unenthusiastic. Murtaugh could see the outdoors held little fascination for her. Once again he was struck by their seeming incompatibility, the muscular boy-man and this ethereal creature with the doe eyes.

Jake and Rebecca. Janis and Rothman. Lindsay and Deacon. Dana and Oakley. Alison and O'Connell. He stopped, realizing that in any list of opposites, he'd have to add the names of Murtaugh and Eve.

They sat him in an armchair across from the overstuffed sectional of guests. Rothman and Florian stood somewhere to the rear, out of his field of vision. He felt like monkey-in-the-middle. The idea reminded him of something Janis had said.

"I hear you're great game players," Murtaugh commented. "Which one is it tonight?"

"Scrabble," Michael Grace replied.

"Trivial Pursuit," Jake said at the same time.

"They're embarrassed to tell you," Rebecca broke in, almost sheepishly, "that it was supposed to be Clue. I hope you won't think us gauche."

Murtaugh couldn't remember ever even using the word.

"Were you posing, Sergeant?" Jake asked, passing him a drink and explaining to the others, "He's being done by the same painter who's doing Rebecca."

The detective felt his ears go crimson.

"No," he said, "not this evening."

"You didn't tell me about any painter," Deirdre pouted, as she cut a sliver of Brie.

"Yes, I did," Rebecca insisted. "Dana Hall, our tenant."

Deirdre let go a little laugh. "Oh, the one with the *clothes*—"

"She dresses artistically," Rebecca said, exchanging a meaningful look that Murtaugh knew meant *not in front of him*. "And she's got such a pretty face."

"Adorable," Deirdre agreed.

There was a short silence.

"You really should bring her to George," Deirdre said. "What he couldn't do with that hair."

Michael snorted, "Well, why not? It takes him long enough."

"Three and a half hours last time, did I tell you?" Deirdre said to no one in particular.

Three and a half hours? Murtaugh looked at the blunt line of her hair. What did he do?, he wondered. Cut one strand at a time?

She turned to the detective and smiled brilliantly. "He cuts one strand at a time."

Jake moved into the circle and sat next to his wife. "You should really commission her, Deir—that downstairs mantel of yours absolutely cries out for a portrait."

"We're in the process of moving across town," Michael Grace explained. "Big old thing on Castle Point."

Murtaugh's heart sank. "The one with the turret?"

Even David Rothman perked up. He moved closer. "Great deal you got there."

"You really must come by sometime." Michael grinned at the detective. "The inside is rather amazing."

Deirdre hit him lightly. "Don't you dare invite anyone until I decorate."

"It's a big place." Murtaugh smiled. "If you ever think of renting out a floor, let me know."

"Joshua is going to have a ball," Rebecca said in a little-girl voice. "All those stairs!"

"The deal was, Mikey gets to live in the old house," Deirdre said, shoving her empty glass at Jake for a refill, "and Deirdre gets a live-in. No way I'm chasing after Josh when I come home."

"Do you have children?" Michael asked the detective.

Murtaugh shook his head, and the young man said encouragingly, "Well, it's never too late. Parenting is an experience everyone should have."

"Give it a rest, Michael," his wife said.

The gin-and-tonic seemed to have gone to the detective's head, but he allowed Jake to freshen his drink just the same.

"They tell me you're a native of Hoboken." John Deacon smoothly changed the subject.

Murtaugh felt all eyes on him. The word "native" sounded untame. He had the sudden image of himself, tattooed and naked, being studied like a freak in a sideshow.

"Yes," he said cautiously, "you could say that."

"Lots of changes." Deacon was obviously trying to get him to talk.

He saw for the first time that all three women wore the same opalescent shade of nail polish. He wondered if George applied it. How long it took.

"Boy, if you knew then what you know now, eh, Sarge?" Jake Florian leaned forward to pass him a plate of bright vegetables.

Murtaugh picked up a floret of broccoli, immediately gave up on trying to eat it, and instead, held it in a dainty napkin on his lap, like a girl's bouquet.

"What's that?"

"I mean," Jake said patiently, "you could've gotten property dirt cheap back then."

"Probably," Murtaugh admitted. "People didn't seem to think much of it, I guess."

Rothman broke in, his face gleaming with perspiration. "It's all part of the cycle," he told them. "This town's on an upward swing now, but not near as high as it's going to go. In ten years, values will be out of sight."

"Bigger than Manhattan?"

"I promise you, M.G." Rothman was downright enthusiastic. "Bigger than Manhattan. I'm talking industry. I'm talking entertainment. I'm talking—"

Rebecca started to laugh. "Obviously, we've just pushed David's button."

"Yeah," Lindsay drawled, "will you can it? Sometimes it gets bor-ing."

Murtaugh was pretty sure Lindsay's buttons sparked other areas, other urges.

Deirdre gave out a shriek. "Where'd you get it?"

Everyone looked to where she was looking: Lindsay's large ring with a rectangular green stone in it. An emerald, Murtaugh supposed.

"You know."

"I thought you said you didn't get anything from him," Deirdre whispered audibly.

Rebecca sounded uninterested. "She got the coat."

"And this," Lindsay said. "But they weren't worth the aggravation."

It amazed Murtaugh that this obvious talk of another lover seemed to have no effect on Deacon, who was happily munching a handful of macadamia nuts.

The detective rose, overriding the protests of the group by saying he had to be up early in the morning.

"So do we," Rebecca told him. "Only it's summer, and there should be a party every night."

The array of wide-awake faces endorsed her words.

"I envy your stamina," he said. "I seem to have misplaced mine along the way."

He shook hands all around, and when he reached Rothman, paused to take another look at Jake's scale model. Some of the tiny buildings had been removed. They lay in a pile on the table.

"What's this?" he asked.

Jake shrugged easily. "Tinkering. An architect's work is never done."

Murtaugh walked to the door with his hosts. "By the way, when you went downstairs on the night of Mrs. Walsh's death, did you lock your door?"

"No," Jake said, after a short pause. "I don't think I did."

His face grew serious. "Any closer to finding the culprit, Sergeant? The way things are, I hate to leave Becca alone."

"I wish I could put your fears to rest," the detective replied.

Rebecca swayed visibly. "Do you mean to say you think there'll be another murder?"

"Only the killer knows that for sure," Murtaugh said. "Thanks for the hospitality."

The television was on in Dana and Oakley's apartment. Murtaugh could hear the tinny sound, see its bluish light in the otherwise darkened room.

He wondered why Dana had not been invited upstairs. Then he thought of her nails, ragged and edged with paint, and the hair that seemed to have a life of its own.

If she'd been there, they could have sat together; and maybe even laughed out here in the night, the way the others were no doubt laughing inside, amidst their clinking glasses and clever wordgames.

It wasn't his cup of tea, but still he had to admit it beat an evening at Paulie's, hands down.

A slight movement out of the corner of his eye startled him.

The lemon cat sat in the window, waiting.

CHAPTER

16

AFTER THE child's funeral, O'Connell and Murtaugh walked for a long while, saying nothing.

The young man was the first to speak. "You were right."

"Huh?"

"Mrs. Cappricio could have been trying to get to a safety deposit box. She had one. But it's going to take a while to find out what was inside," O'Connell explained. "The will won't be read for another couple of weeks. Her lawyer's dead. His son took over the practice, but he's on vacation."

"Where's the nephew?"

"Out Bucks County way," O'Connell told him.

"Oh." Murtaugh lit up a cigarette distractedly.

Of course. No way to get into the deposit box. No way to see the will. No way to prove she was murdered. No sense to any of it.

After sitting through the funeral mass, after hearing the priest's impassioned voice ringing through the church, his meaning more immediate in Spanish than it might have been in English, making Murtaugh hearken back to the days when all masses were in another tongue—after that, what mattered anyway?

A child was dead. No one would ever be able to make sense of that. It seemed fitting that the circumstances surrounding his killing didn't appear to be subject to reason.

Even as he allowed his darker self to ponder this, Murtaugh knew it wasn't altogether true.

As a detective, he knew every crime had motive. As an observer of human nature, he was sure that the murderer had acted with a purpose, however bent or bizarre.

They were just not asking the right questions. That was why the tiny fragments of answers they possessed seemed to get them nowhere.

"I'd lay low for now if I were you," Davy O'Connell said.

Murtaugh glanced sidelong at his companion and saw he was walking with his eyes trained on the pavement.

"That so?"

O'Connell was in earnest. "Word has it you're off the case as of this afternoon. Rourke wants you in-house."

He looked pale. Murtaugh wondered whether the word came from Alison Randall.

"They want you to go through another one of those sessions with the shrink," he told Murtaugh.

The Sergeant only nodded sympathetically, as if it were a problem that the younger man had. "Well, don't worry about it."

"What next?"

"I want you to check out a Michael and Deirdre Grace. I met them last night at Jake Florian's," Murtaugh said.

"I meant for you," O'Connell persisted. "What's next for you, Hunt?"

Thrusting his hands in his pockets, Murtaugh seemed to consider the question for a moment. "Well, I'm not going to sit around playing inkblots with some looney-bin Ben Casey," he told O'Connell.

"Cheer up," he smiled. "Maybe it's time for us native sons to move on."

He left O'Connell with the promise that he'd check in at decent intervals.

*　*　*

It was like playing hooky, Murtaugh decided, as he felt the first rush of freedom wash over him.

When he was little, he sometimes skipped school in order to pretend he was a detective. He'd pick out the target in advance. Maybe the old German who yelled whenever stray balls found their way onto his property, the one who young Murtaugh believed was an escaped Nazi war criminal. Or the beautiful brunette who sold lingerie in one of the fancy shops on Washington and who, in her capacity as the leading lady in all of Hunter's prepubescent fantasies, warranted his attention for reasons other than national security. He'd shadow them all over town, the success or failure of his mission determined by how many times he'd been spotted.

Murtaugh often recalled those afternoons with an ironic smile as he sat in a parked car, drinking cold coffee from a cardboard cup, waiting for some suspect to come out of a bar.

Never, since those days of Dick Tracy tails, had he felt that pounding in his ears as he pressed himself to the side of a building. He'd lost it somewhere, and in its place there was only tedium, fatigue, and cynical banter with the guy who happened to be next to him.

Today was different. There were no procedures to follow, no one in particular for him to see. Murtaugh walked with a slight spring to his step, as though he could, if necessary, disappear into a crevice of the sidewalk or make himself scarce in a crowd.

He knew these people. At least, he knew as much about them as they'd let him know. His targets were selected. Now he'd play detective. A child's conception of what it's like to be God.

And it really made him feel omnipotent, Murtaugh decided. Especially today, as he traced the movements of not only the living, but a few absent parties as well.

He watched Rose Walsh shopping, her thin body leaning over the produce, her bulgy eyes seeking out something over-ripe that might be gotten cheap. He saw her ducking out of the local taverns. He heard her garrulous voice greeting passers-by as she walked the old dog. And when her presence was so tangible to him he could have almost touched her, could have searched those pop eyes for the answer he needed, he let her go back into the recesses of Number 518. Then he began looking for young Tomas.

That was more difficult. For a long while, he stood outside the Quiles' home, feeling guilty for not being inside with the other mourners. Sergeant Hunter Murtaugh had always attended wakes and funerals. It was part of his job, yes, but also part of his life, the way the people themselves were part of it. Often, as in the case of this family, he sincerely cared for them.

He reminded himself that he was really no longer Sergeant Hunter Murtaugh. He'd cut himself off from the title. He wasn't on the outside, observing. He was on the inside, with the lot of them. The way Tomas once was.

His day would have been nothing like Rose's. They'd both gotten up, walked around, and went to bed, completely oblivious of each other, unaware that their lives would someday be connected. In death.

During these summer months, time must have hung on Tomas' hands. He rose early and went with his grandmother and her sister on their round of the local markets, which the Hispanic women made daily, old-world style. After lunch, he was allowed to go to the park, usually chaperoned by one of the family or another mother on the block.

Once a week, on Thursdays, the day he disappeared, Tomas went by himself to a local store on Washington Street to get a Spanish newspaper for his grandfather. The shopkeeper remembered seeing him on that last day a little after noon.

Murtaugh began surveillance of the dead little boy at the park. This sleuthing is beginning to overlap, he thought, noticing the familiar figures hanging around the basketball court. Like a painting by El Greco, Jaime and his friends appeared otherworldish and elongated next to the healthy, sweating adolescents playing ball.

They think I'm following them, he laughed to himself. Little do they know it's not me they have to worry about.

The Sergeant studiously avoided the eyes of a young Puerto Rican detective in a ratty T-shirt who seemed to be interested only in the game.

Relax, he was tempted to call to the boys, I'm tailing ghosts, not witches today. And besides, it's just as likely my presence here will be reported to Bromsky as yours. But deep inside him, he felt something like relief. Sanchez was showing no signs of keeping his appointment with Dana Hall.

The Sergeant cut across to Washington, trying to re-create Tomas Quiles' route to the newsstand. If he were that age, he'd have been sure to take advantage of these few precious minutes of liberty. Several doors down was a music shop. Music blared over outside speakers. Perhaps this was where he'd bought that forbidden album. Farther still, the detective could see a pizzeria, and next to it, an icecream vendor, both surely enticements for a kid with a half hour to kill and an allowance in his pocket.

Murtaugh got a slice of pizza, bringing it outside to escape the oppressive heat of the ovens. A van was parked in front of The March Hare. He watched two men move several cartons of merchandise into the store. Lindsay, in some kind of airy flight suit with squared-off shoulders, stood helplessly in their path.

They pulled away; and Lindsay locked the door, leaving a sign that gave the time she'd be back from lunch.

So Rebecca wasn't in yet, Murtaugh said to himself.

Just as when he'd played this game as a child, every tiny piece of information took on staggering proportions. It made him marvel at the million and one things an ordinary person did in the course of a day. And lurking behind his prey like an afterthought, Murtaugh found each of their actions exciting, provocative.

Would his own life seem interesting to an outside eye?, he wondered.

He threw the greasy remnants of his meal into the trash receptacle, spinning around suddenly to catch sight of someone unexpected.

Oakley Hall dashed out of the record shop, a brown bag in one hand, a briefcase in the other. He weaved around the traffic and managed to make a New York–bound bus.

Murtaugh didn't like Oakley Hall, but it disturbed him to admit it, even to himself. His reasons, he knew, were complicated. And not all of them had to do with the investigation.

On the way back to his apartment, the Sergeant mentally moved the chessboard pieces to their proper places. Jake Florian would soon return on the bus or the PATH. So would David Rothman. Eventually.

He pictured Paddy perched on a barstool; and Madie Quinn,

in front of her daughter's television, yearning for a night at Bingo.

Dana Hall, stirring something from her limited repertoire for the detective's dinner, was probably worried about her overworked husband. Did she worry about anyone else?, he wondered, remembering her words—Murtaugh, I've been thinking about you. Unaccountably, his gut contracted.

More to the point, he reminded himself, except for a cruel, violent act, Tomas Quiles would be sitting down to dinner with his grandparents; while over at Number 518, Rose Walsh nipped from a bottle as she set about to warm up some leftovers. If he closed his eyes, Murtaugh could almost smell her kitchen, hear the mumbling that would later become shrill and angry. And he could see little Anna Cappricio at her window, waving to any friendly face.

The detective changed his clothes quickly and went directly to Number 516. Across the street, it surprised him to see one of his players out of position.

David Rothman was soaping his BMW, half-watching Melissa as she walked a mechanical dog. When she saw the Sergeant, the little girl waved and called, "I'm going to the Barkshires!"

"The *Berkshires*, Melissa," Rothman corrected her wearily. "You're going to the Berkshires."

"I'm leaving Friday night, and I don't even have to sleep in the car if I don't want to," she said aggressively.

The mechanical dog made sharp barking sounds as it traversed the pavement.

"Will you shut that goddamn thing off?" her father demanded.

She switched off a button and sat on the stoop with the toy in her lap. Her self-satisfied look telegraphed to Murtaugh that, even at her tender age, she could tell *he* would never be lucky enough to go to the Berkshires.

"So you're still planning to take your trip," Murtaugh commented to her father.

Rothman was alarmed. "Is there any reason why I shouldn't?"

"No," Murtaugh assured him, "only I thought when your wife wasn't at the party last night that maybe she was ill."

He watched the man weigh the truth against a lie. The lie won.

"Oh, it was only a headache." David Rothman smiled. "Do her good to breathe some country air. And we're taking our girl, Iylish, to sit for Melissa."

"Sounds nice," Murtaugh said. To the child, he added, "Have a good time."

As he crossed the street, he heard Melissa yelling, "And if I want, I can have ice cream every day. You ask my mommy!"

* * *

Dana was more agitated than he'd ever seen her. She asked if he minded posing before dinner; and when he assented, she plunged in with the same energy he'd noticed last time, magnified. They talked very little, and more often than not, it was only about the cat, which persisted in brushing against the detective's legs.

It was Murtaugh who first smelled it. He offhandedly remarked that something was burning in the kitchen and watched her dash, still holding a brush.

By now smoke had begun to billow through the apartment.

"It's burnt," he heard her cry. "It's ruined."

She stood with the broiler open, watching transfixed, as the meal went up in flames.

Murtaugh grabbed a dishtowel and threw the scorched pan into the sink.

Dana Hall sobbed. "I'm sorry," she said. "I'm not very good at this."

210

There was a loud screech from the direction of the window. She rushed into his arms.

"Shhh," he soothed her, "it's only the cats."

Lydia was at the screen, nose-to-nose with the black cat Murtaugh had seen before on Jake's roof. Dana shivered.

He led her to the oak table and let her cry for a few minutes. Part of him wanted to laugh, and yet, really, her earnestness was heartbreaking. Murtaugh knew instinctively it wasn't only the meal. Something else was upsetting Mrs. Hall.

"I'm sorry," she repeated. "Must be lack of sleep . . ."

Meeting his gaze, she explained lamely, "The party upstairs kept me awake."

"Go wash your face," he told her.

Dana made a move to obey and then stopped, with questioning eyes.

"I'm taking you out to eat," Murtaugh said happily.

* * *

He took her to Evelyn's, but they were both discouraged by the long waiting list.

"What about this one?" Dana said, peering through shiny windows reflecting yellow wall sconces.

"I've been thrown out of better." Murtaugh shrugged, pulling her away. He'd also been thrown out of here.

They ended up in his German restaurant, where Dana ordered Italian food, disregarding his prompting in other directions.

She looked better now that she'd splashed water on her cheeks and removed the silly ribbon from her hair so it fell heavily over her shoulders. In fact, sitting there across from him, playing with the buttons on her short riding jacket, he could almost believe Dana Hall was beautiful.

"It's good you got me out of the house," she said, buttering a roll. "With Oakley working all the time, I've got cabin fever."

"He leave early again today?"

She nodded. "Before breakfast. There was a meeting at the magazine." Then, catching his expression, "I told him you wanted to speak with him. Didn't he call your office?"

Murtaugh was honest. "He could have. I was out all day."

Although he hated himself for doing it, he found himself gently pumping Dana about her husband.

They'd met only six months ago, she told him, at an art gallery in Atlanta where one of her pictures was being shown. Oakley was with a newspaper then and he'd interviewed her.

She was struck, she said, by his open nature. Murtaugh busied himself, making elaborate preparations to eat. He didn't look at her, but he heard every word.

There was no romantic subterfuge with Oakley, no cat-and-mouse games. That first day he told her he loved her painting and wanted to take her to dinner. The second day, he told her he loved her and wanted to stay in her life.

Dana had been cautious; but, in the end, Oakley's confidence and kindness won her over. Murtaugh waited for her to say it. The inevitable final sentence. And they lived happily ever after.

Instead there was silence. For the first time in many minutes, he looked up. Her gray eyes were bewildered.

"It's a phase, I guess," Dana said simply. "I don't think he's happy at the magazine."

She continued slowly. "Even when he's home, he's not with me, you know? He'd rather play tennis at the college than talk." The crooked smile. "A shame I'm not more like my neighbor across the street."

Murtaugh was kind. "Your talents are in other areas."

"Like cooking?" Dana seemed to relax. "Well, at least you're not shutting me out. I was beginning to think I—"

"Forget it."

He found himself telling her that they were removing him from the case.

Dana was outraged. "You're not just going to give up, are you?"

They were outside now, walking in the general direction of Castle Point. It was already dark, but the afternoon sky had blushed deep in its last moments so everything was a rich, haunting sapphire.

"Parrish Blue," Dana said. "The color. It's named after a painter—Maxfield Parrish."

She stopped and took a breath of air. "Only when you see it on one of his canvases, you say, no, there could never really be a shade as wonderful as this."

They climbed the hill toward Stevens Tech, and she asked him again if he was going to give up.

"Sometimes you've got to know when it's time to bow out," Murtaugh said.

Dana looked stung. "And what then? Are you planning to roll over and play dead, Murtaugh?"

"You think bowing out is heroic?" Her voice was passionate now, making him wonder whether he'd unknowingly pushed Mrs. Hall's button. "Well, it isn't, believe me." Dana grabbed his jacket. "Heroes keep fighting, no matter what. Only failures give up."

Something, maybe a sudden embarrassment, propelled her forward. They walked apart until they reached the ramparts.

She was right, he knew. But it annoyed him.

The battlements overlooking the skyline were crowded with lovers and students. Since they were neither, he steered Dana on the path leading to the waterfront.

Murtaugh opted for smalltalk. "They're planning to rebuild someday. Doesn't look like much of a seaport now, does it?"

Dana was puffing slightly. They paused, looking out at the docks and warehouses.

"I think it should stay this way. Unfinished." She chose her words carefully. "A hint of past grandeur, maybe, but mostly—"

"Sad?"

"Don't make fun of me," Dana said. "They'll come here, the whole group of them, and tear everything down so they can make a perfect little Disneyland replica of something impractical. Cappuccino cafes. Boutiques for designer shoes. Erotic bakeries . . ."

Murtaugh smiled. They began the slow ascent to Castle Point. He took her past the mansions and was secretly pleased when she told him the one with the turret was her favorite.

He described Deirdre and Michael Grace, talked about the gathering the evening before. Dana was unusually silent, even though he was aware of working, actually working hard, to make her laugh.

Maybe she feels left out by that crowd, too, he thought.

They were in the center of town when he asked, "How'd the sitting with Sanchez go this afternoon?"

"Oh, I had to cancel," she said, not volunteering any more information. "He's coming over tomorrow instead."

Then she turned to him. "Is he still a suspect?"

Murtaugh's reply was succinct. "He's the prime suspect." He fumbled with a cigarette.

"Your friend Jaime is lying, holding something back. That I'm sure of," he muttered. "But then, so are a lot of people."

"I know you don't trust my impressions." Dana sounded tentative. "And maybe they aren't reliable. I don't know. I'm not sure anymore . . . life seems suddenly so—*complicated* . . ."

The word triggered something in Murtaugh. He said, "Try me."

"I've been going over and over things ever since they found

Mrs. Walsh, and there's—" she stopped abruptly and smiled. "Oh, it doesn't make sense. It's only a bunch of images."

"You're an artist," he teased. "Images are your stock-in-trade."

"What's yours?" she wanted to know. "What's Sergeant Hunter Murtaugh's stock-in-trade?"

"Mine has always been," Murtaugh said seriously, "people."

Dana laughed. "Sounds about as unscientific as my images."

Murtaugh agreed. "I'm beginning to think so, too. Especially with the people I've met recently."

They'd reached Dana's block, but kept walking.

"Present company excepted?"

Yes, he wanted to say, from the moment I met you, you were excepted. Instead, he went on, "The point is, someone killed three people—"

Dana blanched. "Three?"

"Mrs. Cappricio was murdered," he told her. "I'm sure of it."

She grabbed the lapels of his jacket again, this time to steady herself. Looking at her upturned face, it was Murtaugh who felt dizzy, felt a surging gravitational pull toward her mouth.

His mind punched out a list of warnings, like a computer readout: you're too lonely, she's too married, this isn't what you think it is.

But all reasons not to were suddenly eclipsed by a fragment of remembered conversation. Does it draw you in, she'd once asked, stir up something inside of you that you didn't even know was there?

This the genuine article, Murtaugh thought. It's no fake. There can't be any false moves.

"Here," he said, awkwardly putting a big hand up to her cheek. Dana's face was feverish. It seemed to burn his fin-

215

gertips, travel all through him, thawing his body in almost forgotten places. "No more shop talk. I promise."

They turned down a sidestreet. A few yards away a restaurant appeared like a refuge. Its windows were studded with hundreds of tiny white bulbs.

He put his hand gently under her elbow and walked her to the door. Dana was biting her lip.

Inside was all lattice and greenery; and everywhere, there were more of the twinkling lights.

Murtaugh held the handwritten menu out at arm's length.

"So it's not that you're forever scrutinizing everybody," Dana said, delighted. "You're just blind as a bat!"

"What's so funny about that?" he asked gruffly.

"Well, anybody who's vain enough not to get glasses," she told him, "has got too much pride to throw in the towel."

They ordered tea and chocolate pie. Afterward, the waitress offered to read their tea leaves.

Murtaugh gave in at Dana's urging. Expecting some kind of fortune cookie platitude, the detective was surprised when the woman paused for a full minute, studying the leaves intently.

"It's strange," she told them. "The leaves are of matching line."

Her voice dropped, somewhat theatrically. "Your lives, your fates, are linked. You're both at a crossroads."

"The portrait!" Dana exclaimed. "Didn't I tell you it was going to make us both famous?"

Murtaugh laughed and let her eat the last bite of his pie.

CHAPTER

17

MURTAUGH couldn't sleep. He prowled around the apartment feeling wound up, and at the same time, deflated.

For company, he put on the television, letting it segue from one program to the next, never turning the channel, never really looking or listening.

It was after three a.m. when he began cleaning. He set a large garbage bag in the middle of the kitchen floor, and emptied the refrigerator and cabinets of smelly milk cartons, grayish eggs, opened boxes of cereal and rice, half-eaten containers of ice cream. Then, for good measure, Murtaugh took the sheets off the bed, rolled them into a ball, stuffed them into the sack, and brought the whole mess outside.

His mind was racing to a blur. He sprawled on the unmade bed, intrigued by a rock video on the tube. The images were disjointed. Color was cranked to the point of unreality, like the vivid greens and oranges of Jake and Rebecca's vegetable

217

platter. The music also seemed unreal, the voicetrack synthetic, unhuman.

Murtaugh found it strangely relaxing. He allowed himself to be mesmerized into sleep.

The telephone rang on the stroke of nine. He went into the shower to avoid it.

Later, as the detective typed letters of resignation at the kitchen table, with his one good hand, the insistent ringing became maddening, so he decided to disconnect it. He would not spring to attention when Rourke summoned. He would return for sentencing in his own good time.

Hours passed. The floor was littered with crumpled paper. Murtaugh the martyr, Murtaugh the bastard, Murtaugh the stoic, Murtaugh the righteous. He never would have believed there were so many ways to ride into the sunset.

So many, that he became distracted and finally bored. Almost before he knew it, he was doodling on the clean white sheets.

Faces, at first. Dana's, in loose, voluptuous lines and circles. Rounded. Curved. But Murtaugh could capture nothing of her, so he tried shapes. Houses. Turrets. Stairs. All ending with a firmly scribbled mark across the paper, and discarded.

He suddenly remembered his promise to check in with O'Connell. It was almost noon, and the basement was unbearably hot.

Ignoring his unplugged telephone in favor of a paybooth on Washington Street, the detective dialed O'Connell's extension. Bonelli answered. Murtaugh could tell by his hushed tones that Lou was afraid of being overheard.

"Hunt," he whispered. "They keep asking where you are. I think they're sending somebody over."

"Any messages?"

"Yeah," Bonelli told him. "The Hall girl. She's been calling since nine. Said it was important, that she wanted to show you something, and we should tell you if you called in."

"Thanks," Murtaugh said, and then, honestly, "I owe you."

He put in another coin, leafing through the book for Dana's number. No answer.

By the time he turned the corner, Murtaugh was running.

In the afternoon glare, it was impossible to tell whether there were any lights on in Number 516. Downstairs, the lemon cat, ever present, jumped softly from its perch.

Murtaugh knocked vigorously. She's not there, he told himself desperately. She's out somewhere.

The door was unlocked. Lydia wove in and out of his legs, making him look only at the floor for a few seconds. It was dark in the apartment, the sunlight that reached not reinforced by electricity; yet when he lifted his head, he saw her clearly in the dull illumination, filtered gray, so that the folds of her sleeves and dress appeared heavy and substantial, like pewter.

Dana Hall had been pinned to her easel.

Murtaugh knew she was dead, had perhaps been dead for hours, but it didn't stop him from rushing to her.

Later, he realized he'd been talking out loud. Words of comfort, words of tenderness. Contrary to all the rules of his training, he slowly, gently, unfastened the long needles, holding her with his bandaged hand. He only knew he was crying by the flat, damp spots he saw on her dress.

She had been pinned to the portrait of a sad, black-eyed boy. Murtaugh carried her to the loveseat. It was really too small. For a moment he considered laying her on the bed.

Don't be crazy, he told himself. It doesn't matter. She can't feel anyway.

The cat hopped onto its mistress as the detective picked up the telephone.

"It's Murtaugh," he said, in a loud, raspy voice. "There's been another one. Number 516. The basement."

219

He hung up, watching Lydia gracefully jump back to the floor. There was nothing there for a lemon cat, Murtaugh thought. Dana was already too cold.

* * *

In the time it took for the others to arrive, Murtaugh found her datebook. Jaime Sanchez was the only appointment for today, at one o'clock, his name written in purple ink. They'll have a party with that, he reflected grimly.

Forcing himself not to stare at her, he went over to the portfolio and leafed through it. Murtaugh rolled up several sheafs of paper. He found a discarded grosgrain ribbon, the one Dana Hall had removed from her bright hair last night, and tied it carefully around the drawings.

While the patrol cars and ambulance screeched to a halt outside, he thought of Oakley. Oakley who was living as though everything in his world was unchanged. Murtaugh tried to formulate the words he would use.

Lowenstein was back, his nose red and flakey. He said nothing to Murtaugh about having moved the body. As the small flat was invaded, the Sergeant picked up the cat and walked into the kitchen, his roll of paper tucked inside his jacket.

The rear door was unlocked.

Murtaugh answered questions, as Paddy Walsh had his own a week before, angrily and with a modicum of cooperation. Bonelli and O'Connell entered together.

Bonelli shook his head. "Why her, I ask you? I should be so lucky if Vinnie brings home a girl like that."

So Lou had met her. Someday they would talk about it.

O'Connell moved through the apartment saying nothing. Murtaugh could feel his eyes, however, when the young man thought he wasn't looking.

Hearing Bromsky, his gut reaction was to cover Dana. If the man touched her, Murtaugh knew he would kill him.

"Do we have to stay?" O'Connell said, out of the blue.

Murtaugh nodded blankly. "I need to call her husband."

"You can do that at Headquarters."

"Good work, Murtaugh," Bromsky boomed. "This wouldn't have happened if you'd helped me nail the little bastards."

"The little bastards didn't do it," Murtaugh said quietly.

"Are you out of your mind? Some neighbor across the street, a Mrs. Libretti, says she saw Sanchez come in an hour ago and run out in a big hurry."

Murtaugh was unimpressed. "He didn't kill her."

"You've really gone round the bend," Bromsky told him. "If he's so lilywhite, then why has no one seen hide nor hair of him since his visit to your girlfriend?"

O'Connell moved toward Murtaugh, ready to restrain him, but the Sergeant was sitting very still.

"One, he's scared. And two, the goon you've got following him would lose his grandmother on her way to the toilet."

Bromsky snarled. "When we find his pawprints all over the fucking apartment, I suppose you'll have another explanation."

Murtaugh walked out of the room. He knew he had to leave before they moved her. He knew he couldn't stand to see her on that trolley, wrapped in plastic like a piece of furniture in Rose's parlor.

"How did she die?" Murtaugh asked Lowenstein.

The doctor's voice was nasal, but curiously kind. Murtaugh wondered how he knew that Dana had meant something to him.

"Strangled with that silk tie."

Murtaugh glanced down. In his frenzy, he'd assumed the long ribbon was just another one of Dana's funny little touches—

old-fashioned and odd, it hung around her neck limply now that the life had been choked from her.

He felt numb. "I'll call you," he said, and he left with O'Connell and Bonelli on his heels.

* * *

He stood for a moment on the stoop trying to regulate his breathing. The muggy air seemed too rich for his lungs.

It was a strange thing, this act of respiring, Murtaugh thought. He allowed himself to experience lightheadedness, the panting dry heaves for oxygen.

Was this how Dana felt as the silk cut into her neck? Or had terror obscured all other sensations until that final lapse into unconsciousness?

Mrs. Libretti's voice acted like a sharp blow between his shoulder blades, knocking the wind loose inside him.

"I told you those kids were animals! I warned you, but you didn't listen!"

"Come on, Hunt." Davy gently touched his sleeve and motioned to a parked car.

Further along the one-way street, Murtaugh heard sirens. A moving van blocked the patrol car. Rourke was putting in a rare personal appearance. Murtaugh knew it was an encounter he must avoid.

"I need to walk," he told O'Connell. "Thanks, anyway."

O'Connell could only watch the slouched shoulders of the man as he, hands in pockets, moved swiftly in the opposite direction.

* * *

Oakley Hall, sitting at his desk somewhere in Manhattan, sounded confused. He interrupted Murtaugh with every few words and repeated them, as though it was a bad overseas connection.

The detective warned him not to attempt the commute back to Hoboken by himself. Oakley said he'd get a friend from the magazine to come with him. Lamely, Murtaugh asked if there was anything he could do. After a long silence, Oakley said no, he would call his family to come north and help with the arrangements.

What about Dana's family? Murtaugh inquired.

He said her mother had died young. Dana never knew her. And three months before she'd met Oakley, her father, also an artist, had shot himself.

Once, Oakley went on, rambling compulsively now, he'd found the suicide letter tucked in one of Dana's portrait books. It was just three words, the young man told him in a bewildered voice, three lousy words to his only child. The man had written: "I'm a failure."

CHAPTER
18

"**Y**OU'RE a good cop," Rourke told him.

Murtaugh considered how ironic it was that those words were the epitaph to his career.

He watched Rourke finger two stacks of paper. The thick one, he knew, contained what was left of almost twenty years of commendations and service. The skinny one was a compilation of complaints, from the Bremmars right through to the mu-mu'd lady.

It was obvious which pile carried the most weight.

"If you weren't a good cop," Rourke was saying, "this would be a piece of cake."

Wordlessly, Murtaugh placed his gun and his shield on the desk.

"Nobody's trying to fuck you over, Hunt," Rourke assured him, magnanimous in his overt relief. "We're not calling for resignation."

He pulled the shield and gun toward him, like winnings in

a card game. "Randall has that information about the program. Give it some time, and we'll talk again."

Murtaugh stood.

"We can put you on desk—"

"I'd prefer the leave," Murtaugh said.

"Good," the Captain told him, "I think that's for the best."

Before he could make a clean exit, Rourke stopped him. "You know, Hunt, there's no reason why you can't hang on here long enough to get the old pension. I'm behind you all the way."

Murtaugh left the door open.

* * *

The boys were sitting very still against the wall. At intervals, Emil turned his head and sniveled onto his shoulder.

"Where's Jaime?" Murtaugh asked.

"We got a lawyer," Ricky looked up. "Says not to say a fuckin' word to nobody."

Murtaugh suddenly realized they were cuffed. He took out a handkerchief and wiped Emil's face. The kid broke into sobs at his touch.

He kneeled, eye level. "I know you didn't kill anyone," Murtaugh told them simply, "but I have to hear about Tomas."

"Don't say shit, man," Ricky warned the others.

Any minute the lawyer and Bromsky would return. It was obvious that Ricky was the leader in Sanchez's absence, so the detective squeezed onto the bench next to him.

"I want to help," Murtaugh whispered. "If you know where he is, get word to him he's in danger. Ask him to give himself up until this is straightened out."

"Oh, yeah," Ricky retorted. *"No me jodas, cop."*

Miguel said something in Spanish. The two argued, then Miguel stamped his foot. "I told him the Hall chick was trouble," he cried. "I told him there'd be a fuckin' catch!"

"A catch?"

"She was too nice, man," Miguel explained.

Too nice.

Think about that later, Murtaugh cautioned himself. There's no time for it now. Consider instead the implications of young boys conditioned to expect kindness as a ruse, a diversion; friendship as a condition with a catch to it. And if you fell for it, there was sure to be pain and punishment.

He heard the sound of approaching voices.

"Get Jaime to come in," he urged them. "Say Murtaugh's going to find the bastard who killed her."

He walked quickly down the hall, leaving his handkerchief on Emil's lap.

Murtaugh was almost out of the building when he felt a tug on his sleeve. Alison Randall stood behind him, tall and elegant, like a piece of frosted glass.

"You might want to look this over," she said, handing him a folder. Inside were the names and numbers of attorneys and psychiatrists who specialized in cops in trouble.

Murtaugh nodded. She started to go, then turned back to him. "I understand she was a friend of yours. I'm sorry."

"Yeah," he said.

It was an attempt to be gracious, but he knew his face was again registering anger.

He hoped Randall wouldn't take it personally.

* * *

The house was only four blocks away, and yet he'd never once, during the many circuitous routes taken to the neighborhood where he spent most of his time in these past weeks, been near it.

That was by choice.

Now, suddenly, it seemed more his home than those awful basement rooms, and Murtaugh was drawn to it for comfort.

He hardly recognized what he saw. The facade, before as plain as a brown bag covering the fine old rooms inside, was washed the palest yellow. They'd put long shutters on the windows, enameled black, and a striped awning lowered, in the way of a glamorous eyelid, seductively over the front door.

The woman was watering her geraniums.

Murtaugh knew he shouldn't linger. It would be a disaster, like the restaurant. These people had erased all touches of Eve about the place; and besides, it was the other one he was mourning. Why come here?

He was being unreasonable, he told himself. Confronting the past, after all these months, wouldn't mean release. What use could a dead wife be when dealing with fresh pain?

It alarmed him when he heard himself speak out loud, "Dana . . ."

The woman with the watering can turned, squinting into the sunlight, "No, I'm afraid you're mistaken." She was pregnant.

Then she smiled. "Mr. Murtaugh, isn't it? Katherine Witt. Come back to see what we've done with the place?"

He nodded, not trusting himself to say anything else.

She continued happily. "We just love it. Of course, you might not approve. We knocked out that wall between the living room and dining room—oh, and," she patted her stomach, "we put in a nursery."

"That's great." His words seemed to come from out in space somewhere.

"Are you feeling all right, Mr. Murtaugh?" Katherine sounded concerned. "You look a little shaky."

Murtaugh grasped the wrought-iron railing. "I've been walking in the sun," he said stupidly.

Katherine didn't appear to notice. "Oh, I know. Eric has fits when I'm in the garden on days like this. Especially now," she added meaningfully.

"The place looks great," Murtaugh said hoarsely. "Take care of yourself."

The woman beamed. "You, too."

He turned mechanically, watching one foot go out in front of the other.

"Mr. Murtaugh!" Katherine Witt called. "Would you like to see how we've got it done?"

"Yes," he said. And immediately, he felt relieved.

* * *

They'd "got it done" in styles and colors so dissimilar to what was there before, Murtaugh was able to be detached and objective.

Katherine took him on a guided tour, not seeming to mind his silence, chatting about swatches and wallpaper, the slow delivery of furniture. She seemed more relaxed and friendly than the times they'd met after that Sunday she'd first knocked on his door.

But, of course, things had changed. It was her door now. She was settled, about to have a baby.

The kitchen was green, in a shade they hadn't liked; and nowhere was there any blue. Eve always teased him that he loved any color as long as it was blue. Even the nursery jarred his sense of the usual.

"Purple is the new way to go when you're not sure of the sex," Katherine explained.

Murtaugh wondered if the choice doomed the kid to a life of sexual ambivalence, or merely above-average flamboyance.

Katherine made hot tea ("Better than cold when you're warm because it lowers the body's temperature,") and insisted on toasting scones.

"They're from Evelyn's," she told him. "Do you know the place?"

Murtaugh said no, out of habit, and listened to yet another

228

endorsement of its culinary attractions. By this time, they were in the living room, as flowery and cluttered as he imagined an English country home to be.

Katherine sat on a wingbacked chair, motioning him to the loveseat, bedecked with pillows. She put the tray of tea and scones in front of him.

"I hope this isn't evoking any painful memories," she said kindly.

"Actually, it's good to know somebody's having a nice life here," he replied.

Katherine passed him a cup. "Well, we had a bit of bad luck when we first moved. Eric's business went under. We almost lost everything."

"Sorry to hear that."

"Thanks," she said. "Maybe it was for the best. Made us think long and hard about what was really important, that kind of thing." She looked embarrassed, as though unsure of why she was telling him.

But Murtaugh was no longer paying attention to Katherine.

Something he noticed, right next to him, jolted him out of this pretty little room, back into the horrible world outside.

He picked up an embroidered pillow and read, " 'HE WHO HAS THE MOST TOYS WHEN HE DIES, WINS.' "

Katherine's embarrassment deepened. "Awful, isn't it? I don't even know why I keep it. It's not very amusing, when you think about it."

"Did you buy this at The March Hare?" he asked.

"No, but funny you should ask. It was a gift from the woman who owns it," she told him. Katherine began buttering another scone. He watched her nervous fingers.

"You're friendly with Ms. Lincroft and her husband?" Murtaugh tried to contain his interest.

"We used to be," she spoke slowly; then with a what-the-hell shrug, she leaned forward. "Eric and I saw a lot of the whole bunch when we lived in Manhattan. It's how we ended up here in Hoboken. Jake and Rebecca were wild about the opportunities for . . ."

Her voice trailed off, and Murtaugh didn't press. Finally, she continued. "When we first moved, we stayed close with them. Until Eric started having problems with his business."

"Fair weather friends?"

"More like we couldn't keep up with the game," Katherine said. She flushed. "I mean, what with us almost going bankrupt, except for Eric's dad bailing us out, and the baby . . . well, we changed, I guess."

Murtaugh nodded. His heart was pounding so fast, he made a move to loosen his tie.

"Oh, dear, you're looking pale again," Katherine said. "Is it too warm without the fan?"

"No," he assured her. "It's fine. It's perfect."

* * *

At the door, Murtaugh inquired casually, "You and your husband off on a Fourth of July trip?"

Katherine laughed. "We thought we'd settle for watching the fireworks from the Tech."

He took her hand. "Thanks for the tea and the look around. It was just what I needed."

She patted her thick waist again, saying, "Now that I'm playing homebody, I'm glad for the company. Come anytime."

Katherine Witt waved as he turned around for a last smile before going up the sidewalk.

Those sad eyes, she thought. Mr. Murtaugh was really a rather attractive man. She tried to remember what he did for a living, and it came back to her all at once. Hunter Murtaugh was some sort of policeman.

The recollection made her slightly uneasy, although she could not have said why; and, in the end, she attributed it to those two scones she'd gobbled so quickly while talking about people she'd just as soon forget.

* * *

Miss Katz seemed not at all surprised to hear from him, as if the fifteen summers had passed in dog's years.

He couldn't help thinking in animal imagery. When he was a kid, they'd called her Kitty, in spite of the fact that her name was Louise. Kitty Katz, everyone's idea of a librarian— each angular, beige part of her neatly tied with pearly ropes from which hung glasses, cardigan sweaters, even keys.

If she disliked children, she loved the child. Come into the Hoboken Library in a group and you were likely to be out on your ear in seconds. Come in by yourself, even at an hour when she knew you were supposed to be in Sister Albertine's geography class, and she'd find you, motion you over with that beaky nose of hers, and hand you a pile of books'd knock your socks off.

That's how Murtaugh discovered *The Black Arrow* and *Treasure Island*. When he first saw the Howard Pyle and N. C. Wyeth illustrations, first read *Northwest Passage* and all of Edgar Rice Burroughs. Later, it was her list of mysteries and detective fiction that made him dream of becoming a cop.

"When the town was so poor the only vacations came from between the frontispiece and the back cover, we kept the library open," Miss Katz said loudly into the telephone. "Nowadays, we close on holiday weekends, they go off in their cars and are henceforth far less well-traveled than beforetimes."

Murtaugh laughed. "I only need you to let me in for a few hours. It's important."

"Hunter Murtaugh," she said, using his full name as she always did, "believe me, there's nothing recently published you should be in such a hurry to read." He waited for her to come around, which she did.

"Of course, if it's research you're after," Miss Katz sighed, "then I shall meet you this morning at eleven. No withdrawals, you understand, and don't you dare eat anything in the stacks."

Murtaugh walked with long, purposeful strides. Strangely enough, he'd slept last night, slept well and long, and was refreshed. Dana's drawings, furled next to his heart, encouraged him on. He stopped at the Korean store for sandwiches and cold soda, rehearsing his promise to Miss Katz about not bringing them into the stacks.

The town was deserted. Only the old-timers and Hispanics remained, and they seemed slightly uncomfortable, like stragglers in an amusement park after everyone else has gone home.

On the sidestreets, a few families were getting late starts, packing L. L. Bean accessories into their BMWs and Volvos. The basketball courts in the park were empty. Murtaugh turned around suddenly to satisfy a notion that Jaime Sanchez was nearby, watching him from some secret vantage point. He saw nothing.

The Hoboken Library appeared bigger, more foolishly Victorian, in an empty neighborhood. Miss Katz stood on the steps, shooing away pigeons. Except for dark Ray Ban sunglasses, which gave her a comical new-wave look, she was much as he remembered, a bit more stooped and beige, perhaps.

"You've aged, Hunter Murtaugh," she said.

He smiled. "Some of us aren't so lucky."

"Stop your folderol," Miss Katz retorted. "You've caught up, that's all, to the time of life when one starts looking like a cartoon of oneself."

She turned the key and removed her Ray Bans, replacing them with bifocals. In the foyer, Murtaugh paused to breathe in the library air, which was different than any other kind.

"Saint Francis of Hoboken," Miss Katz muttered cuttingly,

as she passed the large framed photograph of Frank Sinatra on the wall, "our patron."

It took her only minutes to unlock the doors to the research room, the men's room, and stacks.

"Can't stay," she told him. "Saturday morning shopping, you know."

Murtaugh wondered what her apartment was like, what kind of life Louise "Kitty" Katz had when she left this place.

"I appreciate this, Miss Katz," he said politely, succumbing to that scared ten-year-old in himself that she somehow always managed to summon.

"Well, you should, Hunter Murtaugh," Miss Katz sniffed. "If I find any crumbs around the Coleridge, there'll be something to pay."

She handed him a sealed envelope with a set of keys. "They're clearly marked. Toss them in the bookdrop on your way out."

After she left, it occurred to Murtaugh that she wasn't carrying a shopping bag. Miss Katz, he was certain, would have liked nothing better than to pitter-patter after him all day, but she was perceptive enough to recognize his need to be alone.

He laid out everything. The sandwiches, soda, drawings, and yellow pad. Then he picked up a few books from a cart and put them on the edge of each sketch, flattening them.

Number 516, shown from a variety of angles and perspectives. He passed his hand across the last one in the series, as though, by this, he could magically summon the artist. His movements, however slight, echoed through the empty room. He was totally alone.

Murtaugh looked from one to the other—Number 516, with a wheelbarrow holding a single rose; Number 516, with a pair of old lady shoes slung over the railing; Number 516, with a child's carousel horse leaning next to the front door; Number

516, with a wicker babycarriage filled with petunias; Number 516, with a gilt birdcage acting as a planter for an overgrown fuchsia.

What had Dana Hall seen? He wrote down each of the objects on his pad. He said them out loud.

Wheelbarrow with a rose. Old lady shoes. A child's horse.

Rose . . . old lady . . . child. Rose . . . Mrs. Cappricio . . . Tomas.

He felt that familiar heavy feeling in his gut, as if he'd eaten something which exploded with sparks, and it warmed him.

Rose. Mrs. Cappricio. Tomas. Signals for murder.

But signals to whom? And what about the others? A babycarriage. A birdcage. There were four murders. Was the sign for Dana a bird? Who was the baby?

The theory evaporated before his eyes. It didn't make sense. Didn't fit. As much as he tried to believe, as much as he wanted to believe, he couldn't accept the notion of Jake Florian and Rebecca Lincroft as bizarre cult figures, members of some kind of coven, picking out victims and leaving tokens on their stoop to mark their prey.

Above and beyond their alibis, Murtaugh couldn't buy the profile. Rebecca and Jake were upscale, successful, on-top-of-things. They wouldn't be drawn to the macabre the way Jaime and his friends were. Their passions ran to possessions, toys, real estate.

He allowed the phrase on Katherine's pillow, which he'd pushed out of his mind like a bank account used only for last resorts, to come flooding back. HE WHO HAS THE MOST TOYS WHEN HE DIES, WINS.

Suddenly, he was leaping from the wooden seat, bounding into the reference room. The town, the town, the town . . . He found several volumes, leafed through them, then raced back to the main entrance.

There, next to the portrait of Saint Frank of Hoboken, was

a framed map of the town. One mile by one mile. The Miracle Mile, they used to call it. A perfect square, like a child's gameboard. Or an adult's gameboard.

He saw it now. The way each area was a neat geometric design, leading into the next—Rose Walsh's neighborhood, into Castle Point, into the waterfront.

Murtaugh ran back to Dana's drawings. Five of them. Five symbols, not for murder, but for a game.

He unpacked his sandwiches and took big bites of the turkey with Russian dressing on rye, washing it down with diet soda.

He thought of Rose's property. Three buildings—her own, plus the ones where the man with the German shepherd and that lady in the mu-mu lived. Señor Quiles' home and the tenement next door he'd bought years ago. Mrs. Cappricio's attic space in the house her husband once owned.

Ideas seemed to multiply until the implications were staggering. He recalled playing Monopoly when he was a kid. The rules came back to him, hazy but sure. There were certain desirable properties, he remembered, that could win you the game. Then, of course, there was the Boardwalk.

Translated, the waterfront and the properties immediately flanking it.

Murtaugh went to the card catalogue and looked under REAL ESTATE. He was amazed at the scores of recently published books on the subject. There would be time, later, for more detailed research.

For now, he brought down four from the stacks and sat with his remaining sandwiches, prepared to read until he understood.

* * *

Downstairs, near the men's room, was a pay phone. A nice one with a well-lit booth, a place to sit, and a directory.

He found the Witts' number, and on a hunch, took down the address of one other person, before dialing.

Katherine answered.

"This is Hunter Murtaugh."

"Oh, Mr. Murtaugh." Her voice sounded strained. Katherine Witt had obviously given some thought to yesterday's conversation. She was worried. "We were on our way out."

"This won't take long. It's about something you said," he went on firmly. "About a game you couldn't keep up with."

She expelled a breath. Murtaugh guessed that Eric was standing near, trying to cue his wife.

"Oh, that was only in a manner of speaking, you know," Katherine told him.

"Yes, I do know. I know pretty much the whole story," Murtaugh replied.

"Look, we've really got to—"

He opted for a different tactic. "Mrs. Witt, this information is pertinent to an investigation being conducted at Police Headquarters. Now either we talk over the phone or I can stop by. Or you and your husband could meet me at my office."

He neglected to tell them that his office was, at the moment, a basement apartment infested with maggots.

Katherine mumbled something to her husband, and he took the receiver. "Mr. Murtaugh—er, I mean, Sergeant Murtaugh, isn't it?"

Murtaugh coughed.

"Kathie told me you were asking about Jake and Rebecca, and the others." Eric's tones were businesslike. "Frankly, we've put all that behind us, and since our involvement was entirely legal, I feel that should be the end of it."

"The end of it, Mr. Witt," Murtaugh said calmly, "has been four murders."

There was a strangled cry on the other end of the line, then protest. "That's impossible—for Chrissakes, it was only a game!"

Murtaugh put in another coin. He let Eric Witt's imagination swim during the brief interval. When he spoke again he tried to be kind. "Listen, I don't want to involve you and your wife unless I have to."

Again, he left out the part about not being in any position to involve them at all.

"I just need to know something," he said. "There are symbols, right? Symbols for each player in the game?"

Eric sounded relieved, as if this might not be as bad as he'd expected. "Yeah, sure. Six players. Six symbols."

Murtaugh knew of only five. "What was yours?"

"A top hat."

"And when did you and your wife stop playing?" the detective asked.

"Oh, last part of March, beginning of April." Well over a month before Dana started her drawings.

"One more thing," Murtaugh said, "when you stopped, did another player come into the game?"

"No," Eric explained, "it's set up so that when you go bankrupt, you're out. I literally went bankrupt."

"You were lucky," Murtaugh told him grimly.

"Is that all?"

"For now." Then he added, "Eric, if you or Katherine happens to get a call from—"

"We won't."

He repeated. "If you do, play dumb. Don't mention this conversation. The game got out of hand, and I want you to steer clear of it."

Witt promised.

Murtaugh made a mental note to have Bonelli keep an eye on them.

* * *

As he'd suspected, Davy O'Connell was not at home.

Murtaugh stood outside the swanky condominiums for a long time before giving his name to the doorman.

Alison Randall admitted him, not having had the time to change from the paisley silk robe she was wearing. Davy sat expectantly at the lavender breakfast bar. In front of him were a shiny black art deco coffeepot, a creamer, and matching cups.

Randall's apartment, Murtaugh noticed, like her office at Headquarters, was decorated lavishly, and hung with expensive lithos and those silly Mucha prints. It looked like that trendy restaurant where you couldn't drink without eating.

"I hate to barge in this way," he said simply, without a note of apology in his voice, "but I have nowhere else to go."

She led him to the camelback sofa and let him spread the drawings on her fancy carpet.

CHAPTER

19

—

SHE WASN'T sure why she was allowing herself to get involved.

Certainly, at first, she'd been thrown off by the element of sheer surprise—the sight of Hunter Murtaugh at her door.

Hours later, after the coffee started making everyone edgy and they'd decided to go out for a late supper, Alison still hadn't figured it out.

It wasn't the logic of his argument. She'd stared at those pictures, trying to see what he saw, and yet it was all so nebulous, so improbable.

Jake and Rebecca, as Davy described them, seemed the most unlikely candidates for murderers. They were affluent, bright, attractive. They were like her.

Alison made a point of sitting quietly while Murtaugh described how they'd done it.

Each detail, he said, up until Mrs. Cappricio's death, had been planned. It was part of the strategy, their need to win the game. Of course—and here Murtaugh's smile had been mirthless—they had luck on their side. Jaime and his gang were the perfect scapegoats.

He traced their actions. Rebecca, he told them, was probably alone in the shop when Tomas Quiles came in, as he did every Thursday, to look at the games and unusual toys. She'd put the "OUT TO LUNCH" sign on the door. It was easier than she'd expected it to be, Murtaugh projected, because on this particular Thursday Tomas was acting strangely, maybe even aggressively. He was on angel dust.

Rebecca must have hit him on the head, maybe with one of the antique fraternity paddles, rolled him in a rug, and called her moving men to have them bring a few heavy items to Number 516.

Was Lindsay involved?, Davy asked. Murtaugh thought not. It was Jake and Rebecca's move. What he needed to find out was how far the other players had been willing to go for the sake of the game.

Murtaugh told how Jake, and possibly Deacon, moved Tomas' body from the shed to the Walsh's carriage house. How they came in through the back door and killed Rose. How they put on a tape recording of her voice, an idea unwittingly suggested to them by Dana Hall during one of Rebecca's sittings, put it on so that the three of them could listen to the now dead woman's rantings over tea.

He explained about Mrs. Cappricio's journey to find the policeman she'd seen entering the Quiles home. About Mrs. Cappricio, suddenly wilting and cowering in the presence of a handsome young man who openly chatted about the horrible things that happened to innocent people.

Watching him, Alison could believe that Murtaugh was more unhinged than the people he was speaking about so adamantly, as he rolled up those sketches with such care you'd have thought they were Picassos.

240

Why, then, did she feel this stirring inside her? Partly, Alison acknowledged, it was because of David O'Connell's face. Rapt, intent, questioning, but ultimately . . . happy. Happier, even, than he'd seemed a few hours ago on her ice-blue sheets.

It was almost frightening, the turn their relationship was taking. Alison Randall and a cop. Even an educated cop.

She thought of her father, the president of a major packaging company, a man used to dealing in millions of dollars. She imagined telling him. Saying, Daddy, I think I'm falling in love with a detective. She pictured his face contorting, and then relaxing, as it had when she'd taken this job in Hoboken, as if to say, get it out of your system, you'll come back to your senses. She wasn't sure he'd be right in this case.

Hunter Murtaugh was a man she'd loathed. He was a drunk, Alison knew, and probably sexist to boot. He'd presented more difficulties than the others she'd had to deal with, because, she admitted, he was a cut above. More intelligent. More worldly. If anyone on the Hoboken Police Force could be considered worldly. He was the only one ever to comment about the Mucha prints she had on her office walls, and although the comment was rather derogatory, he had at least known what they were.

And David worshipped him.

That was only partly why, Alison knew, she was feeling vaguely flattered that he'd come back with them after dinner, why she was willing to ignore the mound of ashes dangerously close to overflowing in the virgin ashtrays, the stale smell of cigarettes and caffeine in her centrally air-conditioned rooms.

The other reason was Alison Randall felt challenged. It would be a chance, getting mixed up with a man who'd just been drummed out of the Department, yet . . .

She listened to him courteously enough, but her mind was off and running.

If he was right . . .

Sometime after three, Murtaugh rose and thanked her stiffly, saying he was sorry to have imposed.

The man she was falling in love with was circumspect, noticeably reluctant to commit his services in front of her.

Alison said, "Wait."

Murtaugh stopped at the door.

"You have no real proof," she told him. "What are you planning to do?"

Murtaugh didn't hesitate. He wasn't going to allow Randall the satisfaction of thinking she could stop him. "I'm going to beat them at their own game."

"You'll need me, then," Alison replied.

Murtaugh made a move to protest.

"I can teach you things you'll need to know," she insisted. Davy O'Connell just laughed.

* * *

Murtaugh stayed the night. At five-thirty Alison simply handed him a comforter and sheets still in plastic packaging, and he climbed up into the loft that ran the length of her high-ceilinged living room.

He ignored the ring of the telephone, simply rolling over on the Oriental mat until about nine when the smell of coffee woke him. O'Connell and Alison were already dressed.

They stopped talking as he made his way awkwardly down from the heights of his nest.

"What's going on?" Murtaugh asked, sensing something in their faces.

A brief pause. Alison handed him a cup. "I'm going to take you shopping today."

He laughed derisively. "I'll pass."

She was matter-of-fact. "Look, if you want to establish some kind of viable presence around town, you can't do it looking like that."

Murtaugh shrugged rumpled shoulders. "I own a suit."

A noise came from where O'Connell was unloading the dishwasher, but by the time the detective looked in that direction, Davy's expression was poker straight.

"Trust me," said Alison.

Only days before, the statement would have been incredible, but Murtaugh realized there was no turning back now.

"It's Sunday. The stores are closed," he protested.

Alison deftly sliced a melon as she spoke. "Here, maybe, but who would ever think of buying a suit in Hoboken?"

Murtaugh felt she knew the answer as soon as the words left her lips. She continued smoothly. "A friend of my father's owns a place in the City where you can get some respectable things. It's open until five."

"I don't think—"

"Do you want to do this right or not?" Alison asked.

Murtaugh sat at the lavender bar and ate his fruit and eggs.

* * *

They went in Alison's SL, license plates A L R. She removed the top so there was headroom, even though Murtaugh's knees were pressed up hard against the front seat. He rubbed the bump on his head gotten in an attempt to fold Alison's perfect sheets in the loft space. The detective had a feeling that this breed of newcomers were in general more compact, more streamlined, than he was.

Outward-bound traffic was at a complete stop for the entire length of Washington Street. The driver of a New Jersey Transit bus, also on its way to Manhattan, leaned on his horn. From the opposite direction, they could hear the unmistakable strains of a marching band.

"The Fourth of July parade," O'Connell said incredulously; and for the first time in forty-eight hours, Murtaugh laughed.

During his life, he'd seen more parades go through the center of Hoboken than he could have possibly counted. What was an ever-amusing source of wonder to him was that, more often than not, Police Headquarters was the last to be notified.

The marchers in the holiday parades, the religious feast, and Hispanic Pride Week just congregated at one end of the town and stubbornly started—in the face of whatever moving vehicles were in their path.

This band was particularly anemic. Murtaugh raised himself cautiously in what passed for the backseat.

Someone had thought to call a cop, who, seeing no other way, was now leading the parade. A local branch of the Veterans of Foreign Wars walked solemnly behind him carrying a banner. They were followed by twirlers, and a pretty girl in a red, white, and blue prom gown riding atop a small wagon float. He couldn't see that far, but Murtaugh knew there would also be the Little League and a representative from one of the local parishes taking yet another opportunity to carry their statue of the Virgin through town.

"Maybe I was wrong." Murtaugh had to shout to be heard. Davy looked puzzled.

He explained, "This old place isn't changing so fast after all."

Alison made a sudden, illegal turn onto one of the side-streets.

"Hunt," Davy said, not really looking at him, "Lowenstein called this morning."

The young man hadn't had time to regulate his voice as the Sousa march diminished. The words were overly loud. "Dana Hall was three months' pregnant when she died."

A bass drum rumbled behind them. Alison appeared to

concentrate only on maneuvering around the maze of double-parked cars.

Murtaugh recalled the word "complicated," uttered from that crooked mouth. He'd avoided thinking about it before, avoided connecting it with the mass of feelings pressing him from all sides. Now he realized things had been even more complex for her.

Images—Dana, drawn and tired; Dana keeping appointments with a doctor and canceling them for a sitting; Dana's cheek against his hand—would have to be sorted and gone through, one by one.

With another characteristically impatient movement, Randall snapped on the radio to drown out the pathetic little drum and bugle corps. The sun was so strong it made his eyes tear, and Murtaugh wished he owned a pair of dark glasses.

". . . blue," Alison was saying.

"What?"

"I said, let's try and find something for you in blue," she repeated.

Murtaugh smiled. "Yeah," he agreed, "blue would be good."

* * *

Alison's father's friend was pretty goddamn wealthy by Murtaugh's standards. The clothing shop, which he'd pictured in terms of one of Hoboken's storefronts, only ritzier, took up almost a full city block.

Randall led the two men through it as assuredly as though it was her own apartment. Murtaugh sneaked a peek at one of the pricetags, telling himself he could always be buried in it. The gallows humor hit too close to home.

O'Connell sat while Alison went through the racks, followed by a bewildered, but surprisingly docile Hunter Murtaugh.

It was lunchtime when she finally gave the nod to a conservatively cut navy pinstripe. She trotted off to pick out a shirt and two ties, leaving the detective to turn around and raise his arms for an elegant, silver-haired man with tailor's chalk.

Randall arrived in time to tell the man sweetly, but firmly, that the suit should be ready this afternoon rather than next week. She mentioned the owner by name, with a dazzling smile, and thanked him for doing them both a favor.

While they waited, O'Connell suggested they have something to eat. Murtaugh declined, saying he had an errand to run; and after agreeing to meet at four, they parted company.

* * *

Martin and Richard lived on Fifth Avenue in the teens. It was a building with a television-monitored security system, so if the men were taken aback by Murtaugh's appearance they had time to cover.

"Sergeant!" Fellows seemed relaxed and at-home in his new digs. "We were just mixing Mimosas. Can I pour you one?"

"No, thanks," Murtaugh replied.

The studio was small, but handsome. Richard sat in his robe, feet up, reading the Arts and Leisure section of the *Times*. He waved to the detective.

"So this is, as we say, official business," Martin commented easily, "not a friendly drop-in."

"Actually," Murtaugh told him, "I've come to ask you a favor."

Fellows raised one eyebrow, in the way he'd no doubt seen some film star do. "Ask away," he said.

They sat together at the glass table that was supported on the necks of two great porcelain swans. Fellows poured coffee and prepared himself to listen.

CHAPTER

20

THE QUILES HOUSE was so dark it looked as if no one was at home. Murtaugh wondered if they had already packed up, fled this ghost town, this town of ghosts.

Fourth of July. A holiday. Alison Randall was taking the whole week as vacation. Murtaugh supposed, except for the murders, Davy would have gone off with her in the candyapple-red sportscar.

Only O'Connell was needed, now that the Department was shorthanded; so Alison had driven by herself, not to some resort or private beach, but to a small place called Center Bridge in Bucks County, Pennsylvania.

In spite of Murtaugh's misgivings and a desire to go himself, she'd convinced him there was too much to do here today, too many opportunities to take while others were sailing on the ocean and picnicking in the Berkshires.

Besides, she said quietly, and without a hint of malice, she

247

could honestly present herself as a representative of the Hoboken Police Force. Murtaugh didn't bother arguing.

He rang the bell again. Señor Quiles came to the door, in an undershirt and dark trousers. He was unshaven.

"Go away," he told Murtaugh. "There's no one left to hurt here."

"Señor, I—"

"No," the old man was angry. "I don't dirty this house with the one who lets my boy's murderer run free."

He began to shut the door. His daughter stopped him.

"He can come into my home," Maria told her father, "even if you don't welcome him in yours."

Murtaugh stepped into the front hall. All the shades were down, and inside it was sunless, airless. A vacuum.

Señor Quiles appeared unwilling to allow him to mount the stairs.

"You come to say you have found the monster?"

Murtaugh nodded.

The man grasped his arm. "He will pay, with the others?"

"There is more to this," Murtaugh replied, "more than you know." The man moved away with a grunt of disbelief.

They sat in the living room, where only days ago every inch of space was filled with neighbors and family.

"My mother and my aunt, they are in Union City at my sister's husband's," Maria said, as though apologizing for the emptiness.

Murtaugh paused for a moment, then asked, "What will you and your family do . . . now?"

Quiles rose impatiently. "You come here to ask what we will do?"

The detective pressed on, doggedly. "Will you stay in Hoboken?"

The old man muttered, "Stay where little children and women are killed and no one stops it?"

Murtaugh waited for him to continue. "This daughter of mine, she can if she must, but my *family*," he stressed the word, "my family will no longer remain."

"You'll sell?"

"There were offers, before," Quiles told him, "and when the troubles get bad next door, even then, I think maybe, yes . . . only Tomas, he likes his teachers, and the park, and so I—" His voice trailed off.

Murtaugh wondered what sort of trouble happened next door. Perhaps, he thought, there had been an attempt to sabotage the building before the killers resorted to more desperate measures.

Out loud he said, "The offers came from people in the neighborhood?"

Quiles shrugged. "The banker on this side, first. And after, the architect and his wife with the shop."

"Jake Florian and Rebecca Lincroft?"

"What has this to do with my grandson?" the man demanded. Maria was quiet; but she, too, shot a questioning look toward the detective.

"I wish I could tell you, but I can't," Murtaugh said. "Not yet."

"Then why are you here?" Maria sounded reproachful. "Why do you come to us with secrets in your eyes?"

"I want you to do me a favor."

Quiles began speaking, in a torrent of words. The icy quiet in his daughter's voice sliced through them, cutting them dead. "And for this favor, what do we get in return?"

"Justice," he said simply. Then, taking her hand, "I swear it on my life."

Before he left they promised to do what he asked them.

Señor Quiles walked him to the door, searching the detective's face for some clue. "These people who will come to buy,

249

the ones I tell this lie—they have something to do with my grandson?"

"Just stick to the story," Murtaugh urged him, "and it will be all right." In his own mind, he was hoping desperately that would be so.

Maria put a protective arm around her father, and they retreated back into the darkness of the house.

* * *

The Librettis were another story altogether.

The uneven slope of their venetian blinds clued him into the fact that even now they were watching him. He felt tempted to wave, at the same time intuitively knowing he must put off visiting them as long as he could.

Such a call, however cautiously executed, would be like advertising his moves over a bullhorn all throughout the town. But if the Librettis were talkers, they were also followers. The murderers had taken that into account, he believed, secure in the knowledge that they could be easily manipulated when the time came.

Murtaugh forced himself to concentrate on Paddy Walsh. He bypassed Number 518 in favor of the sure bet of finding the old man at Paulie's. Paddy presented a serious problem.

First, he would sell his own mother's only winter coat for beer money. And second, he was scared.

Mulling it over, Murtaugh decided the old man knew who murdered his wife and why. He'd simply diluted his conscience with alcohol. Occasionally the truth would surface, and Murtaugh had been witness to those glimmers of shrewdness when the owl eyes suddenly focused and the tongue let slip a knowing phrase.

Paulie's was nearly empty as usual. Paddy sat on one end of the bar, nearest to Dominick. On the other side, two stout men in shirt-sleeves were talking loudly in the hopes of being overheard by a woman who sat at one of the tables drinking a pink cocktail, smoking a cigarette, and pretending to wait for someone. She looked up hopefully when Murtaugh entered, as though believing for an instant that this was her nonexistent date come to rescue her.

"Here's our boy-o," Paddy Walsh cried, noticing the detective.

He's still riding the crest of a high, Murtaugh thought. He wasn't sure if that was a good sign or not.

The detective invited Walsh over to a table, off by themselves, after ordering a couple of drinks from the bar.

"What brings you here?" the old man asked when they were settled. "Have you caught the mess of 'em, then, and gotten yourself a day off?"

Murtaugh only smiled. "To be honest, I've got a business proposition for you, Paddy."

"Business?" Paddy puffed up with the vanity of someone never taken seriously in these kinds of affairs, who suddenly was. "Well, now, what can I do for you, sir?"

"I hear you've had an offer on your houses," Murtaugh commented. He slid his own glass closer to his companion.

The gesture was not unnoticed. Paddy swayed toward it, lifting his finger to his lips in that customary gesture and saying, in a stage whisper, "Ahhh, but that's on the Q.T., isn't it now, y'darlin' man."

Murtaugh waited until he'd finished drinking, and their eyes were locked. "They murdered her, Paddy," he told him. "And they know you know."

The old man's face reddened and then closed up, like a turtle, all the vulnerable parts of him out of sight.

"That's crazy talk, and nothin' I care to waste my time with."
He stood on wobbly legs.

Murtaugh didn't even bother raising his voice. "What'd they do? Offer you cash, and maybe a down payment on a little place at the Jersey shore?"

"The Jersey shore!" Walsh sputtered, before he could check himself. "Try Miami Beach itself!"

He'd said it, and suddenly it seemed more important that he should sit again. Sit and drink from this last frosty glass before he went home.

"Now why would they do that?" Murtaugh pressed.

"Cut with your rambling," Paddy wheezed. "I knew there was something daft about you first time we met."

"They want to know where you are," the detective suggested. "Because then it'll be easier for them to get rid of you."

Paddy started to laugh, but the beer went down the wrong way, making him choke. He would have gone to the bar for a napkin, except for this brute of a man holding his arm.

"You're a loose end, Paddy," Murtaugh was saying. "And once things cool down, they'll tie you up, snip you off. Miami Beach, eh? Who'd miss an old man without any family in Miami Beach? They'll make it look natural, like they did with Mrs. Cappricio, and if their lawyer's smart enough, they might end up with a condominium in Florida as a bonus. After all, they'll be paying the mortgage—"

Paddy Walsh was sweating. "Will you stop it?" he whimpered. "I ain't done nothing, so why's everybody got it in for me?"

Murtaugh handed him the other Pilsner glass. "I want to protect you, Paddy."

The old man looked grateful. "Ahh, but you're a grand fellow." He smiled through his tears. "Irish on both sides, aren't you?"

Murtaugh nodded. "I'm going to take care of everything," he said. "Just do as I tell you."

Paddy breathed deeply through his runny nose and took a swig of beer. "Anything," he promised.

Murtaugh prayed the players wouldn't wait too long to act. He might secure Paddy Walsh this evening, but he couldn't count on having a lasting effect on the man. Like the tides and the moon, he was predictable only to the extent of ever-changing.

* * *

The detective skulked about outside the house that had once been his. It was nearly dark when Eric and Katherine emerged. Witt was careful with his wife, keeping a firm hand on her as they went down the steps.

They're really in love, Murtaugh thought. He wondered whether it had always been so. At the closing, he remembered them as aloof and bickering. Maybe it was the baby, he decided, or having come through a crisis together.

"Nice night," he said, matching their stride.

"Mr. —?" Katherine began.

"Hunt," he told her.

Eric tightened his grip on his wife's arm. "Is this necessary? We were going over to see the fireworks."

"I'll try not to spoil them for you." Murtaugh was sincere. "I'd just like to ask you a few questions on the way."

They were silent for a block or so, then Katherine spoke. "I haven't been able to sleep . . . is it true, Mr. Murtaugh?"

Murtaugh nodded. They crossed Washington and began the incline toward Stevens Tech, passing a church that was being renovated into apartments. A large sign advertised the name and address of the architectural firm handling the renovations, and the detective made a mental note.

Skylights were already installed in the slant of the old roof, and on its facade some graffiti artist had spray-painted, "CON-

253

DOS FOR CHRIST." By the end of summer, people would be bidding on townhouses here. Murtaugh wondered if they would name, rather than number the units—The Vestry, The Altar, The Choir Loft . . .

"During the time that you played," he said, matching his words to his gait, "was there any mention of . . . of using . . . extraordinary means to pick up properties?"

Katherine looked at Eric and nodded.

"We thought it was a joke," Witt explained to the Sergeant. "One night we were talking strategies as usual, and Jake said something like, well, as a final resort, we could always kill them." Eric shook his head. "Everybody laughed—I mean, it was so outrageous, you know."

"Was that the only time?"

They paused at the gates of the college. Eric leaned back on the brick and closed his eyes. "No. After that, Rebecca started with the scenarios. It became part of the rules."

"What do you mean, scenarios?"

Katherine said, "When it was our turn, we'd have to pick from the "What If" pile . . . see, like, what if there's a row of houses and the ones on the ends are don't wants—"

"That means the owners will sell," Eric interjected.

"But the one in the middle won't budge," Katherine continued. "And you need all three. So we were supposed to come up with the best plan to get the no sell out of the picture."

Murtaugh felt the hair on the back of his neck stand up straight. "Murder, you mean," he said. "Scenarios for murder."

Eric cried, "We went along with it . . . like it was all kid's stuff. Like it was all just part of the goddamn game!"

The Witts huddled together in the darkness.

Murtaugh asked, "It didn't go any further? Further than talk?"

Katherine answered earnestly. "No. Not while we were playing."

"They'll be calling," Murtaugh said. "Remember. You don't know anything."

The couple began to walk toward the battlements. Murtaugh stopped them with his voice.

"What was the reaction of the others to this new part of the game?" he called softly.

Katherine considered for a moment and then replied, "They thought it was funny at first, I guess. Like Eric and me. Then it started making everybody a little uncomfortable."

"Except Jake and Rebecca," said Eric. "They really seemed to get off on it."

Murtaugh wished them goodnight. He started down the hill by way of Castle Point, hearing the fireworks but never turning toward their brilliance.

CHAPTER

21

Tuesday was a working day, and for the first time in over two years David Rothman called in sick. To be sure, his throat felt a little scratchy, the signs of a cold—Janis had left out his sweaters when she packed for the mountains.

The mere thought of it annoyed him. After all, that was why they had Iylish. But occasionally Janis got stubborn about doing something herself, and there was no reasoning with her. She'd throw a kink into the well-oiled machinery of the household, realize her incompetence, and then sink back into apathy, the state in which she was much easier to handle.

This day, Rothman didn't really mind. His sore throat gave him an excuse not to go to the office. He wasn't in the mood to deal with other people's problems, financial or otherwise. He wasn't even in the mood to deal with Olivia Marsh. And that was unusual.

Maybe you should go through the old GI series, he told

himself, see if you've finally succumbed to the inevitable stress-related ailments of your peers—ulcers or hypoglycemia. In the back of his mind, however, he knew exactly when the trouble had started and when it worsened.

So David Rothman was at home, oddly enough, when the package arrived. He was sitting in the kitchen pretending to read the *Wall Street Journal,* while actually tracing Iylish's pantyline against her tight polyester slacks as she reached to wipe the cabinets with ammonia. He was there to receive it, directly from her arms, after the doorbell rang.

Ironically, he would think later, instead of escaping his worries, he'd set himself up to be confronted by them.

"It's for yourself, sir," she said, with that lilt he found rather sexy.

Harmless-looking enough. A neatly wrapped square box, feeling lighter than he'd expected. His name and address were lettered in upper case on the front.

"Hand delivered?" Rothman asked the girl, noticing there was no postage or messenger label.

The green eyes widened. "No, it was only sitting there, and no one around a'tall."

She wasn't lazy, Rothman thought, but she wasn't too quick on the uptake, either. Still, with some of that hair trimmed out of her eyes, and a few decent clothes . . .

"We should go shopping one of these days, Iylish," he told her, tearing off the paper. "Get you a few pretty dresses—"

He never finished. Under the rolled-up newspapers and tissue was a top hat, shiny with age, yet somehow smart and stylish.

Rothman dug into the bottom of the carton for something, anything, to explain it. Tucked into the inside lining was an index card, with a typewritten message:

CAN YOU COME OUT TO PLAY?

257

"What's this, Mr. Rothman?" Iylish smiled, encouraged by her boss's newfound interest in her. "Is it for a costume ball you'll be going to?"

David Rothman stuffed the paper and the hat into the box, and ran out of the room with it, leaving Iylish to clean up in peace.

* * *

They were meeting at Randall's apartment for lunch. Davy was surprised to see Hunt already there, arguing with Alison over the necessity of a manicure. The Sergeant had a dishtowel tucked under his chin, and the young woman snipped aggressively around his ears with a pair of long, skinny scissors.

"It pans out," the young detective told them, making himself a sandwich. "According to the guy at the Architectural Board, years ago an architect could be drummed out of the corps for getting involved in development or construction. It wasn't considered ethical."

Murtaugh ducked his head from Alison's pointy pursuits. "Don't get carried away."

"Now the trend is toward one company doing both the designing and the building," O'Connell said, his mouth full.

Alison kissed him on her way to the sink. "What about Florian?"

Murtaugh stood, shaking stray locks onto the beautiful parquet floor.

He looks great, Davy thought to himself. And it wasn't just the suit.

"Hard to say," the young man admitted. "These are stiff political contracts, especially in historic districts like harbors where the government comes into play. But FlorDesign has been kissy-kissy with the CDA, and whether they get the final nod or not, Jake would be sitting pretty with all the property he's attempting to accumulate in the neighborhood of the waterfront."

He fed Alison a bite of his chicken salad. "How'd it go with Albert Cappricio?"

"Fine," she told him. "He's not hurting for an inheritance."

"So he'll play?"

Alison laughed. "Listen to us! See how easy it is to get carried away with this game?"

Murtaugh said nothing. He was nervous, and it bothered him that these two, untouched by any real loss, seemed so confident and excited.

"No word about Sanchez yet," O'Connell reported in more somber tones.

Alison pushed open the sliding door of the front closet and came back with a sleek leather attaché.

"Here." She handed it to the detective. "Now you're perfect."

"See you when I see you," Murtaugh said.

"Hunt," Davy O'Connell called. "You know, you might be able to bring all this into Headquarters right now. One of the group's bound to crack."

Murtaugh shook his head. "Can't count on that," he replied. He didn't add that he was looking forward to doing it this way, but he had a feeling that both Davy and Alison knew.

* * *

"He swears he knows nothing about it," Rothman whispered desperately into the telephone.

Rebecca's voice was calm and unruffled on the other end. He pictured her at The March Hare, giving him only half her attention, while she organized a shelf for the busy time that started after three o'clock.

"Of course I talked to her. How do you think I got Eric's number at this flunky new job of his?" Rothman was impatient.

"How *is* Katherine?" Rebecca nearly yawned.

"How the fuck should I know?" Rothman yelled. "The only thing I was interested in was whether they'd sent the goddamn package."

"And they said they didn't, so that's that." It was Rebecca's turn for impatience. "So either it was some kind of misunderstanding or one of your women is trying to get your goat."

"What do you mean?"

"I mean," she sighed, "have you hugged your wife today, or whatever the saying is? Look, I've got a customer."

Rothman breathed heavily into the receiver.

"David, darling," Rebecca said, "calm down. What are you worried about?"

What *was* he worried about?, he asked himself after he heard the dial tone. Certainly he'd done nothing wrong. And nothing had ever actually been said. There was the game, and there were the murders. Why take for granted that there was some connection between them?

But it wasn't only he who suspected, Rothman reminded himself. Deirdre and Michael had been avoiding him. When they'd bumped into each other gassing their cars on the outskirts of town on Friday evening, he'd seen it in their eyes, noted the surreptitious glances, the fits and starts of conversation.

And Lindsay—well, it wasn't easy to tell what Lindsay thought, about this or anything else. Lindsay made a habit of being blithely unaware of details, except the ones that immediately affected her creature comforts.

Deacon wasn't any easier to read. Rothman considered his possible involvement. One thing was for sure. If he'd been asked to do something, to do anything, by either Lindsay or Rebecca, it was a foregone conclusion that the thing would be done.

Rothman went upstairs, left his sweaty clothes in a pile on

the floor, and stepped into the spa. The Jacuzzi always relaxed him.

Where the hell was Janis anyway?, he thought, suddenly remembering Rebecca's innuendo.

His wife would be incapable of such an act, he decided. Not because she couldn't be cruel, but because she didn't care enough. She'd find the idea of a prank boring, not worth the energy of dredging up an old hat, wrapping it in paper.

Olivia, on the other hand, was not so easy to dismiss. She knew about the game. And she was certainly greedy enough, he acknowledged, in the same way he would acknowledge her beauty and ambition—as assets, not causes for alarm.

Yet what would Olivia have to gain by upsetting him like this? When his nerve flagged that last time, hadn't she laid down the law and made it perfectly clear that no more playing the game meant no more playing around either, as far as she was concerned?

Women, David Rothman knew through personal experience, were hard taskmasters. They all came with their own set of demands. No sooner had you gotten a hand up one of their shapely thighs when it hit the fan, that ever-so-gentle whispering in your ear. The further you went (and he wasn't talking sex either), the louder, the more insistent it became.

"You can't expect to—"

"It would be better if you—"

"I think you should—"

But, hey, Rothman told himself, as they say, if you want to play, you've got to pay. That's the way of the world: a price for everything, everything for a price. He'd learned it young, his father being in retail.

The tough part was satisfying everyone. While Olivia never made any bones about what she expected, Janis' demands were left unsaid. She never *asked*, although he understood implicitly that the minute he could no longer supply her with what she needed to get through the day, she'd find someone who could.

Yes, he'd definitely arrange for a GI series. Don't want to fall apart now, not when you can almost feel the brass ring in your hand.

Pressure had been beating his back pretty steadily, like the swirling jets under which he sat. Besides the game, the women, and the job, there was the residual strain from years of being his father's shiftless son: David, the bum.

No one would ever know, Rothman reflected, bitter tears falling into the sluicy waters, what a toll that had taken on his self-esteem; the little humiliations he'd been forced to endure, long after he'd renounced his waywardness and was back on the straight-and-narrow. To this day, he wondered what people found so goddamn funny about Rothman Senior naming his bleeding ulcer "David."

At family gatherings, the routine never changed. "Get out my pills, Lila," he'd say with a belch, "David's acting up again." Cue the assorted chuckles and giggles.

Rothman didn't know which was worse, that or his father's persistent recounting, to anybody who would listen, of how he'd been forced to leave the business to his nephew Gary (who, by the way, the old man invariably added, was doing very well with two new locations) instead of his own son.

But I've proved myself, haven't I?, Rothman muttered aloud, stepping out from the spa. I've got a good job, real estate investments up the ying-yang, a wife and a mistress. I'm a fucking bonafide success.

David remembered his father's reaction when he sold the condo in Manhattan and bought the brownstone.

"Hoboken?" he'd said archly. "Why not Newark?"

In time, he told himself, even Rothman Senior would have to admit his son, the bum, had made a smart move.

Hoboken was only the beginning. He thought about the

drives taken with Olivia on those Saturdays he was supposed
to be working overtime, drives into New York State and out
toward the Delaware Water Gap.

Passing through certain places, David had felt an almost
sixth sense emerging. A curious intuition which enabled him
to discern, like a man with a divining stick, something mi-
raculous underneath the surface, a potential vitality, on the
verge of awakening in an otherwise sleepy town. For future
reference, he always marked the spot on the map with a red
star. At such moments, he felt he knew what it was like to
be Christopher Columbus. To be Lewis and Clark. Ah, fuck
it all, why not say it? To be God.

Olivia was right, he had to stick with the game. Sure, there
was a ruthless, unethical aspect to it which made him queasy,
but was it really any different than Wall Street? Financial
transgressions were, after all, victimless crimes.

(*Oh, please, let them be victimless.*)

His insides felt as if they were ready to split.

Well, he thought, you can always name your ulcer after
dad, or Janis, or cousin Gary. Or the person who sent you
the hat.

Someone *knew*. That was the only sensible explanation.
Someone had figured it out and wanted in.

Rothman heard Melissa downstairs, revving up for one of
her tantrums, but he was rooted in place, unable to move
from this spot in the bedroom. His sweating face in the mirror
looked contorted with something like hate.

"Mommy! Moooom-meeee!" Melissa shrieked.

He ran into the master bathroom and got sick.

* * *

"How do I look?" asked Martin Fellows.

They walked together toward the building where their appointment with the CDA would be.

"Swell," Murtaugh muttered. "Just beautiful." He was beginning to think he'd made a mistake in asking Fellows along.

"I don't mean *that* way," Martin complained. "I'm referring to whether I'm in character." He adjusted his cuffs with the onyx links in them.

"Terrific," Murtaugh said. "Spectacular."

"My, my, my," Fellows chuckled, "someone's got the butterflies."

The sign on the door read Community Development Association, and the inside looked not much different than the offices of the newspaper Murtaugh had visited earlier in the day.

"We're expected," Murtaugh told the receptionist.

Fellows took out a card from a gleaming gold case and left it on her desk. Murtaugh trained his eyes to transpose the upside-down lettering. It said, MARTIN P. FELLOWS, Chairman, Architectural Board of New Jersey.

He put out his hand as if to stop Murtaugh from withdrawing his own, and smiled winningly at the woman. "My associate. Mr. Hunter."

By this time, Murtaugh was sure he had made a mistake asking Fellows along. They sat on vinyl chairs, waiting to be summoned, and the Sergeant's heart raced.

"What fun!" Martin whispered. "I started out as an actor, you know, oh, years ago, before I got into lighting."

Murtaugh picked up a magazine.

"Mr. Fellows?" the receptionist called. "Mr. Delavan is ready to see you now." As they passed her desk, she seemed to remember Murtaugh's presence. "Oh, and you, too, Mr., er—"

"Hunt," Fellows interjected, and he led the way into Delavan's office as though he'd been there dozens of times before.

What had he done? Murtaugh cursed the hunch that had brought him to the lighting designer in the hopes that designers of light would know something about other kinds of designers.

The first few minutes were the trickiest. Delavan sized them up, pulling out techniques from some public speaking course geared to establish common ground. ("Oh really? I'm a Yale man myself.")

Murtaugh worried that the guy might recognize him, as many did, from his occasional photographs in the local tabloid. He combed his memory for all those town fundraisers and police functions where the pols surfaced. But Delavan didn't look familiar, nor did he appear much interested in Murtaugh anyway.

"Yes," he was telling Fellows, "FlorDesign is certainly one of the contenders for the project. Being a Manhattan-based group, with the head fellow actually living here in town, they've been able to stay on top of things all along."

Delavan qualified this statement. "Of course, with any federal project, there are many factors to consider. But, all in all, they seem to have come up with quite a few interesting ideas."

"A shame," Martin commented sadly.

"What's that?"

"This is just between these walls, you understand." Fellows seemed completely at ease. "There have been no indictments, no formal hearings."

"I see." Then, realizing he didn't, Delavan leaned forward. "What sort of indictments are we talking about?"

Martin Fellows sighed and said, "Tell him, Mr. Hunter."

Murtaugh sat straight up, suddenly confused.

"Well, go ahead," Fellows directed him. "Don't be shy, man."

Murtaugh began slowly. "We have reason to believe," he stammered, "that FlorDesign is part of the biggest contracting scam of the decade."

"No!" Delavan sounded both shocked and curious.

"Yes." Fellows clucked his tongue.

Murtaugh began again, this time more confidently. "We understand from your assistant that FlorDesign is making a formal presentation to you sometime this week."

"True." Delavan nodded. "You're aware of how these things go. Takes years to actually get started, but we've been trying to pull together our proposal for the fed people. You know, find out how many highrise and lowrise they're going to allow around the waterfront, that kind of thing."

"The adjacent properties will be an issue?" Murtaugh wanted to know.

Delavan seemed puzzled by the question. "Obviously, they always are," he responded, "but as far as most of the community is concerned, renovating the harbor is still at the talk stage. We don't want to stir up too much attention. Let people know what they're sitting on, eh?"

"Isn't it the truth?" Martin laughed. "Well, we won't tell your secrets if you won't tell ours."

This last comment came out a bit coquettish, Murtaugh felt. He cut in, "Hopefully, you can nip your relations with FlorDesign in the bud and save yourselves the embarrassment later."

Delavan thanked them profusely. They went out the front door, took two stairs at a time, and kept up the pace until they reached Washington Street.

"My dear Sergeant," Martin Fellows said, laying a hand on the sleeve of Murtaugh's new pinstripe suit, "you wouldn't happen to have a Valium on you, would you?"

* * *

Deirdre Grace knew she shouldn't be drinking wine after the Valium she'd taken, but it bumped everything up to the proper level of unreality. Because that was the way things seemed to her now. Unreal.

The murders, for instance. Not so bad when she'd first read the reports in the papers, but leaving a sick, dizzy feeling after they were digested, like the pills.

Then there was the telegram, arriving at the exact moment she'd stepped in the door: THE GAME'S GETTING GOOD STOP I LIKE PLAYING FOR KEEPS STOP

Her first thought was it had been sent by Jake and Rebecca. She'd dialed Michael's number at the ad agency twice, because her fingers kept jumping.

"Ask them," Deirdre ordered her husband.

"It's better not to," he said, his voice uncharacteristically strained. "I thought we agreed, we'd just pretend nothing has happened."

"I can't," she wailed. "I need to know. If you won't call them, I will."

In the end, Michael had promised to touch base with Jake. He told Deirdre to take something and lie down. Luckily the live-in was working out. She and Joshua were watching the Disney channel in the room adjoining the nursery.

"He says it must be some kind of joke," Michael told his wife when he got home. "Not to worry."

"What a relief!" Deirdre muttered sardonically. It was then that she'd uncorked the first bottle of wine.

It had been a fitting end to the day when that detective Murtaugh turned up at their doorstep. The unreality heightened as she watched him tramp through the house like a tourist in a museum, oohing and aahing.

And now, sitting in the room Michael so pretentiously called the conservatory, Deirdre was in a downright festive mood.

"What's the news on the Rialto, Sergeant?" she asked him. "Caught all those nasty murderers yet?"

Murtaugh looked uncomfortable. "Like I said, this is purely a social call, to take advantage of your husband's kind invitation the other evening."

"Oh," Deirdre gushed, "But we're so interested in your work, aren't we, Michael? *So* interested."

The detective bowed his head a little, looking from under knitted brows. He really has lovely eyes, thought Deirdre. "To be honest with you, I've been removed from the investigation." He smiled weakly. "Removed from my duties completely, if the truth be told."

Michael relaxed noticeably. "What a shame."

"But what will you *do?*" cried Deirdre, as though she cared. "More wine, Sergeant? Oh, and what do we call you now, anyway?"

"Hunt is fine," Murtaugh said. He allowed her to fill his glass, knowing then she could more easily justify doing the same to hers. "I'm considering relocating. That's partly why I stopped by."

"Sorry, Sergeant." Michael clapped him on the back. "We're not thinking of selling."

Murtaugh laughed. "No, I don't think my bank account's up to this place, anyway. But Mr. Florian and Ms. Lincroft mentioned you dabbled in real estate, and I was hoping you could—"

Michael interrupted. "Jake and Rebecca told you that?"

Deirdre began to giggle, low and throaty. "So like them," she croaked. "Overly modest about their own accomplishments."

"Wasn't that Joshua?" Her husband turned toward an imaginary upstairs noise. "You'd better check."

"Oh, he's with the new woman," she reminded him, bobbing her individually cut coiffure. "Besides, I want to stay and hear your pep talk to the late—or do I mean ex?—Sergeant . . ."

Michael shrugged at Murtaugh apologetically. "Perhaps some other time, Hunt," he said. "I think I'd better tuck my wife in for the night."

"Ohhh, bedtime stories!" Deirdre exclaimed. "I'm sure this nice man would enjoy them, wouldn't he? All about earnest money, and reconstructed cap rates, and amortization—so exciting!"

"Thank you for the wine and the tour," Murtaugh said at the door.

Deirdre grasped his arm. "The secret is commitment, Sergeant."

"Is that right?" The two men exchanged patient glances.

"You bet your life," she shouted. "Now you go home and you draw up a contract with yourself, promising to make such-and-such a fabulous amount of money this year."

The woman leaned forward and whispered into his ear, "And then you make it *happen*. Get it? You just figure out how to make it happen!"

Murtaugh politely disengaged himself from the woman and walked outside with her husband.

"I'm really sorry," Grace told him. "She seldom overdoes the booze, but I'm afraid she's making up for it tonight."

"No problem. Thanks again."

"Oh, and good luck with your new ventures," the man called as Murtaugh descended the drive.

"Yeah," the detective called back. "You, too."

Deirdre was still downstairs, collecting the empty bottles and glasses. Meticulous to the last, Michael thought grimly. Compulsive cleaning and compulsive shopping, that's what makes my wife tick.

He remembered once showing Deirdre a magazine, two glossy pages filled from left to right with rows and rows of the satin shoes which had formerly been owned by a dictator's wife. "Say, Deir," he'd said jokingly, "how'd they get a picture of your closet?"

The shocked expression on her face had surprised him. For a moment he really thought he'd touched a nerve. "Don't compare me to that woman," Deirdre told him, obviously highly offended, "*I* have *taste*."

Now she turned to him, and he saw she was weeping. "Those bastards. They're trying to turn it around, pin it on us."

"We don't know that." Michael sounded unconvincing, even to himself.

"Maybe not yet, but we will." She moved toward the telephone.

"What are you doing?"

"I'm going to tell them," Deirdre insisted. "I'm going to get their dirty game out into the open."

He caught her hand and replaced the receiver. "Listen," he said earnestly, "that's the last thing we should do." Deirdre's face was streaked with expensive makeup.

He took her shoulders, shook her gently. "Promise me. We say nothing to any of them. Then, when everything cools down, we'll get out."

She surveyed the sumptuous room, looking as if she was going to retch. "I'm tired," Deirdre said, as he led her up the mahogany staircase. Then, "I wonder if they're sleeping?"

"Who?" Michael asked her.

"They probably are," she nodded. "The bastards! Sleeping like babies."

CHAPTER

22

Janis sprinted up the center of the court, shuffled right, and backstepped to the end line. Her muscles were toned, her legs tanned and strong. Janis Gillmore Rothman was in as good a form as when she was doing it for a living.

"Missed you yesterday," Murtaugh said, coming up behind her.

She spun around, startled.

"Did you get a chance to play over the holiday?" he asked in a friendly voice.

"What are you doing here?" the woman demanded.

The detective patted his gut and laughed. "Look a little out of place, do I?"

She strode toward her canvas bag, and not even stopping to wipe her glistening face, she moved off the court, saying, "I don't have time for you."

Murtaugh thought to himself, Gillmore, that's one of your

271

problems. You've got too much time. Time is overpowering you.

He said, "They're killers, Janis."

She kept walking. He had to jog to keep up with her. "Your husband included."

Janis was defensive. "I told you," she yelled. "He was home watching television with me."

"And that makes him clean?" Murtaugh taunted. "Ever hear of Charlie Manson?"

Janis scoffed. "You can't be serious, comparing—"

"Why?" He was on a roll now. "Because they're not shabby? Not droolers or wackos? They're rich, and smart, so they're somehow better?" He grabbed her arm. "Let me tell you how Dana Hall died, lady. How the kid looked when they finally rolled him out of the rug."

Janis pulled away, stood there, with her hands over her ears.

"Help me," he asked her.

"Fuck off," she said. She sank onto the grass, crosslegged.

"It's all the same to you." Murtaugh talked down at the golden-streaked head. "Just let it happen, right? Life can't get any worse."

He kneeled next to her. The grass was still morning wet. "Well, think again, because you're wrong." He kept on going. "That scandal when you threatened the player, when they caught you packing your gym bag with cocaine and a little something extra—that was rough? It ain't squat compared to what you'll go through when this hits the fan."

Murtaugh rose. "There'll be no shielding you this time, kid. You're not a minor anymore, are you?"

Janis raised her face. It was hard, and brown, and filled with rage.

"Get away from me," she shrieked. "You think you can play me, but you're out of your league, old man. I was the best—

the best! You'll never know how that feels. So get going, before
I call a *real* cop!"

Murtaugh nodded. "Don't worry about getting in touch. I
can always find you."

Looking over his shoulder, he saw Janis Gillmore Rothman
lying prone on the grass, her face defiantly arched toward the
sun.

* * *

Only blocks away, John Deacon was rolling out of bed. It
was almost eight. He'd be late again, not a habit to get into
when you were an accountant. Precision, punctuality, those
were the prerequisites. But somehow, for the past couple of
weeks, he couldn't seem to get it together.

Lindsay was still asleep, sprawled over a good three-quar-
ters of the bed. She slept like she made love—aggressively,
selfishly, with her whole body. Not the best lover he'd ever
had. That honor went to Rebecca during their brief affair a
couple of years back. No, Lindsay only looked to everyone
else like the best lover they might ever have, and that was
important to Deacon.

He turned on the coffeemaker. Showered and shaved quickly.
Then he opened the front door to get the *Times*. Within the
blue plastic liner was an index card, typed neatly:

> HAT'S OFF TO YOU. BUT REMEMBER,
> IF YOU WANT TO PLAY,
> I'M THE TOP.

Deacon felt his knees buckle. In one action he balled up the
message and closed the door.

No sense showing it to Lindsay, he said to himself. Why
upset her? He poured himself a cup of coffee.

In fact, he told himself as he downed his vitamins, why
upset yourself?

It was a joke. Rebecca, probably. She was the cool one. And who knew better than he that she was the top? His heartbeat slowed to normal.

Still, he wouldn't bother Lindsay with it. If things were going to work with her, he'd have to take charge, handle responsibility. She was used to powerful men. Her father owned a large chain of family hotels, the sort that Lindsay wouldn't be caught dead in; yet it had made him fabulously wealthy. Deacon knew what it would take to keep her.

They'd been together over a year, except for those times she disappeared without warning, calling him as high as a kite from a hotel in Paris or sending him unsigned postcards from some beach in South America. One whole year, and yet she knew absolutely nothing about his background, where he'd come from, who he really was.

Occasionally he wondered whether it would even matter to her that his name had originally been DiFascio, that he'd legally changed it to Deacon upon graduating from college. The name change was simply the knockout punch which had finally toppled his lousy birthright.

Yeah, John thought, I'd trained for that moment for years.

It hadn't been exactly a cakewalk either, erasing every tell-tale Nicky Newark characteristic from his speech and dress, but he'd done it. Of course, inheriting his mother's Neapolitan coloring helped. It was the only genetic legacy which had ever worked in his favor.

When he entered that courthouse he was Johnny DiFascio, another punk from the Ironbound District, and when he came out he was John F. Deacon. He never once looked back. No one had ever questioned the biography he'd so painstakingly created for himself—the decent little prep school, the maiden aunt in Connecticut who'd taken care of him after his parents were killed in that tragic boating accident—well, no one except Rebecca the first time he'd met her, at that swank loft party in Manhattan. By then he'd told the story so often he almost believed it.

"Is that so, Johnny?" he remembered her saying, widening those incredible eyes until he felt stripped naked, right down to the swaggering "goomba" inside himself.

At first, Deacon admitted, it had freaked him out. Later, as he got to know Rebecca, he realized that was just her way. She let you know she'd guessed all your secrets, and then made a point of never mentioning them, so you found yourself feeling incredibly grateful to her, without being able to say why.

Under her guidance, he'd come a long way, longer, in some respects, than the bumpy road he'd traveled from DiFascio to Deacon. Because of Rebecca he'd even moved to Hoboken, although it was a little too much like going back to the old neighborhood for his liking. But he'd made a commitment. More than a commitment after the events of these last days.

He wouldn't let himself think about that night. Carrying the inert little bundle over the fence. Watching while Jake did those things.

The mind was a wonderful thing. It could focus and unfocus like the lens of a camera. And if it had been wrong, he hadn't actually done it himself. And if it kept him awake at night, or made him late in the morning, it was only temporary.

Rebecca had said it best. Consider the Eskimos, she told them. When an Eskimo becomes a burden, or threatens the general good, the group simply leaves him on the icy tundra to die. So the others don't have to share what they've worked so hard to get for themselves. That way, the best and the strongest can grow better and stronger.

Deacon had tried, really tried, to regard what happened as an act of euthanasia. Maybe he would have succeeded, had it not been for a few stupid things he couldn't get out of his mind: the smells in the old woman's kitchen, the sofa, and the holy pictures on the wall—it was like walking into his grandmother's house. Like it was Grandma.

For the hundredth time, he banished the thought, forcing himself instead to consider the ways in which that awful night would strengthen his bond with Lindsay (and Rebecca). Not only because of the money and the property—other men could give Lindsay plenty of that—but because of the element of danger. Lindsay was addicted to it.

Putting the crumpled message into his briefcase, John Deacon left for work. He didn't bend over to kiss the sleeping, naked woman before he went. There was no room in their relationship for tenderness.

He would call Rebecca from the office. Rebecca would straighten out his fear about the card. And then, for the first time in years, he'd call home.

* * *

Rebecca thought if another person called her and said, We have a problem, she'd scream.

It was bad enough having to keep up the collected facade when talking to John and Rothman. Now she was even having to do it around Jake for fear he would start to lose it.

"What is it this time?" she asked him, with all the disinterest she could muster. "I've got a business to run, you know."

"I stopped at the Quiles' on the way in, like you said." Her husband sounded panicked. "And get this—he's already accepted an offer on the buildings. Yesterday. Wouldn't tell me his name, only that it was a middle-aged guy, real distinguished type." There was a pause. "Do you think it's him?"

"Him?"

"The top hat. Whoever he is."

Rebecca laughed. "Do you really believe some Fred Astaire character in tails is going around buying up our property?"

Something was wrong, though, she admitted to herself. Very wrong.

"Sounds crazy, I guess," Jake said uncertainly. "But I spoke with Eric and Kathie myself, and they swear—"

"Did you call Bucks County?" she asked.

"No," he replied. "I thought I'd wait until after lunch."

Rebecca made little tears in the local paper that someone had left on the glass counter. Probably the new salesgirl. She would have to be replaced. Those clothes she wore! The only passable one she'd had on when Rebecca hired her—

Suddenly she saw it. A small ad, blocked off, and in tasteful print.

I BUY PROPERTIES.
GOOD PRICE. GOOD TERMS.

There was a number, and a small logo. A top hat.

"I'll call you back," she told Jake.

Rebecca dialed the number, and a voice on the other end said, "Coroner's office."

*　*　*

Alison Randall crossed another item off the posterboard list on her kitchen cork board.

"What next?" she asked Murtaugh.

He was preoccupied. Lowenstein had just informed him that Dana's body was being released to her husband. Oakley Hall was taking her to South Carolina for burial.

He thought of Dana traveling all alone to a place she'd never even lived. For one impulsive moment, he wanted to book passage on that plane. Stay with her.

"The ad looks splendid," Alison said, cutting it out with yet another pair of scissors. "I told you Bryan does lovely work."

The bell rang.

277

"That must be David." She pressed the intercom button and asked for identification.

"Louis Bonelli," the voice came back, over-enunciated, over-loud.

Randall buzzed him in. A few minutes later, Bonelli knocked on the door.

"Uh, O'Connell was called out," Bonelli told them, after awkwardly shaking Murtaugh's hand. "They found the Sanchez kid, right smack out in the middle of daylight. Your neighborhood, Hunt."

"Is he okay?" Murtaugh wanted to know.

"Yeah," Lou nodded, "but still not talking." He shifted his weight. "I coulda called, but O'Connell said you might be here, and I wanted to say hello, you know."

"Thanks," smiled Murtaugh.

"Have some lunch," Alison invited him.

"Naa." The man shrugged. "I gotta get back."

But when Murtaugh asked him, Bonelli gave in. It was strange seeing Hunt talk to the Randall woman as if he didn't half mind her, Lou thought. Luckily, everybody steered clear of business. So he didn't have to feel guilty one way or the other.

*　*　*

When you gonna fuckin' learn, man? Jaime asked himself. When you gonna learn that you can't trust any of them?

Murtaugh's okay, Mrs. Hall had told him. If you're in trouble, Jaime, she said, go to Sergeant Murtaugh and he'll take care of you.

So he waits, seems like days, outside the cop's place, man, and he never comes back, never comes at all. Then one of the neighbors spots him from his picture in the paper and he's screwed.

Ricky was right. People like that, they can't do nothing for you, he thought. They just get themselves killed, or disappear, and you're worse off than you were before.

Besides, who's to say if you did find Murtaugh that he woulda believed you anyway? You gave the kid the dust. Hey, man, you really think he's gonna believe it ended there?

It was all fuckin' Emil's fault. Wanting to bring another kid in, a younger kid. Wanting to play the big man for a change. You knew he was trouble, man, with those namby-pamby eyes and his fuckin' babysitters watching every step he made.

Try him out, Emil had said. So he finally gave in. He'd shown 'em—nothing bothered Jaime Sanchez, no babies, no babysitters, nothin'. Then the kid went and got himself wasted.

That was the worst part.

I mean, Jaime's thoughts raced ahead of him, yeah sure, death's the ultimate. Like the music says—badder than sex. He didn't know much about sex, except it was as lonely and dirty as everything else. Death had to be better.

Only Tomas Quiles' death was different. It wasn't like them animals, and the churches. It wasn't like psyching each other out with stories about digging up graves, and what they'd do to what was inside. He'd had control over those things.

There was no controlling Tomas' death and what happened afterward. Instead of you digging stuff out of the ground, it was like a long sucking wind at your back, with the stuff pulling you in. Into the tomb with Tomas, having to feel his baby hands; and that crazy lady next to you, smelling of beer and rot; and now, even pretty Mrs. Hall.

He didn't want to think about Mrs. Hall, being there, inside with them.

She'd told him Murtaugh was all right. Murtaugh, the guy who seemed to know your head, who tried to get you to say things about your connection—and that kind of ratting was worse than death, for sure. Only Mrs. Hall had this way of making you believe, even if you knew it was probably gonna

279

nail you to the wall in the end. And you did it. Because for her, you'd do anything.

Oh, fuck. Jaime stifled a sob.

The cop made him swivel in the chair, from face forward to profile, the way she used to do when she was drawing his picture. He heard a click as they took another photograph. It was a sad little sound, so sad it made Jaime Sanchez want to cry.

* * *

"Excuse me, but didn't you read the sign on the door?" Rebecca asked. "No food is allowed in the shop."

The Spanish woman stared uncomprehendingly.

"No ice cream," Rebecca repeated, raising her voice and pointing to the double-dipped cone, thinking, Christ, this one doesn't speak English, let alone read it, "No. No. *Nada*."

She should try living off that fat like a camel, instead of feeding her hump, Rebecca thought, watching the woman beat a lumbering, shuffling retreat.

An attractive customer in a well-cut jade linen suit who'd been browsing through the book section flashed her a sympathetic smile.

"To each his own nasty little compulsion," Rebecca sighed.

"I guess you must meet all kinds."

"Let's put it this way." As a businessperson, Lincroft knew the value of friendly chatter when building the right clientele. "It's not easy running an essentially New York City shop in Hoboken, New Jersey."

The young woman laughed. "Well, don't give up."

"I won't. Something's got to give," Rebecca replied in a firm voice, "eventually."

Lindsay's been messing with the volume control again, she thought, the music is too loud.

In the office, she found Lindsay sitting over a steaming

plate of stir-fry vegetables and a copy of *Interview* magazine.

"Want some?" she inquired, offering Rebecca her chopsticks.

It had been an unusually busy day. Rebecca decided to let Lindsay close, knowing in advance that tomorrow everything would be in chaos. Before she left, she checked to see if the woman in the suit wanted to make a purchase, but Alison Randall was already gone.

She'll be back, Rebecca said to herself. She's just our type.

She closed the door, tuning out the shrill cascade of little bells, while pondering exactly what that meant—"our type." Was Lindsay their type? Her total inability to do the simplest things was confounding; but then again, the bimbo had one real talent. Lindsay could always manage to find someone to do what had to be done for her.

That prospect bored Rebecca Lincroft. She was an achiever. A doer.

When they started the game, the others hadn't enough nerve to knock on a stranger's door. (Heaven forbid, the door of a widow!) It was she who spurred them on. She took the game out of the parlor and put it into their lives.

Even then, with the first little snag, they put their tails between their legs and ran. After those crude attempts at sabotage in the Quiles' prewar failed, Michael actually suggested they cut their losses. It was a blow to Rebecca. She had hoped that the scenarios she'd so carefully developed for the "What If" pile were teaching them to be more creative in their thinking.

They were children learning a grown-ups' game, trying to bend the rules, even resorting to telling you they didn't want to play anymore. Until they got on a roll. Until they were able to lovingly stack their winnings, all in a row. Like houses. Then they laughed and waited eagerly for the time when it would be their turn again.

281

Could they really be so self-absorbed that the pattern escaped them?, she wondered. Rebecca understood its rhythm intuitively, the way she understood the rhythm of sex.

First, there was the bait. The carrot. The candy. An object which brought saliva to your mouth, made your private parts sharply contract and softly release. Whatever the thing was—a building or a piece of property—you wanted it so bad you could taste it. That others wanted it, too, only sweetened the sugar, until you didn't just want it, you desired it, you needed it, you couldn't live without it.

Next came the set-up: the game. The game drew out pleasure, prolonging it, like foreplay. At times, it was an orgy: senses on overload, teasing one another with every move, juices flowing, highly charged and revving. At other times, it had all of the intimacy of a one-on-one encounter—as though there were nothing else in the world but you, the board, and those exquisitely proportioned pieces that fit glovelike into the palm of your hand.

Afterward, when you'd completed a deal, the awful letdown feeling poured through floodgates from which, only moments before, exhilaration was shooting like a spray of champagne.

Rebecca could almost read their minds—did I pay too much? am I over my head? why did I want this in the first place? The bait, that object most lately prized, suddenly seemed as old hat and unexciting as an opened Christmas gift—something to be stored in a drawer and forgotten.

But that was no reason to quit, she wanted to scream, no more than you'd join a convent just because getting laid never measures up to your expectations. (There were exceptions, Rebecca smiled to herself. After all, she'd hardly cultivated Johnny D. for his sparkling wit.)

Of course, no one ever actually quit. There was the usual bitching and moaning, the edginess, and depression—all easily conquerable with only a little resourceful prodding from Rebecca. And Jake. Jake always followed her lead.

They didn't quit because they couldn't. The game was a high to end all highs. It was in their blood.

As Rebecca made her way down Washington Street, the same fat Spanish woman walked by, eating from out of a small brown bag. Her immense ballooning breasts brushed the young woman's arm, causing her to shiver in disgust.

At least with my nasty compulsion, Rebecca thought, I don't wake up in the morning hung over, obscenely bloated with yesterday's garbage. I *have* something, and if the high is gone, there's always my next move to consider. My move on the board. My move on the block.

Rebecca couldn't say for certain when she'd first realized the game would lead to murder. The idea seemed to present itself gradually, so that by the time it became a viable strategy, she was already comfortable with the implications. It was as though killing Tomas and Rose had been a part of the game all along, on some higher level of play which required a degree of expertise she'd only now achieved.

There was no painful deliberation, no dark night of the soul. That they'd have to die came, instead, like the anxiously awaited answer to a nagging question, leaving her serene and resolute. Because she finally understood the game in all its complexities. The game wasn't simply about acquiring. It was about building, reconstructing, beautifying.

An incident from her childhood came back to her, clarified with new meaning, like a dream that suddenly makes sense. She remembered old Helen, hated housekeeper and sometimes Rebecca-keeper. Helen, fired and driven away in ignominy for stealing money that Rebecca had taken herself.

At some moments it was easier for her to picture those skinny, rounded shoulders disappearing into her father's Mercedes for the last time than it was to conjure up her parents' faces. She felt no guilt, then or now. Young Rebecca had known all about Helen—how she drank from a perfume bottle in her purse when she thought she was alone; how she took handfuls of macaroons from the cupboard, not caring if the child would be blamed; how she sometimes sat barefoot, her crooked taloned toes on an embroidered footstool, and watched soap operas until the Lincrofts came home. Maybe Helen hadn't stolen that fifty dollars, but she deserved to go for other reasons.

It was the same with the boy and the old woman. In evolution, they called it natural selection. As the species progressed and developed, the weak fell to the wayside and died. In sociology, Rebecca reasoned, the term was "gentrification."

The reshaping of Hoboken wasn't just the renovation of its buildings. It meant pushing out undesirable elements from the heart of town, pushing them farther and farther toward the city limits.

Jake had been a slow study. For weeks on end, she patiently explained the obvious: that the murders were catalysts, triggering what would eventually happen anyway, if left to time and chance. But time was of the essence, and they could make their own opportunities. It was quite simple. Two target groups, two victims. A Puerto Rican and an Irish or Italian. Just a little grease, she'd smiled, so the wheels of change might turn on their own.

But Becca, he'd protested, *you're talking about murdering people—*

Stop thinking that way, she ordered, the first of many times. They're not people. They're drunks. Dope addicts. Losers. They're accidents just waiting to happen. Do you really believe they'd think twice about mugging you, or raping me, or cheating us of what we've worked so hard to achieve?

They would simply be orchestrating the inevitable. Like weeds, certain elements had to be removed before the garden could grow. There was a positive and a negative way to look at the revitalization of any city. But in the final analysis, she assured Jake, they'd be more agents of life than death.

Rebecca was aware all along that she'd have to commit the first murder. She approached it pragmatically, as she did everything else. Her strategies weren't formulated overnight. They took thought, and more than that, observation.

She laughed to herself, remembering Dana Hall's rambling speech about an artist's perception during one of their sittings. With characteristic self-discipline she had smiled and said, isn't that fascinating?, while her thoughts took another, more reckless direction: you know, Dana, I've been watching our neighbors and I've perceived a perfect design for murder. You'll appreciate this—it's got classic composition, fabulous subjects, original technique. And I've even got several candidates lined up to pay for it when I'm finished.

An artist's perception! Where had an artist's perception gotten Dana Hall?

No, perception wasn't the ticket. The ticket was commitment. And every Thursday when Tomas Quiles came in the shop, Rebecca's commitment had grown stronger, more directed.

She let herself be bothered by him. She allowed his little reedy voice saying, "Lady, how much is this?" and "Lady, how much is that?" to wash over her. She studied the prints his little brown hands made on her clear glass display cases (What was that? Pizza?). The scent of him, the oil from his hair nauseated her, so she bent as closely as she could, following his greedy black eyes as they darted over her expensive merchandise. She opened herself up to revulsion.

When the day came, *that* day, she had a piece of luck. The boy was acting strangely, talking to himself. Rebecca felt herself vindicated before the act. Hadn't she called it? Weren't they all just drunks, drug addicts, losers, accidents waiting to happen? One day, this same boy might wait for her on a dark empty street. There would be no mercy then, why show any now?

As usual at that hour, the shop was empty. The kid never noticed Lindsay putting the "OUT TO LUNCH" sign on the door. He was toward the back of the shop, putting his soiled hands on one of her marionettes, on the virgin velveteen of its coat.

Rebecca had no recollection of the blow that knocked him down. Two thoughts ran through her mind simultaneously. First, that she should have had music playing, in case he screamed. And second, that she'd been foolish to strike him where blood might have ruined the toys. But he hadn't screamed, and he only bled onto the faded old carpet. She and Lindsay inserted the pins carefully, as though they were mending a doll.

Yes, luck had been on Rebecca's side.

Except in her decision to include Lindsay.

"It's like the scene where they kill the Yankee soldier in *Gone with the Wind*," she'd whispered as they rolled up the carpet.

Inexplicably, Rebecca had felt herself lose control. For the first time, she realized her hands were shaking. "This isn't a goddamn movie."

Lindsay widened those naked blonde eyes of hers. "I know," she said petulantly. "It's a *game*."

It annoyed Rebecca how Lindsay always managed to trivialize things.

The events of the last weeks came back to her as she walked home, and it suddenly hit her how tired, how mentally fatigued she was. More so because she knew she couldn't let it show. She was almost disappointed when she saw the light on in Paddy Walsh's house.

Before, it would have given her a surge of energy, a high,

just to know she was going to have the opportunity to deal, to make things happen.

Tonight Rebecca was tempted to pass it by, go home, put a movie on the VCR. These were the times, though, she knew, you had to give yourself an extra push. The times when you could actually accomplish the most. The conditions were perfect. Any onlookers would think it more than natural—the concerned neighbor checking on an old man, newly a widower.

Paddy came to the door in his undershirt and trousers. The sight of his toneless, kneady arms disgusted her. Rebecca forced herself to smile.

"Can I come in for a minute, Mr. Walsh?" she asked sweetly.

He shook his head vehemently. "No," he nearly shouted. "Can't do it tonight."

Drunk as usual, she thought. First rule, be firm. Take positive action. Rebecca stepped inside the screen door.

"I wanted to find out how you're doing," she said.

He retreated down the hall. Fine with her. Now she was in. "How are you doing?" Rebecca repeated.

"I'm not doing nothing," the old man replied cryptically.

Out of habit, Rebecca surveyed the place. Her mind knocked down walls, stripped woodwork, washed everything white in one crisp flash of the imagination. The smell, too, of grease and booze and mothballs would gradually be erased by lemon detergent and furniture polish.

"I spoke to our lawyer today." Rebecca followed him into the kitchen. "He seems to think we can wrap up the details by next week."

"Can't," Walsh mumbled, his back to her as he poked in the filthy refrigerator.

"What's that?"

"Somebody else's buying 'em." The words spilled out of him, and he stood cringing as though he expected to be hit.

She would have hit him, too, if she could have. Instead, she regulated her anger. "Somebody else? But we had a deal. We left a hundred dollars as a measure of our good faith—"

Paddy shuffled to the utensil drawer and took out a wad of bills. "It's here," he whimpered. "Most of it. I'll go to the bank tomorrow for the rest."

Rebecca made no move for the money. "Who was it? Who's buying you out?"

He hunched his shoulders. "Told me not to say."

"Was he older—older than me?" The man nodded. "Distinguished? With a hat, maybe?"

Paddy wiped his nose on his stringy, white forearm. "So that's that."

"I want you to promise me something, Mr. Walsh," Rebecca said. Her tone was meant to convey that she was talking business. "Next time this man comes around, you call me. You have my number.".

Walsh nodded. Rebecca turned and walked quickly down the hallway, and let herself out. When he heard the latch click, Paddy Walsh tucked the wad of uncollected bills back into the drawer, thinking that maybe things would still be all right.

*　*　*

Jake must have come home in the interim, because Rebecca noticed the lights were on. As usual, he hadn't checked the mailbox. She picked up an envelope. No address. No stamp. Without waiting until she got inside, Rebecca ripped it open. The index card read:

IT'S MY MOVE.
PHILIPPINE DESICCATED COCONUT CORPORATION.
MIDNIGHT. FRIDAY.

On the bottom, someone had drawn a cartoonish top hat.

Rebecca walked inside. Jake was sitting on the sofa with a drink. He jumped to his feet when he saw her.

"I know," she stopped him. "We have a problem."

"Cappricio said some guy—"

Rebecca handed him the note and sank into the comfort of the cushioned sectional, looking up at the dangling oddities.

"Put out the birdcage tonight," she ordered him. "It's Rothman's turn to have the game."

* * *

"Absolutely not," Alison Randall said.

O'Connell shook his head. "I'm afraid I'll have to agree with her on that."

"Go to Rourke with what you've got." They were eating in his German restaurant, Alison's first time, and Murtaugh noticed she'd cleared her plate of the wiener schnitzel. He himself had ordered Italian tonight.

"We'll back you up," she was saying. "Let him take it from here."

Murtaugh shook his head stubbornly. "They're prosecuting the kids. They've made an airtight little case against them. All I've got is a couple of drawings and a frigging bunch of twitching neurotics."

"What about the testimony of the people they tried to buy out?" Davy questioned.

"No law against real estate, and even if there were, face it. Paddy Walsh? Think he'd stand up under scrutiny? How about the Libretti woman? Or a Puerto Rican half crazed with grief?" Murtaugh needled him.

"But you—"

"Yeah, me," he chortled, tearing off another piece of bread. "Last week they looked me over and told me I needed ten more minutes in the oven." Murtaugh dared the couple to prove him wrong. "Yeah, they'll be wildly enthusiastic about what I have to tell them."

Alison was undaunted. "Explain about the meeting. Have Bromsky check it out."

"No law—"

"Against people meeting in an abandoned warehouse in the middle of the night? Maybe not, but it'll look pretty suspicious."

Murtaugh paid the check, over their protests. Randall had been shelling out food during the last four days. They walked to the SL together.

"I want to be wired," Murtaugh mentioned easily.

"For Chrissakes, Hunt," Davy cried, "this isn't fucking make-believe."

Murtaugh laughed. "You may not have realized it yet, but cops don't get wired that often in Hoboken. This might be my only opportunity."

Without a word, Alison drove past Number 516. Downstairs was dark, locked up tight. In front of Jake and Rebecca's door hung a brass birdcage. It looked like giant ribs, highlighted as it was by the lamp over the entrance.

Alison slowed the car and turned to face Murtaugh. "There's something about this I can't understand." He could see, even in the darkness of the car, the goosebumps on her thin arms.

"They want the property. Okay, fine, that makes sense. What doesn't make sense," she insisted, "is how apparently otherwise sane and intelligent people could rationalize killing innocent human beings."

The Sergeant took his time to respond, and when he finally did, he paused between each word as though framing his thought for the first time. "In a strange way, I think they believed they were just making this town a better place to live, for people like you."

Alison covered her face with her hands.

"You all right?" Davy asked.

She ignored him, turning once again to Murtaugh. "They've killed four people for the sake of a lousy game," she said. "You won't make them blink an eye, you jerk."

Randall put the car in gear and sped down the street.

* * *

Two sets of calls. Players who didn't feel up to playing. Deirdre, Michael said, was getting the flu. And Rothman was afraid he couldn't have anyone over with Janis in one of her moods.

Rebecca, however, had insinuated that this was a command performance. The group assembled by nine o'clock.

Jake didn't want to bring the board, but his wife insisted. He was in no shape to argue.

The presentation at the CDA had shaken him badly. FlorDesign was a heavy contender for the waterfront project, he knew. To find Delavan so cool and distant, so ultimately firm about not hearing their proposal, was an unexpected blow.

It led him to hazard that rash guess—humiliating, in retrospect, letting that man see him grasp at straws.

"Has someone been talking to you, sir?" he'd asked. "Middle-aged guy. Distinguished . . . ?"

Delavan's face gave him away. "I'm sorry," he told Jake, "I can't discuss that." He had rushed him out the door so quickly that he hadn't even had the chance to ask about the top hat.

As he set up the board, Jake caught a glimpse of himself in the ornate mirror hanging on the Rothmans' wall.

Not bad, he told himself. The tan looked a little faded, but all in all, he was holding up nicely. Rebecca would be pleased.

Keeping a composed demeanor, she'd told him at dinner,

was half the battle. Take the top hat man, whoever he was. From all indications, the guy was ice, cool and slick. We can't let ourselves get rattled, Rebecca warned, he's bound to be the type who can smell fear from a mile away.

Would the group pass muster?, Jake wondered.

Rothman was playing host, running from this room into the kitchen as though it was some kind of relay race. Deirdre had already downed two drinks. Otherwise, things were much the same as ever.

"There's a new player in the game," Rebecca said, when everyone was settled.

"It's Eric and Katherine," Deirdre cut in. "The more I think about it, it has to be—"

Jake interrupted. "Forget that. They don't know anything."

Rothman wiped his brow. "So what?" he said, comfortable in the role of arbiter. "If there's a new player, let him in."

"Not that simple," Rebecca reproved him, thoughtfully sucking on a Godiva chocolate. "You see, he wants everything. Everything we've . . . worked so hard to get."

Michael Grace said, "Maybe he'll compromise. We've all made compromises in the past. Deirdre and I got Castle Point for that church David wanted . . ."

"He knows about the murders."

Rebecca's words were like a douse of icewater, making everyone squirm in their seats.

"I don't see what they have to do with anything." Deirdre poured another drink.

"Of course you do," Rebecca told her matter-of-factly. "We all do. The question is, our next move."

She picked up those small precious buildings off Jake's model and busied herself with the pile of houses, not saying anything but letting the others see. One for you. One for me. One for you. One for me. One for you . . .

Jake spoke up on cue. "Well, let's play."

"Just like that?" Deirdre shrieked. " *'Let's play'?*"

"That's what we're here for," Jake said. Then turning to Rothman, "It was your move, wasn't it?"

"What if we don't want to play tonight?" Deirdre asked. "What if we don't want to play anymore?"

Rebecca stood. "You know the rules. You play until you go bankrupt." She looked at their pile of winnings, as though making a cursory count in her head. "There's no other way out."

"David?" Jake nodded toward the board. Rothman was frozen, a tall, moist plant growing out of the plush pile of the carpet.

"I'll roll for you." Rebecca tossed the dice. They clicked lightly, like fingernails on the board. "The 'What If' pile," she read.

Jake picked up the card for Rothman, took a look at it, then held it close to his chest, without referring to it again.

He recited, "A competitive buyer shows up on the scene and threatens to take over all of your waterfront properties. He makes an appointment to meet you at a deserted warehouse, late at night. What do you do?"

There was silence. Everyone looked at David Rothman, but he still hadn't moved a muscle.

"We can open this one up," Rebecca told them, "to all of the players."

Deacon's response was prompt. "Get rid of him."

"The only way," Jake agreed.

"And how do we do that?" Deirdre's voice kept climbing decibels. "Kill him, bang-bang? Throw him in the river?" She was almost laughing. "Or make it look like the others?"

"The boys who did the others," Rebecca reminded them gently, "are in custody."

Lindsay piped up, "I guess your first idea's the best, Deir."

"I don't believe this is happening." Deirdre Grace looked

around the room, from one to the other, but everyone was suddenly occupied with a glass, or a shoe, or a napkin. "I won't be involved in this. I refuse to be—"

"Sit down," Jake told her. "You already are."

Michael, embarrassed for not defending his wife, tried another tack. "Who the fuck here even owns a gun, for Chrissakes?" He managed a snicker. "I mean, we're the generation that doesn't believe in the things."

"I own one," a voice said plainly from the foot of the stairs. "You could have mine."

Janis Gillmore Rothman looked calm, and for once, totally straight.

CHAPTER

23

IT LOOKED as though it might rain, but that hadn't stopped Janis Rothman from practicing on the courts. Jake noticed her walking back from home, sweaty and sullen, as he ran to catch the morning bus. They nodded to each other, and Jake smiled, flashing the old dimples. Janis merely walked on, as if last night had sapped all of her energy.

Not that it mattered, he thought. She'd done her part. He could handle it from here.

The idea made him both proud and a little sick at heart. The pride was from a sense of being experienced. Tonight Jake would be the expert. Rebecca, too, of course, but the others would never really consider her. They weren't sexist. It simply wouldn't occur to them that Rebecca had been anything more than the talker, the engineer.

He was sure they were trying to figure out how he'd established an alibi for himself on the day the boy was killed, when all along she'd planned to do the first one herself.

To give you strength and courage, Jake told himself. And a little black voice inside him said, to dare you.

The sick of heart part came into play whenever that black voice spoke up.

Rose hadn't been too bad. She was a miserable old bitch just as Rebecca said, and they'd gone through the motions together hundreds of times, so when the actual moment came, it was almost like a dream. With Deacon on the verge of tears, it had made him, Jake, suddenly sure of himself. Everything— the smell of the filthy kitchen, the look of her watery pop eyes, the touch of the vinyl dustcovers—sickened him to the point of rage. He'd ordered Deacon to straighten the path into the parlor so he could begin the pins himself.

And he'd remembered so many details! Deacon, he knew, was impressed. They hadn't been able to talk about it. It was still too fresh, too dangerous a memory, but someday, when, in Rebecca's words, the dust settled, they would.

No, not Rose. Rose had given him that nervous edge, like when he'd just closed a great deal. And Mrs. Cappricio, well, Mrs. Cappricio did them a favor by expiring without any assistance. True, he'd gone up to kill her, walked up those stairs with a box of candy, after he realized she'd been spying that night.

There was no other way, even though Rebecca had freaked when he told her. Called him sloppy and stupid. Still, no harm had been done. The old lady's ticker stopped. The police didn't suspect foul play. And if any of the other players did, it worked to their advantage. Helped them realize the scope of the thing they were doing.

FlorDesign was on the East Side. The sky looked downright threatening. Jake decided he'd better cab it.

That twinge of whatever it was inside him persisted. He knew the only way to rid himself of the feeling was to explain it away.

He would have been fine, he was sure, if Rebecca hadn't insisted that Dana Hall must go. She said Dana was asking too many questions.

"She thinks if she opens those eyes of hers wide enough when she's nosing around I won't notice," Rebecca had told him.

Jake tried to say that it was just the way she was. Sweet. Friendly. Like with the detective.

Rebecca laughed, told him not to be so naïve. "She's sleeping with him. Isn't that obvious? He's there more than Oakley is."

The notion upset Jake. He'd always liked Dana. Not enough to cheat on Rebecca, but still, she was so . . . different.

Different than the people he knew.

But Murtaugh! I mean, Jake couldn't help being incredulous, Dana could do a lot better than that drunken has-been. No, he was worse than a has-been, he was a never-been. Jake didn't believe Dana would fall for someone like Murtaugh. She was into fidelity anyway, he decided, remembering how she'd ignored those little overtures he himself had made.

I handled the old Sergeant pretty smoothly though, Jake thought, in spite of the fact he really pissed me off. It was as though he thought he was smarter than everybody else.

Jesus, Dana, he swore silently. Why'd you have to press her? Why'd you have to ask Becca about the way she decorated the door, and all? Why'd you have to make up that silly story about wanting to run something off on our tape deck? You must have known she'd see through that.

Jake overtipped the driver, as usual. It was kind of a superstitious thing with him—seeing those flat, foreign faces posted in the front seat, with their names and serial numbers under them, never failed to make him thankful that he'd been born who he was, and not by some cruel twist of fate into some fucking Iranian, or Russian, or Haitian family. The thought horrified him: Jake Florian, appreciator of the finer things in life, mired by insurmountable circumstances.

He smiled at the poor bastard and slammed the door.

Leave it all outside, Jake warned himself. The baggage you're carrying. You don't want to have another day like you had yesterday.

He went to the newsstand for a paper, telling himself that Dana's death was necessary. She was the last. The last except for this one tonight, but the one tonight was different.

No, Jake winced, as he pushed the button for the elevator. She was the one who was different. Something nagged him. Not the worry that somebody would find out he hadn't made it to the site in Jersey City on time that morning. Something else.

As he had bent to strangle her, as she'd struggled, her amber hair was pushed flush to his nostrils. It smelled spanking new, and clean, like a fresh sheaf of paper. He could smell it now.

Jake Florian stepped into the car and let the doors close on that last image of her face. But the fragrance went with him.

* * *

She was reminded of one of those awful ethnic jokes that all run along the same lines: How many yuppies does it take to make a murder?, Deirdre asked herself wryly. And what, in fact, does one wear?

Not funny. Definitely not funny. Yet Deirdre Grace more and more found herself on the verge of hysterical laughter. She sat at her desk, surrounded by the proofs of the calendar they were publishing, and tried to keep her shoulders from shaking.

Yesterday, she'd called in sick. Now she buzzed her secretary, "Beth, cancel that meeting with Ed. I'm going home."

Better bring these with, she thought, stuffing the proofs

into her large eelskin portfolio. Not that I'm going to do home-
work, but I might as well look as though I am.

Pictures flashed through her head. Seven people in leather
trenches and slouched hats, walking through the fog. A piece
packed neatly away in someone's Gucci clutch.

A weary voice says, "Well, now that's been taken care of,
how about a late supper?"

And Deirdre sighs, "Not tonight, loves. Thought I'd just
head straight home and go over my proofs for the wildlife
calendar."

She gulped back the giggles as she stopped to give Beth
instructions on where to re-route her calls. Poor dear, she
thought I was going to be whoops all over her desk. Deirdre
smiled to herself as she headed for the elevator bank.

What was she going to do? she wondered. Surely not go
back to the house, to that breathtaking mausoleum on Castle
Point. She counted the hours to midnight, considering how
to fill them.

Movies, maybe. Thrillers. Murder mysteries. Spy films and
adventures to psych herself out. She could open her journal,
sit in the dark, and take copious notes with a Cross pen.

As bizarre and unbelievable as it might seem, they were
going to kill a man.

"Are you all right?" asked one of the secretaries who was
riding down to the third floor. Deirdre guessed she must have
been laughing again, but after the woman got off the elevator,
she discovered her cheeks were wet.

* * *

Rothman called the house, something he never did, twice.
The first time Janis answered. She seemed all right, not talk-
ative, but then that was normal for her. As far as he could
tell, she wasn't having any second thoughts about what she'd
done the previous night.

299

Her action had terrified him, coming as it did from out of the blue. After, when everyone left, the terror subsided into a kind of sensual thrill making him want her, like he hadn't for months and months. They had sex, or rather he had sex, Janis letting him. Still, it was exciting.

It was like those first times. Him—skinny, not terribly attractive David Rothman—in bed with Janis Gillmore. *The* Janis Gillmore. And so what if, even in the old days, he knew deep down he was nothing more to her than a way to rebel? Rebel from the overbearing parents who pushed her into tennis as soon as she could hold a racket; from her coach; from all the pretty boys with the bodies who lusted for her.

The incredible thing was that she had chosen Rothman to express her discontent. Rothman and his powderwhite mounds of magic. At that point, he hadn't known for sure which she wanted more. He'd known cokeheads before, but nothing like the way Janis was with the stuff. When she snorted a line, it was as though she was breathing a soul into her empty body.

At first it just made her wild. Wildness he liked. From that, she progressed quickly into unpredictableness, and then finally to violence.

It was an out for her, Rothman had often told himself. She went out at the top, and she went out with a bang. Almost.

He'd stayed with her, not out of guilt or any illusion that they loved each other. He'd stayed with her because she was still *the* Janis Gillmore. Sometimes he wondered why she'd stayed with him. Maybe it was because he made it easy for her to hate herself, and that's what Janis seemed to want, more than anything else.

Still, they were in the game together now. They were a couple again. She'd made no requests, except that Melissa be sent to her parents in Florida for a few days. She hadn't said, in case anything goes wrong. For that he was grateful. Instead, she told him she didn't want the child to overhear any talk. Rothman had readily agreed.

So the second time he called, Iylish answered, telling him Janis had already taken Melissa to the airport. She'd left word to ask if he would be home for dinner.

This tidiness, this orderliness on the part of his wife—even when she was high or depressed—amazed him. Rothman said yes, yes, he would be home. (He'd canceled with Olivia early in the morning.)

He wondered why Janis had suddenly, and so dramatically, decided to acknowledge herself a part of the group. There was that dangerous side of her, it was true, but Rothman had a feeling, deep down, it was her way of wiping the slate clean. He'd stayed with her through a sticky situation once. She was turning the tables.

The sentiment pleased him. Not for the only time, certainly, but for the first time in a long while, he felt justified in having married her.

* * *

Randall had pulled every string she could think of to get the equipment. She and O'Connell worked in the warehouse while, for the most part, Murtaugh stood by helplessly.

"This isn't smart," Alison warned him. "Too much can go wrong with so many people around. If something happens, we won't be able to get to you in time."

Murtaugh nodded. When she was right, she was right. In the old days, he would have felt invincible. He was the good guy. Now he was beginning to believe being good simply invited death.

He shook their hands. Told them he'd see them when he saw them, and left.

* * *

301

It kind of ticked Deacon off that everyone had so readily agreed Jake would use the gun. After all, he had been just as involved in the other murders, in a way, as Jake had. More involved, at least, than any of the others. And this was his chance to really do something, with Lindsay right there to see.

He'd told her it wasn't necessary to come, knowing full well she wouldn't miss it. They hadn't even slept together after the meeting, reinforcing the special nature of the coming event—like being apart the night before the wedding.

. Now that it was finally dark, Deacon felt an aching for her. Maybe not even for her. For anyone.

He thought of Jake and Rebecca. Deirdre and Michael. It had to be easier, in pairs. Even Rothman, the poor bastard, wasn't on his own. Janis wouldn't be there—everyone knew how erratic her behavior was, at best, and no one wanted to tempt fate—and yet, she'd play a part in it, for a change.

Casting Lindsay and himself as the young lovers, the ingenues, in tonight's scenario had a calming effect on Deacon. An act of derring-do. The inevitable reward of riches and a maiden's hand. A chance to once and for all prove that he belonged.

If only Jake wasn't going to get to use the fucking gun! This way, he'd have to watch the bad things again. And Deacon was afraid—terrified—that he didn't have it in him.

* * *

This warehouse was closer to the water and had a more vandalized, bombed-out appearance than any of the others. The Philippine Desiccated Coconut Corporation.

Sounded to Deirdre like some kind of reggae band.

They walked kindergarten style, using the buddy system, and there was something of the field trip about the entire experience. Hushed whispers to be quiet, Deirdre's nervous giggles, stopping and starting.

Rothman wished silently that he'd remembered to go to the bathroom before he left. That wine he'd had with dinner seemed to be flushing everything from him. He envied Janis, at home, in front of the television set where he'd left her.

"It's fucking locked," Deacon hissed.

Only Rebecca had thought of flashlights, although it seemed everyone had deliberately chosen a dark, loosely cut outfit. God knows why it should matter, Deirdre wondered, but they matched nicely.

Jake trained the beam up against the building. There were lights on inside. Someone was already there.

"Try another entrance," he ordered, taking charge in a way he knew couldn't help humiliating Deac.

They tramped, en masse, around to the other side of the structure, passing the walls where the company's name still loomed in faded paint.

"I feel we should be singing 'A Hundred Bottles of Beer on the Wall,' " Deirdre twittered.

"Shut up." It was Michael, disciplining his wife.

She should have been allowed to stay home, like Janis, he thought bitterly. Why did Rebecca have to make such a stink about her coming along?

The rusted lock had been pried open on this set of doors. Rothman and Deacon pulled them open, creaking, until they could all slip into the cavernous interior.

As Rebecca feared, it was difficult to distinguish shapes and images. Piles of debris, discarded cartons, and pieces of metal were the perfect places for someone to hide. She halted suddenly, causing the line of people behind her to jam up.

On the corroded floorboards was an object. A top hat, worn almost completely through at the brim.

"Oooh, a souvenir of the occasion," Deirdre whispered. They hushed her all around.

Jake was already holding the handle of the gun. He'd used one before, long ago. Hunting at home with his dad.

Dammit to hell, he scolded himself, why'd you have to think of the old man now? To erase him from his mind, Jake stepped boldly toward the center of the warehouse.

Behind him, Deirdre hummed the theme from those James Bond movies. Dun-dun-dun-dun-da-da-da, dun-dun-dun-dun-da-da-da.

Jake spun around, angry. "Jesus Christ, Grace, if you can't control her, take her outside—"

A click. Then the sound of a voice on tape. Muffled. Background noises, knocking and hissing, but still easily identifiable. It was Rose Walsh, yelling in her kitchen. Mostly the words were indecipherable, just a lilting the way Rothman imagined Iylish would sound if she were upset. Then suddenly, there would be a barbed phrase. ". . . don't fool me." ". . . know what you're up to." The recorder clicked off.

Rebecca called out, "All right, you've won. You've won the game. You can come out now—"

Deacon felt the vulnerability of their position. Like being monkey-in-the-middle.

He yelled, "We've come here in good faith! What do you want from us?"

From behind a freight elevator, someone approached. Well-cut suit. Squared shoulders. A light passed over his head, trimmed, salt-and-pepper hair.

They saw his face for the first time, and Deirdre laughed. If the truth were told, it was exactly what Jake felt like doing.

"Not you," he said, his voice as friendly and natural as it always had been in the presence of the detective. "*You* didn't figure it out."

304

Murtaugh tossed something next to Deacon's feet. A small tape cassette. "Ain't it a bitch?" He smiled.

Rebecca was thinking fast, but her mind went in too many directions. All she could manage to say was, "What now?"

"Same as if I'd been anyone else," Murtaugh told her. "I want some of the toys."

"You've already taken them," Rebecca reminded.

"Oh, that." Murtaugh shrugged modestly. "You don't think those checks I wrote will clear, do you? Unfortunately, I've got a cop's bank account."

Rothman gulped audibly. "Just let him in, right? All he wants is in."

"Why?" Rebecca's doe eyes narrowed.

"I like the way you live," Murtaugh suggested.

"I don't believe you," she responded easily.

He nodded. "It's the game. I'm good at the game."

Michael felt encouraged. "You'd be willing to divide, wouldn't you?" he prompted. "To compromise?"

"Absolutely."

Does not compute, does not compute, Rebecca's mind was saying. Remember his girlfriend, Dana Hall.

She shook her head. "It makes me nervous. You have everything on us. Compared to what we have on you."

"We'll have something in common," Murtaugh replied. "Mutual distrust. An asset in business, I'd guess. Although you'd know better."

"We'll need something in writing," Rebecca said. "Jake. Give him what we discussed before."

Michael Grace, who had momentarily relaxed, saw in a split second what was about to happen. He lurched forward. Too late. Rebecca and Lindsay had sidestepped together, like in a dance step, as Jake whipped out the pistol.

Someone screamed. Not Deirdre, strangely enough, but

Jake. The gun discharged. Once, twice, hitting Murtaugh in the chest. They watched him clutch the pinstripe suit, saw the panicked look in his eyes as he appeared to search the rafters for something, saw the damp red splotches on clothing and fingers before he fell.

Deirdre screamed now. Out of the corner of his eye, Jake, in that special state which allowed him to notice everything, caught a glimpse of Rothman. His dark clothes were so soaked it almost looked as though he'd wet his pants.

"You killed him," Rothman yelled. "You killed a fucking cop."

"The closest path to the river is out that door," Rebecca told her husband. "You and John carry him down. You, too, David." She turned to Grace. "Shut her up. It's all over."

"I can't go," Rothman stammered. "I'm going to be sick."

"Look," Rebecca said, "I'm only going to say this once. Two more minutes of distasteful work, we all win the game. Not just one player, all of us."

"But the murders," Deirdre sobbed, "they weren't our—"

Jake nodded. "Don't look a gift horse in the mouth." He commanded Rothman, "Come on."

Deacon was already kneeling by the body, so it frightened him the most when Hunter Murtaugh sat straight up, grabbed his collar, and shouted into the heights of the warehouse.

"That a take?"

Another light snapped on. They all saw the woman clearly. She held out a video cassette and waved it in the air. "Yes, sir, Sergeant!"

From another direction, a young man's voice shouted, "Police. You're under arrest."

Murtaugh said softly, "Do not pass go. Go directly to jail."

He wiped his hands on the new suit and threw the blood capsules onto the dusty floor.

EPILOGUE

IT WAS the first time he'd been back. The hiatus brought changes to Rose Walsh's neighborhood.

There was a SOLD sign in front of Number 518. All the windows were open, blackened screens heaped in a pile on the meager front lawn. As Murtaugh passed he could hear shrieks of laughter, and looking up, he could see its source.

A young woman was chattering to her comrades-in-renovation, painting in what used to be Paddy's bedroom. The detective heard, ". . . and I swear, beer cans stacked in the closet!"

Across the street, the Rothmans' house was dark. Shuttered and shut like an out-of-season resort.

Janis was planning to sell. She'd told him on the only occasion they'd seen each other, the day before she left for an exclusive convalescent facility—translated rehabilitation center.

Melissa would be staying at her folks for a while, Janis said.

Murtaugh never asked about her husband or referred to that night in the warehouse. The look on her face was enough to telegraph she wasn't ready to talk about it.

He recalled her resolutely set mouth when they met at the tennis courts the morning before the players were to gather for the last strategic move.

"I want to stop it," she'd told him. "I want to stop everything."

He'd known then that she wasn't only referring to the game, to the violence. Janis Gillmore Rothman wanted to stop the self-destruction.

The downward slide. The wasting of her life. It had taken incredible self-control, and a good amount of courage, to come to such a decision.

The gun was the key in so many ways. Janis must have considered it a fitting end to her relationship with Rothman. It had been the beginning, in a way. After all, it was after she'd been introduced to him, and simultaneously introduced to drugs, that she'd begun carrying the weapon in her purse.

Murtaugh could well imagine what role it had played in Janis' cycle of self-hatred and despair. Even at the height of her paranoia, when her coach and friends feared she might take her own life, or the life of someone else, the gun was simply a private shame, reinforcing her feeling of being a fake, an imposter.

It had never been loaded with anything but blanks. And for a perfectionist such as she, that was the ultimate failure.

Murtaugh was glad she could let it all go, be rid of the gun and what it had come to represent. Later, at Christmas perhaps, he would write Janis in care of her parents. He hoped to hear she was playing tennis again.

The thought of Christmas made him suddenly wilt inside. First, Murtaugh reminded himself, you've got to get through today. Then you can consider the future.

At the other end of the block, he saw that there were new people living in the Quiles house. Bonelli said Maria, refusing to move with her family, was living in her father's building next door, acting as superintendent. It was presumably under her supervision that the tenement had been given a fresh coat of paint. He wondered if Maria enlisted the help of some young and able workers—like Jaime Sanchez and his friends. But maybe it was too soon for that. Maybe that could never be.

Paulie's was boarded up. They were probably going to turn it into that health spa Dominick had talked about. As a matter of fact, the Librettis seemed the only constant. He knew she was watching him, from behind her venetian blinds, as he knocked at the door of Number 516.

Oakley called out, telling him to come right in. He was packing his belongings. They shook hands tentatively.

The young man said, "You look different somehow."

"It's probably the glasses," he replied.

We need her here, Murtaugh thought, to smooth this over. We need her hovering around us, smiling and gently nudging us together.

"I hope you don't mind if I keep working," Oakley said. "I'm taking a plane out tonight."

"For good?"

He nodded. "No reason to stay."

Murtaugh balanced his weight against some cartons. "I know the feeling."

"I called your office a couple of weeks back," Oakley told him. "They said you were on leave."

Murtaugh nodded, thinking of the trip mapped out for him by Martin Fellows and Alison Randall. "I rented a car. Drove through the Berkshires. Ever been up there?"

Oakley shook his head. They had nothing in common, Murtaugh decided. Nothing but her.

"They'll return the drawings to you as soon as the trial is over," the detective said lamely. "That tape of Rose, too."

"I know."

There was an uncomfortable silence. Oakley was sweating in spite of the cool September weather and the dankness of the basement apartment.

Finally Murtaugh spoke, "I came to apologize."

The young man shook his head wordlessly, but would not turn.

"I wanted it to be you," the Sergeant said. "I knew you'd lied. And I thought she was too good for any kind of liar."

"You were right," Oakley's voice was filled with self-reproach.

"No."

Oakley kicked a pile of books and they flew in several directions.

"You were right," he repeated stubbornly. "If I'd been here instead of researching that, that pathetic excuse for a novel, they wouldn't have—"

Murtaugh interrupted, "It wasn't your fault. It was mine."

"*I* was her husband," Oakley told him. "She was my responsibility." The statement stung the detective with the antiseptic bite of truth.

Oakley laughed ruefully. "Want to know the worst of it? Turns out I'm a pretty second-rate writer. Not in her league. Never was."

"What will you do?"

Oakley shrugged. "I'm going back to newspaper work. Try to figure out what I can salvage from what I used to believe." As an afterthought, he asked, "And you?"

Murtaugh replied noncommittally, "Oh, I'm keeping my options open."

Oakley picked up two panels, one payon, one acrylic, from the paintings lining the walls. "They're yours."

Murtaugh held up his hand. "I couldn't—"

"Take them," Oakley insisted. "She . . . she cared for you. I thought at first it was because of the thing with her father." He stopped, choked with emotion, then began again. "Now I know it was more than that."

Murtaugh took the portraits. The study was a finished piece, strikingly complete. The one she'd painted on the last night of her life was only a spectre of a picture, but somehow it was the one Murtaugh preferred.

The lemon cat ran out from the kitchen, scurrying past its master and coming to rest at the detective's feet.

"I'm not sure what I'm going to do about Lydia," Oakley sighed. "Friends kept her while I was away, but they can't do it permanently." With the trace of a smile, he admitted, "I—I don't think we were meant for each other."

Murtaugh shook hands with the young man. At the door, he turned and saw the lemon cat sitting forlornly by the easel.

"If you'd let me," the detective said, "I'd like to take care of the cat."

Oakley nodded. "That would be good," he said slowly. "That would be right."

Murtaugh walked down the street one last time, trying to balance the portraits under his arm. From inside the carrier, Lydia yowled.

The block had changed, he thought. Much of the old guard was gone. And, ironically, so was much of the new. Once he would have felt the need to divide these buildings into camps, to tally the scorecard as though his future depended on it. But he had changed, too. What happened to the people who lived here was up to them. And what happened to Hunter Murtaugh was up to Hunter Murtaugh.

On the other side of town, exterminators and painters tramped through his basement apartment readying it for the next occupant.

311

Davy O'Connell had offered him the use of his place until he decided what to do. The young detective was spending more and more of his nights with Alison Randall.

"It's all right," the Sergeant told Lydia in a soothing voice. "We're going to find ourselves a home."

Murtaugh could feel the cat relax, curl up within the metal box, and by the time he reached the end of the block, he was sure she was asleep.